DOOMSEEDS

Book Two in the Botanicaust Series

TAM LINSEY

Cover art by Tam Linsey

Print Version

ISBN: 978-0-9859013-4-9

Created with Vellum

The Tox
Cannibal Wastelands

The plains stretched as far as the pilot could see: undulating poisonous amarantox weeds broken by an occasional jutting rock or umbrella-like yuvee tree. Along the river, gray-green tamarisk with deep roots resisted the competing growth. Beneath the canopy, cannibals stalked each other with ferocious tenacity.

The com crackled in her ear. "Uma, movement starboard, riverside."

With one lazy hand, she tapped the attitude controls and the duster swiveled in the air to follow a bend in the river. In the back of the aircraft, her team clung to the open doorway, flame guns ready.

Her job was easy—keep the duster in the sky. The other team members had the task of flashing every living thing beneath them. They had to make sure the cannibal hordes never reached the Burn–the desolate circumference of scorched earth surrounding the city.

A concussive burst from the flame guns told Uma they'd found their mark. She steadied the duster, glancing through the window on her right at the curls of yellow smoke as tamarisk caught fire. Never comfortable with the pitiful writhing of cannibals caught in the flash, she lifted her gaze to the sky. If only the mongrels would surrender once in a while.

The duster bucked once, and she frowned, returning her attention to the controls. Normally these dusters almost flew themselves. Behind her the team shouted warnings, and the flame guns took up a steady roar. On her dashboard, the mag-gauge flashed erratic numbers.

The team lead poked his head into the pilot chamber and clamped a hand on Uma's shoulder. "They're firing at us!"

Cannibal spears and arrows would barely dent a nuvoplast duster shell. She spared the man a glance. A smear of blood marred the green skin of his cheek. "Wha–?"

"These mongrels have guns!" he shouted. "Get us out of here."

Uma swore as the duster rocked left and she fought to maintain thrust. She yanked emergency lifters as cries of "Fire! Fire!" came from the back. The port thruster sputtered and the duster twisted in a lazy spin. She compensated with front and rear auxiliaries, but the duster was sinking fast. She tapped her com to access Command. "Mayday, mayday. Duster six delta four November. We've been struck by what appear to be bullets coming from—"

The forward thruster gave out and the nose of the aircraft plunged toward the smoking ground. Her face slammed against the windshield. The rest of the crew screamed as they slid toward the short wall separating the cockpit from the main cabin. The last thing Uma saw before passing out was a crush of brilliant green amarantox leaves against the windshield and the crimson splatter of blood.

Chapter One

The Holdout
Protectorate Territory

With the nervous crowd skittering across the hard-packed earth, the skeletal trusses of the barn reminded Eily of a ribcage picked clean by hungry vermin. A familiar keening drew her attention to a figure balanced high on the barn's roof ridge. His slender green arms shone brightly in the autumn heat as he raised a glinting blade toward the sun.

The Knife Song.

Beside her, Brother Michael sucked his teeth then spat, his tanned face as impassive as ever beneath the brim of his straw work hat. "Ijon says if you can't get him down, they'll take care of it."

Her gaze flicked toward Ijon, the Haldanian Protectorate liaison, and his aide, their naked green skin gaudy against the modestly dressed, milky-skinned crowd. At least Ijon made a small attempt to respect the Holdout Order's sensibilities and wore a sleeveless tunic and short pants. His aide wore only a breechcloth. The aide's skin was drab, almost muddy, rather than bright jade like Ijon's, the result of genetically modified chloroplasts mixing with existing pigmentation on dark-skinned cannibals. The very few members of the Holdout who'd elected to undergo genetic modification had emerged with emerald-green skin, giving them a defining look opposite the cannibals.

One of Eily's few vanities was that her cannibal heritage had presented as a tawny green; if she wanted to, she could pass as a Native Haldanian, genetically modified as an embryo before implantation.

Although the aide had once been a cannibal, like herself, converts were often the hardest on each other. She knew what Brother Michael meant by "take care of it." The Protectorate thought nothing of euthanizing reversions—cannibal converts who were viewed as troublemakers. Her job as Reversion Remediation Specialist was to help those who couldn't acclimate to life in the city to conform to the rules at the more rural Holdout. She was their final chance.

Swallowing, she examined a ladder scaling the half-finished barn. "I have to climb up that?"

"Perhaps it'd be best to allow them to step in this time."

With a firm shake of her head, Eily pulled the back of her skirt up between her legs and tucked the hem into the waistband of her apron. Today was supposed to be a time of celebration—the first barn raising since she'd come to the Holdout. Everyone would take a death as a bad omen, and if the death happened to be one of her cases, the Holdout might revoke asylum for the rest of the reversions.

The crowd quieted as she approached the nearest ladder. She was used to the gawking. For years, she had been the only converted member of the Holdout—the green-skinned girl in the Old Order dress. The people of the Holdout used to avert their eyes, knowing she'd once been a cannibal, fearing her green skin was the Mark of the Beast. After her baptism, she'd gained some acceptance among them, but many still watched her with distrust.

She gripped a rung and then pulled back to wipe her sweaty green palms against her dress. Barn raising was for men, and she'd never been up a ladder, let alone to confront a knife-wielding patient.

Climbing the rungs turned out to be easy, but when she reached the slatted trusses, her muscles weakened. The dusty ground looked very far away, so she turned her gaze upward. On the composite beam above, Lisius raised a slash of silver to the sky, his Knife Song taking the final turn before death. She'd seen what came next several times in her previous life, her cannibal life. She'd urged the song on with joy and anticipation of the flesh-feast.

"Lisius," she croaked, then in a stronger voice called out his cannibal name. "Alisis. Hold your song."

The singing faltered and she pulled herself up onto the slats.

Lisius spoke in a dead voice. "Don't come closer. I'll jump and take you with me."

She stopped, hands in a death-grip on the truss. Lisius had removed his suspenders and shirt, so his trousers hung low around his scrawny green hips. His face glistened with tear tracks. He was younger than she was, a new convert genetically modified with the Protectorate's green, photosynthetic skin. She'd had more than six years to acclimate to her new skin, her new life.

"Taking the Knife is a waste here." She spoke Cannibal, in spite of the Protectorate's insistence that all things of the past must be left behind.

"Everything is a waste here. Why don't they let me go?"

"Why would you want to go back out there? There is no Hunger here. No fear of hunters. Shelter from wind and rain—"

"And the sun now makes us sick."

Eily blinked, her world spinning for half a second as she was reminded of the alkaloid drugs drifting through her system. She had learned to ignore the "high," a side effect of the photosynthesis. The sensation would still be new to Lisius. Some converts liked it. Some insisted it dulled their survival instinct. "You'll get used to it."

"I don't want to get used to it. I don't want to let them tell me what to do. Or these Holdout people, either." He sneered at the pale-faced crowd below. The people at the Holdout had made a bargain with the Protectorate: no forced conversions, no euthanizations, and the Protectorate could maintain a peaceful base within the electric fences. Many still viewed green skin as the Mark of the Beast.

"They've done you no harm."

"The girls won't even look at me. And the boys—pfft—they're worse than the girls. I'd be a man in the tribe now. Here I'm treated like a child before his naming day."

"You have to earn their respect, the same as in the tribe."

"How do I do that? They won't even fight back!"

"They're pacifists. Earn their respect by following *their* ways."

His nostrils flared. "They wouldn't survive the Tox."

She sighed and looked over the horizon, past the electric fences and the scorched perimeter to where the poisonous amarantox grew thick. *Only cannibals call it the Tox.* Uncle Levi and the rest of the Order called it the Amarantox Plains. Aunt Tula and the Haldanians called it the Reaches. Whatever it was called, outside the fence was dangerous. "Lisius, look around you. They *have* survived. Their ways take getting used to, but they're good. They don't have to take the Knife here. Their god keeps them safe."

"The Flame Runnas keep them safe." He used the cannibal name for green people.

"The Protectorate," Eily corrected automatically. Even she had trouble keeping things straight sometimes. Haldanians, Flame Runnas, converts... the Order called them Blattvolk. And then there were the few green-skinned people called reversions, like Lisius. They all lived under the thumb of the Protectorate, along with the unconverted members of the Order at the Holdout.

"How did you come to the Holdout?" Lisius asked.

She turned her face from the horizon to look up at him again. "I let go of my past a long time ago."

He crossed his arms, and a sneer twisted his upper lip. "I bet you're not even a convert. Just another Flame Runna trying to rule the world."

The muscles in her neck tightened. "I'm a reversion, like you."

The sneer didn't fade, and she knew she was going to have to tell him her story, even though she'd worked so hard to forget it. He was only her fourth charge since the Protectorate began sending reversions to the Holdout, and she was sure she'd have to tell her story many more times in the years to come.

She leaned her torso against the beam she was clutching and rested her chin on the wood. The story was as uncomfortable as she was. "When I was converted, the Protectorate still killed reversions. There were no second chances. My sister and I were condemned, but instead of being killed, we were sent to the Fosselites, who tortured us, harvesting our chemicals against our will. Tula and Levi broke us free." All the new converts knew Tula; she was the doctor who oversaw the influx of cannibals the burn operatives brought in from the Reaches for conversion. "The Protectorate didn't yet know about the Holdout. They were chasing Tula, who they thought had reverted. We led them here."

She trembled. The day the dusters had appeared over the houses still lived fresh in her memory. The Protectorate's mission was to convert or kill every cannibal, and they'd assumed the Holdout was more cannibals. They'd burned several buildings along with the people in them before Tula convinced them to halt. And afterwards, a compromise had been a long time coming. "Because of Tula, reversions have a second chance. All the Order asks is that we respect their ways and earn our keep. The Holdout is your last shot, Lisius."

"Does your sister live here, too?"

Tears she'd thought long dried filled her vision. "No." She turned her face to the distant Tox, laying her cheek against the rough wood. "She sacrificed herself to hunters to give the Holdout time to open the Gate so the rest of us could get inside."

Lisius's voice cracked. "Then she wasn't wasted."

Hot tears flowed down her cheeks, and she trembled, her grip on the beam so tight her arms burned. Outside the fence, grief was part of the flesh-feast when a loved one took the Knife, but hunger dulled the loss. Hunger dulled everything out there. Here, with no need for the flesh-feast, death seemed sharper.

You've become one of the Order more than you thought.

She pulled herself together, gulping at the breeze that carried the tang of the hog barn from three fields away. The smell had been overpowering to her when she'd first arrived, but now it was a familiar sort of comfort—a promise of sustenance. She wiped her eyes against her forearm.

Lisius lowered himself to his belly along the beam so he

could lean close to her, his face long and serious. "I'm sorry you didn't get to share her flesh-feast."

Eily sighed. She had a long way to go to bring him into the Order. "She's with God, now."

"Do you believe in their god?"

She dreaded the question, but every reversion asked it. "With all my heart," she said. Then she lowered her voice to barely above a whisper. "But you do not have to believe. Only comply. They do not honor the flesh-feast. Taking the Knife would be a waste."

The admonition not to waste, so critical to cannibal survival, seemed to reach him, even if her assurances about God did not. He slumped against the beam, arms dangling on either side, knife glinting in one hand. She stretched out a hand, and he gave her the blade.

They carefully descended the ladder, Eily's legs trembling with each downward step. How could going back be so much harder than the climb up had been? She let out a huge sigh as Lisius reached the ground safely next to her. The crowd hung back, allowing her to right her skirts and direct the boy toward the shade tree and the barrel of cool water brought there for the workers. He thrust his chest out, suspenders still dangling at his sides, and strutted, glowering at everyone he passed, even children, who cowered at their mothers' skirts.

But at least he wasn't dead.

Gideon's voice caught her attention as he limped his way through the throng toward her. "Eily! Eily, are you all right?" He still wore his occulus strapped to his blond head, straw hat resting askew above the lens. His beardless face with its hideous crisscrossing of scars looked even paler than usual. "I came as soon as I heard."

"I'm fine." She reached up to relieve her fiancé of the electronic magnifier, taking a small liberty to smooth his tangled curls. He shied away, eyes sliding meaningfully to the attentive crowd as he replaced his hat. Public displays of affection were minimal among the Order, but Gid took the restriction too far. *Because you are an outsider. A Blattvolk. A cannibal.* No, not a cannibal. Not anymore. But the Order—even the New Order—still attached a stigma to anyone not born in the Holdout.

Gid turned his gaze to where Lisius slurped water from the barrel with both hands while the women in charge of the picnic lunch wrung their dark aprons uncomfortably. Edging over to block her view of the boy's posterior peeking above the waistline of his pants, he said, "Eily, why don't you quit now, before you get hurt? You could focus on wedding plans."

She let her head fall back to look at the branches of the walnut tree above them and bit her lip. Always with the wedding. Yes, they were to be married in two weeks, but that didn't mean it had to be her whole world. "Gid—"

"You won't be working anymore once we're married, anyway. What's a couple of weeks?"

Her heart shriveled at the reminder. Married women did not work outside the home. She kept hoping to find a way to be the exception. Cannibal women shared equal roles on the Tox. Why not here?

"Gid, there are no other advocates for reversions here. Even once we are married, I'll be called to help. I might as well get paid for it." The Protectorate gave her a small stipend for the time she spent acclimating the reversions to life in the Holdout. She would have done it anyway, but the income was nice since she didn't own a birthright in the Order's co-op.

To her right, a man cleared his throat, and Eily turned to see Ijon gazing at her with deep-set eyes. As far as Haldanians went, he was okay. He even wore a tunic and short pants in deference to the Order's modesty, unlike the other nearly naked

Haldanian observers. But he still followed Protectorate protocol. "I'll have to take him in," he said.

She stood straighter. "He's in a precarious state of mind right now—"

"The Protectorate has been discussing changing our policy on reversions." He rocked back on his heels, the nuvoplast sandals on his feet squelching against his skin.

Her stomach tightened. "Give Lisius more time to acclimate. He'll be fine."

He held up a hand. "I don't want to argue. The Board's talking about it. I just wanted you to know."

"He's not a danger to anyone but himself, here. Let me do my job. I'll help him figure things out."

Ijon scrubbed his face with both hands. "This was too public. The incident report will come back on me."

She glanced at the small crowd of green-skinned Haldanian tourists watching from the end of the dirt lane, bedecked with beads and baubles that did nothing to hide their nakedness. Haldanians embraced their photosynthesis with a vigor the Order found more than shameful. Eily had no issue with the human body, but although she had photosynthetic skin, she wore the full and modest dress of the Order, right down to the bonnet over her hair. She didn't need to expose her skin to photosynthesize as long as the Order could feed her.

Turning her attention back to Ijon and his aide, she caught sight of Gid watching her, face closed to emotion in front of the Blattvolk. An idea came to her. She locked her gaze with Ijon's. "Are you familiar with the tradition of barn raising?"

He and his aide exchanged a blank look. The Order was closed about its religious practices, and Haldanian sociologists were infatuated with what they considered a primitive belief system. Ijon asked, "Is there a ritual involved in this process?"

"A new barn is an important event. Lisius volunteered to be

part of the roof-raisers, but misunderstood some of the process. The height frightened him, and he could not come down with the others. I'm just glad I got here before he passed out and fell."

"We would be interested in this ritual—"

"You know how secretive the Order is about their practices."

The liaisons again exchanged glances, lips pursed in disapproval. But the agreement the Protectorate had with the Holdout protected religious rights. Ijon tilted his head toward the Haldanian tourists. "What am I supposed to put in my report?"

She grimaced. She hated writing reports. "Why don't you let me write it for you? You'll have final approval, of course. But that way the matter is handled delicately—and you'll get some inside information."

Ijon rolled his eyes. "All right, then."

Chapter Two

The Tox

Jubal brushed his fingertips over a palm-print the color of dried blood: the mark of the Red Hand Tribe. How long had it been since he'd seen that symbol? At least three winters, maybe more. The sign on the rock wall hadn't been there long enough to flake or fade. His chest tightened. *Home.*

The nanny goat next to him bleated and bumped her head against his hip. He clutched one of her short horns to hold her at bay while he squinted toward the opening he'd cut through the wall of amarantox leaves.

"Rann, Pops, Red Hand camped here," Jubal called as his father emerged from the trail onto the sandstone beach. The old man's back hunched even without a pack. Pops refused to ride in the cart, but damned if Jubal would let him carry a load. Behind Pops followed a tether of more goats, top-heavy with items from the Sunset Shore. "Where's Rann?"

"Fighting the wheels." Pops limped to a ledge of stone and

sat, one leg out stiff in front of him. The left side of his mouth drooped in a perpetual grimace, his left hand curled against his thigh. When the pain got too bad, he would take the Knife and feed his family, but Jubal was in no rush to honor his father's flesh-feast, especially on the trail. Pops spoke toward the river. "Give me my pack, and leave the damn cart. Autumn trade will be over before we get there."

Jubal glanced back to the opening. A man in a pack could walk the Tox without much need to clear the trail, but the cart required more room. They'd used a machete to widen the path, lopping the towering amarantox stalks at the base so the cart could pass, and Jubal's hands were sticky with the milky sap. All that work, and the goats wouldn't even touch the stuff. He tied the nanny close to a stand of bulrushes she could nibble and lowered his pack. "I'll go help."

As he slipped back down the tunnel-like trail, the metal shards suspended from his trader's staff jangled in rhythm to his footsteps, the discordant melody an announcement of Peace. He was not prey. Traders were not sacred like the Knowing, but as long as they paid the tolls, they were off limits to hunt. The only ones who didn't honor the Peace were the Flame Runnas, green men who shot fire from the sky.

He found the cart canted to one side while the attached goats contentedly chewed cud. "Rann?"

Rann's unshaven face popped up from behind the mound of goods, and he wiped his mouth with the back of his hand. "Figured you might miss me eventually. Drink?"

He held out some bitters they'd traded for with the Rice Tribes. The bota looked half empty.

"What did I tell you about using the inventory?" Jubal had been hoarding goods so Pops could buy a place among family at the Red Hand, so he could live without fear of the Knife until he was ready, hopefully a long time from now. But keeping Rann out of the potent drink was like keeping the sun from rising.

Jubal examined the tilted cart. Other than the half empty bota, the rest of the cargo looked intact. Blocks of salt from the Great Salt Sea. Shell necklaces from the Sunset Shore. Red clay pots from the high country tribes to the south. They were wealthy men.

Together, the brothers freed the wagon and helped the goats pull the load toward the river. As they emerged on the bank, the old man got to his feet, the ornaments on his staff clattering. "Might make the Taguan by nightfall if the wheels don't get stuck again."

Rann groaned and dropped to his knees at the edge of the water to slosh it over his hair and face. He shrugged out of his pack. "We need a break."

Pops worked his mouth in that way that meant trouble. He'd made this run for decades, moving from nomadic tribe to nomadic tribe with an unerring sense of season and migration. "You want to miss the trade? The Red Hand could be packing to leave right now."

Rann reshouldered his load and rose, dripping water and grumbling. This time Jubal kept a close eye on the cart, helping it over rocks and debris littering the river trail. The sun hovered low when the path opened onto a long beach where children chased each other, screaming. Adults sat and worked in the shade on either side of a cave opening in the cliff.

"The Taguan." Rann let out a relieved breath behind him.

As they approached, children gathered around them, chattering with excitement. Parents raised their heads and stopped their chores to greet the newcomers. The stench of garbage, sewage, and other odors of human living made Jubal wrinkle his nose, but he covered it with his trader smile.

"Jubal!" A familiar voice rose out of the crowd, and a petite woman pushed forward, a young child on her hip.

"Rodi!" he exclaimed, bending for a hug.

"Uncle Nido! Rann!" She greeted Pops and Rann in turn.

"We're glad to find the Red Hand still here. Where's Adrul?" Pops's gaze sifted through the crowd.

Her lips pressed into a line. "We celebrated his flesh-feast two autumns ago after he was killed in a Flame Runna attack. Everyone at the Taguan has suffered. Red Hand got swallowed up with Long Branch, One Eye, and many other tribes."

Rann put a hand on her shoulder. "I'm sorry, Rodi. I liked him."

She patted Rann's arm and smiled. "We all go to the Mother eventually."

Jubal tickled her child under the chin, eliciting a giggle. "He looks just like Adrul."

The boy leaned out of balance, trying to reach Jubal's necklaces, so Jubal took him. The little one put the end of the necklace into his mouth and looked up at Jubal with sleepy, dark eyes.

Rodi put her weight on one leg, cocked a hand on her hip, and looked around pointedly. "Why no woman yet, little cousin? Seems a man who takes to children like you do is bound to attract a wife."

Jubal shook his head, his gaze sliding toward Pops. *Was he breathing too hard?* "I don't need some woman using up my goods."

She shook her head. "Stingy as ever. Come on, then. You can all stay at my fire."

"What're you cooking?"

"Whatever you brought me." She grinned and turned on her heel.

Inside the Taguan, Jubal paused behind Pops to allow his

vision to adjust. Haphazard walls of loose stone marked a corridor to the back of the cave. The sides of the wall were broken in places, leading to small living areas or to halls with more openings. The last time he'd been here, the cave had only had boundary stones around each hearth.

"Who constructed these walls?" he asked. The child squirmed from his grip and ran to his mother.

"Things have changed," Rodi said, lifting the child back to her hip. "Keep your head down, and I'll tell you over the fire."

After about a hundred paces, the main hall ended, and the area opened into a high-ceilinged room illuminated by a central fire. Smoke hazed the air despite the hole in the ceiling where the first evening stars peeked through. Against the far wall stood two wooden cages. A natural opening in the rock led to another section of the cave. Between mounds of bedding, the floor swarmed with people preparing food. Many of the men had piercings, and Jubal's skin tingled at the thought of being surrounded by so many proclaimed hunters. Rodi skirted through the crowd like she was avoiding them in a game of tag.

Jubal slowed behind Pops, who limped slightly but kept his shoulders back and head high. He was one of the oldest traders still doing business, and people greeted him as he passed. *Pops will do well here if I can convince him to stay.*

Nearest the fire, on a natural rise in the stone floor, a bald man marked with the ritual raised scars of a healer sat on a tamarisk-branch throne. Chin high, he gazed out over the crowd like a father at his child's naming day. Beside him reclined a dark-haired woman adorned in nothing but layers upon layers of beads. The man turned his face toward the newcomers as they wove through the milling people.

"Visitors! Let us welcome you with a kiss, Cousins."

Every eye turned toward the bald man, and a hush fell over the crowd. The woman on the dais rose. Light from the fire painted her body a deep brown, and Jubal caught the subtle swelling of her stomach beneath the beads. She sauntered over and stopped before the traders.

Away from the firelight, her skin was as green as freshly budded amarantox. Jubal's mouth fell open, and he fell back half a step before regaining his poise. "A Flame Runna?"

She kissed Pops's mouth while he stood rigid, then moved to Jubal. Jubal darted a glance at Pops, relying on his father's greater experience. Pops hadn't objected, so Jubal allowed her to put a hand behind his neck and rise on her toes to bring her face to his. He didn't recoil as her tongue drew a line between his lips, but he sucked in a startled breath. She smelled like fresh rain among the needle trees that grew in the high country. A twirl of dizziness swept over him, as though he had stood up too fast. He trembled. It had been a long while since he'd been with a woman, and his groin stirred in response.

She pulled away to give her attention to Rann, leaving Jubal swallowing and blinking to clear his vision.

Rann groaned softly, hands sliding from her pregnant belly as she sashayed backward and returned to the dais.

"What was that?" Rann moved forward eagerly, his attention never leaving the Flame Runna as her beads swayed against her legs like wind through the amarantox.

"This is the power of the One Tree. Spirit healing. I'm called Sefe, creator of the One Tree. Some call me King." Several nearby pierced men cheered, and Sefe waved them down. "It's my honor to protect the Taguan. Come, sit." Sefe pointed to some mats near his chair.

Jubal looked to Rodi, but she didn't meet his eyes. Rann was already in pursuit of the woman, with Pops close behind.

"You'd better go." Rodi's mouth barely moved, and she turned without another word, carrying her son from the cavern.

Jubal lifted his chin and strode to where Rann and Pops had already lowered themselves to the cattail mats.

Pops sat straight, his gaze on the bald man, but Rann's eyes roved the Flame Runna woman without any attempt at subtlety. Once Jubal had settled in, Pops spoke. "Tell us how you came to own a Flame Runna."

"Not one. Two." The man swung an arm to indicate the cages at the back of the cavern. One appeared empty, but the other contained a mound of bedding. "And we'll have more. I brought the tribes together, many branches of the One Tree. I recognize you." He nodded to Pops. "You're Red Hand? You are part of the tree, and welcome here."

A woman set a woven platter before the King—flat, gray cakes piled high and steaming amidst a circle of roasted cattail roots. The King gestured to his guests to help themselves. "Meal cakes from the manna beetles. You've heard of them? They grow with great abundance among the amarantox here. We haven't had to declare a Hunger in four winters."

Jubal took a cake and sampled the familiar sweet flavor reminiscent of fresh-caught trout.

"Four winters is long between Hungers." Pops pulled the bota off Rann's shoulder and offered it. "We bring a taste of bitters from the Rice Tribes to the south."

Sefe set the bota aside without tasting. His dark eyes danced with the light of the fire as he stroked the back of his hand along the Flame Runna's shoulder to her elbow. "This is Ana. She was born of the tribes." His hand came to rest upon her rounded abdomen. "Her skin is green, but Ana is not a Flame Runna. The Spirits freed her from them so she could show me the way. You felt the power of her kiss?"

Jubal nodded along with his brother and father.

"All Flame Runnas have the gift of spirit healing," Sefe said.

Ana looked away, her hands tightening into fists.

Sefe glanced at her and laughed. "Do not fret, my Ana." He returned his gaze to Pops. "And have you heard of the Blood-Eye men in their mountain cave?"

"I have traded with the Blood-Eye. Fosselites, they call themselves," Pops said. Jubal had gone there once at the beginning of his apprenticeship, helping Pops carry goods into the dark tunnel with the huge door. The man inside had indeed had eyes of blood, and the small bottles of medicine he gave them had traded for much with the tribes in the west.

Sefe nodded and lifted a metal tube that gleamed in the firelight. "They provide us weapons—guns—to make the flying craft fall from the sky. These guns shoot farther and faster than any spear or arrow. The problem is, when the Flame Runna craft hit the earth, the Flame Runnas die. We've brought down two flyers, and the flesh-feast was glorious. I would show you the power of the weapon, but it would collapse the Taguan upon our heads."

Several people nearby laughed, nodding forcefully.

"All the Blood-Eye want in return are a few prisoners from the Flame Runnas. Yet we've only captured one alive." Sefe gestured to the cages, and one of the men prodded the pile of mats and blankets inside until a figure emerged. A pitiful green woman backed up to the wall, unable to escape the poking. The guard leered at her and she spit at him.

Pops shook his head. "We don't deal in slaves."

Rann laughed around a mouthful of food. "I'd keep her for myself."

The king gave Rann only a glance, then directed his words toward Pops. "I don't need you to trade. To the east, there's a place surrounded by a lightning wall. The people inside look like us but don't fight like we do. Their wall keeps them apart from us."

Pops nodded. "I've traded there, many years ago. They ask for salt and for metal parts from the Before."

"Flame Runnas now live there among them. Flying machines can be seen coming and going from inside. One with a trader's staff would be granted access. Might take some men inside with him. We could capture many."

Jubal stared at Sefe, trader smile forgotten. "You think the Flame Runnas will honor the trader's staff?"

"Another trader who came through here has been inside."

Pops worked his mouth. Jubal kept silent. Pops could handle this so-called king. "We don't take part in wars between the tribes. It's bad for business. We honor trader law."

Sefe rose, casting a huge shadow on the rock wall behind him. "This is no war between the tribes. Flame Runnas are monsters, not men, and they must be rubbed from the earth if the tribes ever hope to find peace. Even Ana wants her revenge for what they did to her."

Jubal sneaked a glance at the green woman, but her face remained placid. The one in the cage sat with her back to the wall, bruised knees drawn up against her chest, and glared in their direction.

Pops brushed his hands together, as if the matter was over. "Our route takes us south, where the Marsh Tribes await our return."

"You're Red Hand. Your people are in danger."

"We're traders. Of the Red Hand no more. We wish the One Tree prosperity." Although they had barely touched the offered food, he clambered to his feet. "Forgive us, we have a long day of trade tomorrow. Thank you for your food."

The few bites Jubal had eaten churned in his stomach. Trade would likely not go well tomorrow. *And it might be impossible to settle Pops here after that interaction.* The next trade stop was half a moon away. An unrelated tribe would ask for more goods to keep an old man, plus once Jubal and Rann moved on, there would be no blood relation to advocate for him.

Jubal hurried after his father, smiling automatically at the people he passed. Rann caught up to him in the corridor. "We should talk to Pops about this. I mean, that kiss... bet Sefe'd have offered us a night with one of those Flame Runnas if we agreed to help him."

Jubal kept walking. "Is that all you think about?"

"It might be a good trade!"

"Traders can't get involved in wars. Even if we get through the lightning wall, there's no guarantee we could figure out how to get Sefe and his men past."

"All I'm saying is that we should agree to try."

They emerged from the darkness of the Taguan into the star-filled night, and Jubal rounded on his brother. "Try and what? Get ourselves burned to crackles, our bodies wasted on the Tox? The Flame Runnas have never traded with the tribes. And we have bigger things to consider. What about Pops?"

"Pops has traded with the people behind the lightning wall."

Jubal found himself chewing his lips the way Pops did. "Rann, you're an idiot." He stalked back toward the river camp.

Rann's voice echoed behind him. "You're just like Pops—too wrapped up in the rules."

Chapter Three

Jubal unrolled his sleeping mat next to the tents where their goods were stored. Tonight, Rann and Pops would sleep at Rodi's hearth. Well, Pops would—Rann could hardly stop talking about his time in the main cavern, gambling with Sefe's men and spending his earnings on time with the captive Flame Runna.

"There are plenty of willing women, Rann. Why do you want time with a Flame Runna?"

"It's not just the sexing, Jubal. The best bitters can't compare with the feeling. Come with me."

Jubal shook his head. "A waste of trade shares."

"What good are shares if you refuse to spend them?"

Jubal stretched out on his sleeping mat and looked up at the stars. The cool night air felt good after a long day of trade in the sun. "I don't plan on finding myself short one day when we run into hunters on the Tox."

"You own enough to pay tolls for the next two years even if you never make another trade."

For a heartbeat, Jubal considered. It had been a long time

since he and Rann had let loose together. But then he thought of his father. "What if Pops gets sick again and needs a place to stay? If we have to seek protection for a season and not fear the Knife?"

Rann's eyes glittered in the silver moonlight. "One kiss from this Flame Runna, and you won't care about the Knife. I'll treat you tonight. You'll see. Her kisses are like nothing you've ever experienced."

"No." Jubal crooked his arm over his eyes to hide his brother from his sight. "Do as you please. Just don't come running to me when you need a toll on the Tox."

When he looked again, Rann was gone. Half full of regret, Jubal rose and paced around the camp, checking the tents where they had stored their goods, reassuring the goats as they lay chewing their cuds, gazing across the moon's reflection on the river. Tomorrow they would pack up and be on their way, away from the Flame Runnas and their magical appeal. Things could go back to normal.

He lay down and closed his eyes, ears attuned to the gentle rustling of contented animals as he dozed.

A sound like a rock exploding in a campfire, only louder, drove him to his feet. At the edge of the water, the goats stood in a clump at the end of their tethers, bleating in confusion. From the other direction, toward the Taguan, shouts echoed off the rocks. Someone cried out for a Healer. He left the goats behind, terrified Pops had fallen again, but Pops met him partway, leaning on his staff, his breath heaving.

"Jubal, bring the goats. Now." His mouth twitched as he lumbered in an arc to return to the Taguan.

"Pops?"

"Now!" Pops didn't even look over his shoulder. When he made a demand like that, he meant business, and his instincts were never wrong.

Jubal sprinted back to camp and gathered the goats' tethers in both hands, urging the reluctant animals to follow him. The youngest skipped into the air, bouncing over her neighbor and tangling the line so Jubal had to halt and reorganize. He glanced at the tents of goods and scanned the immediate area for thieves. The items would likely be safe. Pops needed him.

Leading the line, Jubal arrived at the rocky ledge before the entrance of the Taguan to find what seemed to be the entire population of the One Tree amassed and angry. Many carried torches, and a handful held the Fosselite weapons. When the warriors saw him, they pointed the guns in his direction. Jubal's breath caught, but he pressed on. In a wave, the crowd stepped aside. Jubal did not want to enter that mass of people. He longed for the protection of his trader staff, but he'd left it propped against one of the tents. *Pops is in there.* Attempting a smile, he led the goats into the throng.

"You owe us a Flame Runna," one gunman growled in his face as he passed.

At the center of the crowd, Rann hung from his arms and legs on a tamarisk pole, each end supported on the shoulders of one of Sefe's warriors. Jubal's stomach lurched. His brother's hind end dangled nearly to the dusty earth without making contact. Blood dripped onto the rock, painting the surface red like the mark of the Red Hand.

But this was not the Red Hand.

And even if it was, Rann, Jubal, and Pops were no longer part of the tribe. They had only trader amnesty here, which could easily be broken.

Pops knelt at the feet of the king. Sefe leaned on his spear as if it were a walking stick.

"King of the One Tree, I beg you. My son had nothing to do with this."

"He was the last to enter her cage."

Jubal marched toward them, the goats following so close that their tethers threatened to trip him. "What did he do?"

Sefe raised his gaze from Pops and took a moment to look Jubal over. "Our captive Flame Runna has disappeared. Your brother helped her escape."

Glancing at Rann, Jubal fought the fluttering panic in his chest. "Why would my brother do that? There is no profit in letting her go."

Sefe scowled. "She did not free herself."

Pops remained on his knees. "Sefe, let us pay his toll, and we will be gone. These goats are more of a flesh-feast than three Flame Runnas. Take them. Let us pass in peace."

"My warriors are searching for her trail. No one goes anywhere until we find her."

As if on command, warriors swept in from the crowd and pulled Pops to his feet, yanked the goats from Jubal's hands, and prodded both men to enter the Taguan. Jubal and Pops were shoved into an empty cage in the main room, and Rann was dropped, still trussed, on the floor outside the bars.

Jubal paced the tiny confines of the cage. A crack of sunlight crept across the cavern floor from a hole in the ceiling as the sun rose. Outside the cage, people ate, napped, came and went. The crack of sunlight slid slowly toward the opposite wall. Rann woke and moaned in pain. Pops and Jubal begged to tend him, but Sefe refused to loose his bonds or allow the traders out of confinement. Instead, the Flame Runna called Ana got to her knees and kissed Rann. He relaxed into slumber.

When she rose, she looked to the cage and said, "I'm sorry you'll lose your brother."

Groups of men came and went, reporting to Sefe, and the king's scowl deepened. The cave grew darker, and someone stirred the central fire to life. The main cavern overflowed with people, and the walls echoed with murmurs.

Finally, Sefe rose on his dais and shouted above the noise. "There is no sign of the Flame Runna." He stepped down, and the crowd cleared a path as he advanced toward the cage. He stopped several paces from Rann and pointed the butt of his spear at him. "This man came under the Peace of a Trader's Staff. Then he stole from us. The punishment must be the Knife."

The crowd roared.

Pops pulled himself up to the bars, his voice stronger than Jubal had heard in a long time. "We owe you a Flame Runna. Give us a chance to replace it."

Sefe raised a hand in dismissal. "All you own cannot replace what we have lost."

"We will get you another Flame Runna."

Jubal grabbed his father's bicep and hissed in his ear. "Pops, what are you saying?"

Ignoring him, Pops shouted again. "We can get past the lightning wall."

Sefe roared for the crowd to hush and stalked over to stand nose to nose with the older man. Jubal's heart threatened to jump from his chest. With the flickering light of the central fire behind him, Sefe looked like an avenging spirit. "You will take my men inside?"

Pops shook his head. "Traders travel alone unless they are slavers, and the people of the lightning wall do not trade in slaves. But we can bring you a new Flame Runna."

"Why should I trust you to come back?" Sefe crossed his arms.

"My sons will go. I will remain."

"Pops, no!"

"Hush! He's your brother." Pops's gaze never wavered from the king.

The cave rang with arguments among the people gathered.

Sefe crossed his arms. "You are close to the Knife already, old man. You might die before your sons return."

"They will bring you two Flame Runnas."

Jubal remained stiff, his throat tight with repressed arguments. Slaves? Pops always refused to deal in human life.

The king rubbed his chin but said nothing.

Pops added, "If I die, you keep the goats. It's a gamble, but at least you won't lose everything. And my sons will travel much faster without me."

"Pops," Jubal hissed, unable to restrain himself. "We can't trade behind the lightning wall without you."

The glance Pops gave him told Jubal all he needed to know. Pops didn't intend for them to travel to the lightning wall. He wanted them to take their goods and flee.

Sefe swung his gaze toward Jubal. "I will attempt to keep him alive until you return. Be back within a moon or never show yourselves among the One Tree again."

Jubal gritted his teeth, his attention still on Pops. "I won't sacrifice you because of Rann's careless choices."

"I cannot avoid the Knife forever. Would you travel the Tox alone?"

Jubal had considered many times what would happen when Pops died, always shying away from the final conclusion. Rann kept himself in check largely because of Pops's firm hand. Once their father was gone, there was no telling what he might do. "I won't leave you here."

Pops squinted at his son, jaw thrust forward as he worked his lips over his teeth. "He's your brother."

The king placed his fists on his hips. "It seems keeping the old man is the wise choice." He twitched his head and two warriors opened the cage. When Jubal didn't move, one of them grabbed his arm and jerked him toward the door.

Jubal struggled against the warrior, but the second man took his other arm. Sefe shut the cage door.

"Pops... don't do this, Pops."

Pops's mouth spasmed, his eyes glistening in the firelight. "Take care of your brother, Jubal."

Rann could barely walk, let alone help pull the cart or carry goods. The weapon called a gun had created a hole straight through the muscle of his thigh, like a spear.

"Why were you trying to run?"

"You'd have run, too, if the warriors had accused you of stealing."

"Too drunk to realize you'd freed her."

Rann scowled and shook his head. "Everyone was drunk. It wasn't me."

Jubal rolled his eyes and sneered, but didn't argue. They had to pack up and leave, and because of his wound, Rann was no help. He sat propped against a rock, sipping bitters to numb the pain while Jubal picked through what they would leave behind, trying to decide if there might be a way to tuck one more thing into his pack.

He could pull the cart himself, with a lot of effort, but had opted to leave it behind in favor of speed. Pops might not have intended them to fulfill his bargain, but there was no way Jubal would leave him here.

Rodi circled the cart, jostling her son on one hip, a frown cut deep into her face. Goods formed lumps beneath the hide tent Jubal had tied over the cart. He'd also taken time to cache other, more valuable merchandise in various places to await his return. But Rodi only knew about the cart. He hoped it might serve as a decoy to would-be thieves while he was gone.

"I'll do my best to keep it safe, Jubal. But I can't promise."

"Take what you need to pay for guards. The boys love the plums. I know this takes you away from the manna harvest, so if you need to take a few things to trade, go ahead. Or if Pops needs anything. These goods are his." He looked into her worried eyes. "Take care of him."

She swallowed and looked at the ground.

"I'll be back within a moon. I promise." Jubal nudged Rann with his foot. "Let's go."

Rann opened one eye—the other was swollen shut—and sighed. But he struggled to his feet without complaint. Jubal helped him into his pack. Rann wobbled under the weight, leaning hard on his staff.

Jubal fought the hollow helplessness spreading in his chest. How were they going to acquire Flame Runna slaves? It was hard enough to take regular slaves. But he knew he had to try.

Rann steadied himself and took another deep swallow of bitters, then corked the bota. He lifted it to shoulder height before dropping it with a gurgling slap against the hard earth of camp. "For Pops."

Then he turned to limp down the path.

Inside Jubal's hollowness sprouted a seed of hope.

Chapter Four

Haldanian Protectorate
Med Ops

Councilman Rael paused at the top of the stairs to allow his eyes to adjust to the florescent lighting below the Leibert Building. Up top, noontime sun flooded the halls and offices, but down here, the only light for photosynthesis came from pools of fiber-optic light installed in each office. The smell of antiseptic and the sweat of caged cannibals floated down the long hallway, but he veered into a conversion lab before reaching the large concrete room at the end.

A gaunt woman rested in an autosurgeon chair, her green body covered with a thin blanket. Tubes and wires connected her to the telomerase drip, and her bloodless lips were stretched thin in a rictus of endured pain. A tech sat in front of a computer at the other end of the room. He looked up as Rael entered.

Rael nodded grimly in greeting. "Is she well enough to talk?"

The tech shrugged, eyes narrow with worry. "I can wake her, but she's in a lot of pain. She's been overwhelmed by UV exposure. We're trying to augment her liver function. Her kidneys are at ten percent, but I'm not sure the damage is repairable."

Although Rael hated to make the woman suffer, the pilot was the only survivor of the latest duster crash. *The only survivor of any of the crashes.* "Do it."

The tech rose and tapped some commands onto the autosurgeon console. "Sir, she's been mumbling about cannibals. Are the rumors true?"

Two weeks ago, a garbled distress call had sent speculation about cannibal attacks through burn-operative ranks, forcing the Board to clamp down on the information before panic spread citywide. Quite a few operatives refused to fly until the situation was resolved, and the Board had placed them on "extended leave for alkaloid recovery," hoping to blame the paranoia on UV overload. But the rumors still spread. Rael crossed his arms and asked, "What's your clearance?"

Swallowing, the tech straightened. "Sir. Beta one. It won't leave this room."

"See that it doesn't."

The poor woman shuddered and opened her eyes. Her pupils were so dilated, the irises looked black. The muscles of her face twitched, and the blanket trembled as her body fought the chemicals coursing through her.

Rael pulled up a stool and leaned close her. "Hello, Uma. I'm Councilman Rael. I'm sorry to wake you, but we need answers." He resisted saying, *before you die.*

She didn't speak, just nodded.

"I understand cannibals held you prisoner."

Again Uma nodded, closing her eyes as a tremor shook her.

He reached out to take her hand, then thought better of it. Physical contact during an overdose could be painful. "Are you the only survivor?"

"A reversion is with them. O-one who escaped the Fosselites."

Rael pinched the bridge of his nose. *Great.* They'd believed all those escaped prisoners had been accounted for. News of one successfully living in the Reaches would cause a new upsurge of reversions. But he couldn't think about that now; he had to take this one problem at a time. "What caused your duster to malfunction?"

"N-no malfunction. Th-they've got guns."

"Surely not guns." Spears, he'd believe. Maybe bows and arrows. A metallic arrowhead fired directly into one of the mag-lifters could cause a malfunction. Bullets were beyond cannibal technology.

"I saw the weapons."

Rael's skin turned cold. Had the cannibals found an old weapons cache? The Protectorate had discovered a few ancient military sites during exploration of the Reaches—nothing worth salvaging. Even so, how could the mongrels know how to use them?

In an attempt to assuage both her and the listening tech, he said, "We can handle a few guns. Cannibals are nomads. Their savage lifestyle keeps them from banding together."

"They—" her voice choked as she spasmed in pain.

The tech glanced at the numbers on the autosurgeon console. "I'm not sure how much more she can take."

Rael gritted his teeth but nodded, wishing he'd been able to learn more. Maybe he could have some analysts backtrack Uma's route and deploy scouts with heat sensors on a high-altitude scan. He'd have to talk with Panone at Burn Operations about new shielding for the patrol dusters. Until then, they'd need to curtail all sweeps beyond the Burn. He began making a mental checklist as he rose to go.

As he stood, Uma whispered, "They're trading with the Fosselites."

He froze halfway off the stool, unsure he'd heard correctly. The tech whirled to stare at her, his back against the console.

Rael lowered himself back onto the seat. *How are the cannibals even aware of the Fosselites?* The scientists never came out of their underground complex; the longevity treatments that had allowed them to live for centuries also caused severe skin photosensitivity. The Protectorate had always traveled to them to trade. Six years ago, when it was discovered that the Fosselites had been harvesting escaped reversions for anti-dementia chemicals, the Protectorate had cut off all interactions. Rael and the rest of the Board had assumed the citizens of the Protectorate were safe. No more converts—reversions or otherwise—could be harvested by those monsters.

But the Fosselites had found another way. They had savages hunting Protectorate citizens. He caught the tech's wide-eyed stare.

"This cannot leave this room," Rael said. "You understand?"

The tech bit his lip and, after a moment, nodded.

He can't be trusted. No one could be trusted.

It was time to go on the offensive.

The Holdout

Eily glanced over the vehicle as Gid slammed the hood. The mini looked nothing like the sleek, gleaming dusters of the

Protectorate. In addition to lifters, it had huge tractor wheels. Welded seams connected the panels with warty lines, the metal darker there from the heat of the torch. Inside, a panel of toggles and gauges faced the driver's seat. A plate of transparent nuvoplast across the front protected the operator from the elements, while a roll bar over the pilot seat gave the canopy an ugly, boxy shape. After the combine accident had given Gid a permanent limp, he favored safety over aesthetics.

"All set." Gid rubbed his dirty palms on the front of his trousers. The scars on his hands mimicked the weld lines on the mini duster.

"We'll stay close to the ground?"

He dropped his shoulders and cocked his head at her in exasperation.

Her heart pounded fiercely. "At least a kiss for luck?"

His gaze lifted to the surrounding field. "Someone may see."

"There's no one here. And we're to be married soon. What's the harm?" Her chest ached as he shook his head and turned back to the mini to climb inside. They'd agreed to marry for practical reasons; his scars repulsed the girls at the Holdout, and her green skin kept suitors away. Every time she saw other couples sneaking glances or discreet touches, she longed for the same. But that wasn't his nature. She accepted that. She planned to lavish all her affection upon their children once they started a family.

She took a breath and climbed in the opposite door. He fastened her seat harness and then his own before he engaged the engine. Although smaller than a Protectorate duster, the mini was nowhere near as silent. It rumbled like a tractor. Gid grinned at her, giving her a thumbs up. He wanted to finish testing before the wedding next week. Eily nodded at him, clutching her apron against her thighs.

He pulled back the throttle, and her stomach lurched. The

mini wobbled alarmingly as they rose higher than the lights along the electric fence. She craned her neck to look at the ground. Bits of debris kicked out below them. In the grass where the mini had taken off, only a dark circle of bare soil remained, and the scent of crushed plants blasted toward her. Gid wouldn't be pleased about the damage to the pasture. His intent was to use the mini in field applications, but it was worthless if it shredded crops to bits.

The machine dipped sideways, and she cringed until he regained control and circled the field. He turned to look at her, smile as wide as the sky. "Hold on!"

He tapped the throttle and the mini shot forward. Air surged through the cab and caught her bonnet. The white scrap of fabric whipped out the side window. "Oh! My bonnet!"

His face creased with apology, then brightened. "I need to test the landing, anyway."

The world dropped out from under her, leaving her stomach behind as he sloped the vehicle into a rapid descent. A squeal escaped her lips. "Giiiiiid!"

The barren soil of the small Burn surrounding the Holdout approached with terrifying speed. Gid's fingers danced over the controls, and the mini bounced against the ground, huge wheels rumbling as they rolled to a stop. Dust choked the air. He cut the engine and disengaged his harness. "Your bonnet landed just over there."

He exited the cab and limped across the desiccated ground. Eily clutched her skirt, heart racing from the ride. And something more. *We're outside the fence.*

She hadn't been outside the fence since she'd arrived. Since Ana had been taken. She darted a look around, senses she'd long forgotten coming alive. The whisper of the breeze, the scent of dust, even the way the shadows fell across the rocky ground jabbed at her awareness. The urge to unbuckle her harness tugged at her, but she resisted. *He'll be back in a moment, and we'll be in the air again, out of range.*

She waited. And waited. Craning her neck to the rear, she spotted Gid circling behind the mini, eyes to the ground. If he needed to run, his limp would slow him down. He didn't belong out here. *He's not even aware of how exposed we are.* With a flourish, he swept something from the ground, raising a hand high with its prize. Eily heaved a sigh of relief as he limped back to the cab and took his seat.

"Your bonnet, milady. And I shall raise the windows."

She forced a smile and took the dusty headpiece. "My hero."

He strapped himself back in and pushed the starter.

Nothing happened.

He frowned and pressed the ignition again.

"What's wrong?"

He shook his head and unbuckled before reaching into the back to retrieve his toolbox. "Probably something's come loose."

"Gid, we're totally exposed out here."

"I know. I'll have us running again in no time." He climbed out and raised the hood, blocking her view of the horizon.

This time she let her instincts take over. Yanking the seatbelt off, she scoured the cab for some sort of weapon. But of course there would be nothing. The Order believed violence —even in self-defense—was a sin. She hopped out of the cab and scurried to where Gid had his head buried in the engine compartment. His toolbox sat on the ground, open. She bent and picked up a large crescent wrench.

Placing her back toward Gid and widening her stance, she surveyed the horizon. Waves of ghost-like heat rose from the hard, pale soil of the Burn. The amarantox was only a hundred paces away. Her stomach churned with memories of her past. Of her flight to this place. Of her loss.

She began murmuring the Lord's Prayer as she watched the horizon. "And deliver us from evil, and deliver us from evil, and deliver us from evil..."

Chapter Five

The Burn
Outside the Holdout Compound

From beneath the protection of the towering amarantox, Jubal gazed across a stretch of open land at the hazy line of what had to be the lightning wall.

Rann held a broad leaf aside with one hand. "I don't remember Pops talking about all this open space between the Tox and the wall."

"Flame Runnas've been burning." Jubal pointed to where new growth sprouted amidst fire-blackened amarantox stalks at the transition.

Taking a small step backward into the concealing foliage, Rann huffed out a breath. "We can't do this. Pops wouldn't want us to do this."

Jubal whirled to face his brother. "You're the reason we're here, Rann. We have to do this. You owe Pops."

"I told you, I didn't free that Flame Runna."

"Maybe not on purpose, but your drunkenness caused

all this. Now come on." Jubal readjusted his pack and took a firm step onto the hardpan, belying the terror of his thundering heart. Without the surrounding amarantox leaves, his skin crawled as if a thousand eyes focused on him. Heat from the cracked red soil pierced through the hard leather of his traveling sandals. He plunked his trader staff against the earth, rattling it with each step, wondering if Flame Runnas even knew what such a symbol meant. The clattering metal of Rann's staff sounded behind him.

Halfway across the expanse, a strange noise, like the rapid pounding of a woman's grinding stone, caught Jubal's attention. A flash of metal in the sky drew his gaze, and he stumbled to a halt.

Rann croaked, "Flame Runnas."

Jubal's legs turned weak. They would never make the edge of the Tox in time. He dropped to the ground, the dusty bulk of his pack hopefully concealing him. Rann sprawled directly beside him. The flying machine dipped and wobbled in the air, then sped toward them, the rapid beating sound growing louder. As the craft passed nearby, it wobbled again and dove for the ground. It contacted the surface and rolled like a runaway wagon, kicking up a cloud of dust before coming to a stop a few hundred paces away.

"I thought flying machines were supposed to be silent?" Rann whispered.

Jubal squinted across the sun-drenched space. He thought so, too. But then, he'd never been through a Flame Runna attack. "Just watch."

A man's figure emerged from the craft. He limped in a meandering loop behind the wagon, then bent and lifted a fluttering white cloth from the ground. He thrust it into the air as he hobbled back to the flying machine and disappeared inside. A few moments later, he reappeared, and a woman joined him at the front of the vehicle.

Two Flame Runnas, one wounded, or at least limping. Jubal looked at Rann. Perspiration carved rivulets down his brother's dusty face. Jubal's pulse thundered in his ears. He covered his nose and mouth with one hand, attempting to filter out the dust choking his lungs. What if more Flame Runnas arrived to help? He squinted toward the sky.

Rann clambered to his feet. "Maybe we can take these two before help arrives."

Jubal thrust out an arm to stop him, but Rann had already paced forward. By the Knife, Rann was determined to get them both killed. *Keep up trader appearances before you're caught skulking.* He scrambled to his feet and loped to his brother's side. No going back now. He hoped they could get these two back to the cover of the Tox before help arrived.

"Gid. Men are coming." Eily kept her voice level and chose the word *men* rather than cannibals. If Gid was close to finishing, they had time to board and get airborne before the two figures approaching from the amarantox reached them.

"What?" Gid raised his head so quickly he slammed it against the mini's hood. "Ow!"

Eily's fingers hurt from gripping the wrench. She took a shuddering breath, longing for the protection of Haldanian guns. Some of the Order owned guns for hunting. She could have brought Samuel's gopher gun, but she'd never dreamed they'd find themselves outside the compound.

Over her thundering pulse, the tinkle of metal and bone reached her. Where had she heard that sound before? She backed up a step.

"Are those cannibals?" Gid whispered.

She nodded, unable to speak. She felt the pressure of his gaze as he looked at the wrench she held upright beside her.

He put a calloused hand on her arm, attempting to lower the weapon. "Eily, you mustn't. I'll talk to them."

She fought the pressure of his hand as she spared him a sharp glance. "We can't let them take us."

"If it's Gotte's Wille—"

"Don't give me that! God didn't force us to cross the fence. You have no idea what's in store."

The jangle of metal sounded again, purposeful and rhythmic. Eily squinted at the approaching figures. Sunlight winked off shards suspended at the top of two tall staves. The music of a trader's staff. The air lightened, and she began to laugh. "Traders!"

Gid took the opportunity to remove the wrench from her grip. "Let me talk to them. Get in the mini."

"Gid, you don't speak Cannibal." He barely spoke Haldanian, and it was akin to the Cannibal dialect.

"It's not proper for you to speak to them. Now go, woman." The thin line of his mouth told her she'd better obey.

She took her seat, but left the door open so she could hear. Women in the Holdout did not speak to the salt trader when he visited. They barely spoke to Protectorate tourists inside the compound. *A good wife obeys her husband.* She folded her hands in her lap and squinted through the dust-covered windshield at the blurry images outside.

Gid placed the wrench back in the toolbox, then straightened his spine to face the oncoming men.

One of the men called, "Keep the Peace!"

Excitement thrilled up Eily's spine as she recalled trade days with her tribe. She'd only been a girl, but those words meant small treats and new stories.

When Gid didn't respond in kind, the men slowed to a near halt. Eily leaned out the door and shouted, "Gid, repeat the greeting. Raise your hands, palms out."

"Geep de Peace." Gid raised his hands. With all her willpower, she pulled herself back into the mini, but not before catching a glimpse of sun-browned torsos and hair worn in traditional bone beads.

The sound of the staves filled the air as the men continued forward. The taller of the two gestured at Gid and tilted his head. In spite of the language barrier, they seemed to come to an agreement, and Gid walked back to her open door. "Can you steer? They'll help me push."

Eily nodded and slid across the bench to Gid's control panel. He shut the door and retreated to the back of the vehicle. The carriage dipped as the traders loaded their packs onto the back bed. She swallowed and looked at the steering wheel. She knew how to ride a bicycle or guide a horse team, but driving the mini daunted her.

"Release the brake!"

She found the brake lever and popped it loose. The mini began to move.

Jubal strained against the grounded flying machine, Rann on one side and the man on the other. The dust on the glass prevented him from getting a good look inside, but he could tell the woman was green. *One Flame Runna.* One wasn't enough.

Then there was the other issue; the man named Gid bore evenly spaced scars on his face and hands. One of the Knowing. Jubal couldn't read the marks, but they were unmistakable. As a member of the special class, the stranger was off limits.

Gid didn't speak their language very well, but he was

obviously distressed that his machine would no longer fly. Jubal offered their help pushing it back to the fence. The wagon was heavy, but the toothed wheels gripped the ground well, and soon they were moving at a good pace. In spite of an obvious limp, Gid urged them on, faster, until they were running behind the wagon. He shouted in his strange language to the woman. The machine sputtered, and a loud rumble shook the frame.

Jubal and Rann jumped aside, hands raised to protect themselves. The wagon continued to move, and Gid hopped onto the back.

Without them.

"Flame Runna trickery!" Rann cried.

Gid beckoned them with an arm, shouting, "Come! Come!"

Jubal's feet felt stuck to the ground. "He's not a Flame Runna. His skin isn't green."

"The one inside the wagon is. They'll take us prisoner."

Jubal grimaced. "Our goods are on that wagon."

"Or what if it flies away?"

Without their staves and merchandise, he and Rann might as well be dead on the Tox. "We have no choice."

Heart racing, Jubal sprinted forward, caught the edge of the wagon, and swung himself up next to Gid. Rann followed a moment behind.

Once they were sitting atop the wagon bed, hands clutching a rail along the side, the wagon picked up speed faster than Jubal thought possible. Gid threw back his head and let out a whoop. Rann laughed and joined in. Jubal watched the looming wall of wire links, too worried about what they would face inside to revel in the speed.

They slowed as they neared the fence. A gray wooden plaque with white marks pointed out the entryway, just as Pops had described. Jubal didn't know his letters, but he'd encountered writing before, during their trade route along the

Sunset Shore. Many people used these symbols to talk without using words, Pops said.

They stopped at a wide gate and Gid hopped off. He faced the fence and shouted, waving a small white cloth above his head. Jubal and Rann dismounted and retrieved their packs and staves.

"Be ready," Jubal said, although he had no idea for what.

Another man came out of a small stone house about fifty paces inside the fence and hollered back, then disappeared. Gid grinned and gave Jubal a thumbs up before tucking the cloth into a pocket in the back of his pants.

Jubal looked overhead at the wall of metal netting. *This is the lightning wall.* The top of the weave was decorated with more coils of wire, but Jubal had the feeling it was more than decoration. The man reappeared from the stone house and waved. Gid pulled the gate open, allowing the flying wagon to rumble through. Gid followed, gesturing furiously for Jubal and Rann to do the same.

"Do we go?" Rann asked.

Jubal's limbs trembled so badly, he thought he might collapse. Did the lightning wall keep men in as easily as it kept them out? "Pops has traded here."

Rann looked to either side, then moved forward through the gate.

With a last glance toward the barren soil surrounding the fence, Jubal followed. Gid drew the gate closed, throwing down a latch and stepping back before yelling something toward the house. Jubal and Rann stood close enough to brush shoulders as the man in the stone house emerged again and began walking their direction. A straw hat shaded his face, but he wasn't a Flame Runna, either. *Have we come here for nothing?*

The door to the wagon opened. Small, booted feet swung to the ground. A calf-length brown dress. Black hair mussed from the wind. Then the face of the Flame Runna came into view. A face burned into Jubal's memory as she'd leaned over his unconscious brother.

Rann jerked and almost lost his balance under his heavy pack. "Ana?"

Her smile disintegrated into an open-mouthed stare.

Chapter Six

Eily froze, matching their stares. There were others called Anne or Anna or even Hannah in the Holdout. Heard in conversation, the name had stopped jarring her long ago; she no longer expected to be confused with her twin sister. But these men spoke Ana's name directly to her face. Her insides quivered. "What did you call me?"

The men looked at each other then back at her. The taller one stepped forward, his smile transforming his handsome face into a stunning visage as he put a hand in front of him, palm down. "Our mistake. We thought we knew you."

The cadence of the Cannibal language sounded strange to her after six years at the Holdout. The reversions were only allowed to speak Haldanian. She studied the traders' faces, trying to place them. Not much older than she was, with smooth, sun-darkened skin, traditional beads in the hair and around the neck, and chicory-brown eyes. They were obviously brothers. If they thought she was Ana, then they must have known her and Ana as children, but she had no recollection of them. How could they recognize her after so many years, not to mention her green skin? "I'm Eily. Are you from the Under Stone tribe? My sister and I were with them during our early years."

The tall one shook his head at his brother before speaking. "We're traders, not of any tribe. I'm Jubal, and this is my brother Rann."

"I'm sorry, I can't recall your faces or names." Eily swallowed past the lump in her throat. "My twin sister Ana died many years ago. Taken by hunters."

The one called Rann grinned like a dog after a run, exposing every one of his teeth. "Twins!"

Jubal elbowed his brother, hard.

Rann shrugged away, scowling. "What? She should know her sister's alive."

Spots of light exploded across Eily's vision, and she thought her heart might actually leave her chest. *Ana's alive?* How many times had she repeated that over the years? She'd stopped believing it a lifetime ago. The air felt too thick to breathe.

The tall trader put a hand out again, as if to placate her. She swayed, and he put an arm around her waist to keep her from falling. Her hand flew up to catch herself against his bare chest, and she sucked in a breath at the solid, warm contact.

Gid finished speaking with the gatekeeper and rushed to her side. Brows lowered in disapproval, he took her elbow and gently urged her away so he could address the traders. "Welcome to the Holdout," he said in clumsy Haldanian, which was close enough to Cannibal to be understood. "Thank you for help. We trade soon."

Eily clutched Gid's shoulder to steady herself. He turned and caught her under both elbows. "Eily?"

"Ana's alive." Her voice cracked. After a few moments of his puzzled stare, she realized she'd spoken Cannibal. "Alive," she repeated.

He shook his head, still not understanding. "Go sit in the mini. Ijon is sending an Ops team. I guess he's not happy about our adventure."

Her mind swam with longing for Ana's shared laughter, the feel of her twin's hand in hers, the bond of glances that spoke more than words. She silently thanked the Order's God for answering her prayers. Behind the traders loomed the very gate where she'd last seen her sister's thin green legs hanging over the shoulder of a retreating hunter.

Eily sidestepped her betrothed and stumbled toward the traders, clutching at the beads hanging from Jubal's neck. "You have to take me to her. Please!"

The crunch of wide tires on gravel forestalled his answer, and he stared over her head, eyes wide and pupils tight. From behind her, she heard Ijon's voice. "What's this I hear of an uncharted lift? I know you people believe in self-sufficiency, but you could have caused a serious accident."

Gid said, "Eily, come away!"

Rann focused on her with an intensity that made her shudder. He reached out and cupped the bare skin just above her elbow. The hint of a smile played at the corners of his mouth. "We'd be happy to take you to Ana."

Ijon joined the group. "Gid, is this your vehicle?"

Gid greeted the liaison without taking his eyes off Eily. "I apologize, Ijon..."

Eily let go of Jubal's beads, pulled her arm from Rann's grasp, and turned to the Protectorate liaison. That Ana was still alive was a miracle. Ijon would help. He wouldn't leave one of their own people out there alone. "Ijon, they've seen my sister! Ana's alive!"

The liaison's brow creased. "How can that be?"

"They knew her name. We have to find her!" She had no

idea how Ana could be alive, but she wasn't going to question how when the real issue was where.

He looked at the traders in horror. "Is she a prisoner?"

Jubal shook his staff so the baubles rattled. "We come to trade, not to create problems."

Ijon's mouth turned into a hard line. "The Board will insist on speaking with you."

"We only saw her in passing."

Ijon signaled two Burn Operatives who'd traveled with him. "Help these men with their things. They'll be our guests for a while."

Rann slid a foot backward. "We carry the trader staff."

Eily flapped her hands, grimacing as the tension escalated. She placed herself between the traders and the oncoming guards. "Wait! They said they would help! You don't have to do this. They'll take me to her."

Ijon shifted his gaze between her and the traders. "You can't leave. If we let you leave, we have to allow every reversion to do the same."

"Eily!" Gid barked. "You're breaking the *Ordnung*."

She trembled, but didn't budge. Each breath shuddered in her chest. *Please, Ijon*, she begged with her eyes. "She's one of us."

"There's more at stake here than your sister. If the traders cooperate, we won't delay them long."

She clenched her fists. There was no fighting the Protectorate machine. They would have their way. *Ana has survived this long, another day or two won't matter.* But the reassurances did little to slow her racing heart. She looked to the traders. "He won't harm you. Tell him what you know. Please."

Jubal had taken a step back as the guards approached. "We're traders. We can't take sides in tribal disputes. Your sister is safe. Her man's a big man. He takes good care of her. They're expecting a child."

A wave of nausea forced Eily to swallow back bile. UV alkaloids were toxic to unborn fetuses, and there would be little, if any, protection from the sun out on the Tox. "She's pregnant?"

Jubal lifted his brows and nodded, his attention flicking between her and the guards.

Fighting tears, Eily turned to the liaison. "Ijon, if Ana's pregnant, every moment in the sun counts. We have to get her back here and into one of the Gardens immediately."

Ijon scowled as he looked over the traders. "Does your tribe have more than one Flame Runna?"

Rann thrust out his chest. "No."

The muscles in Jubal's jaw twitched, but he shook his head silently in agreement.

Ijon rubbed his forehead. "Take a duster team."

Eily smiled and closed her eyes a moment. Ijon was a good man. "Thank you."

"Duster?" Jubal asked.

Eily said, "Flying machine."

Jubal shook his head slowly, mouth pursed. "We won't show Flame Runnas where the tribes gather. Only you."

Ijon snorted. "Impossible!"

"She would never go alone," Gid said.

Eily's vision swam for what felt like the hundredth time that day. *Of course they won't take you to their camp. You're a Flame Runna.* The Protectorate was the enemy. Even the people at the Holdout, who lived under the Protectorate umbrella, didn't trust the regime. But without a duster, she'd have to walk the Tox, protected only by these trader's staves. Would their amnesty be enough to keep her—a woman marked as a Flame Runna—safe?

Ana sacrificed herself for you. It's your turn to take a chance for her.

She looked past the traders to the barren ground surrounding the Holdout. Voice shaking, she said, "I've already lost my sister once. I won't lose her again." She turned to Jubal. "Can we leave in the morning?"

Despite Eily's protests, the Flame Runnas escorted Jubal and Rann to a dome that looked like an enormous drop of water. Jubal gawked at his own reflection before being ushered inside, where he stared once again; the walls from this side were not reflective but translucent, allowing a view of the broad fields and brick houses. The rear wall was an opaque gray, broken in the center by a passageway deeper into the structure. To one side, a large, rectangular panel danced with pictures of moving Flame Runnas that shifted angles and faces like magic. Several Flame Runnas lounged on seats watching the panel but rose when the entourage entered.

Jubal startled as the weight of his pack lifted behind him and one of the Flame Runnas slid the shoulder straps down his arms.

"Wait, you can't—"

Another guard wrested Jubal's staff from his grip. Jubal snatched at it, but the man retreated down one of the passageways. Beside him, Rann sputtered with indignation as his items were taken as well. Jubal thought about chasing down the man with his staff, but with ten or more Flame Runnas watching, he decided against it.

"What's going on?" one of the spectators called out. "Are we under attack?"

The man who called himself Ijon put on what Jubal would call a trader's smile. "Of course not. These men are our guests."

A guard behind Jubal pushed him—not roughly, but not gently, either—toward the passageway. Jubal's pulse raced. Flame Runnas had no respect for the Peace or trader laws. *Just play along*. He let out a shaky breath and entered the corridor. At the end, a Flame Runna opened a door and thrust him into a small room with a single, translucent wall. He spun as Ijon entered and closed the door behind him. Two guards flanked the exit.

"If you don't give us our goods back, we'll be sure no trader ventures to this place again." Among the tribes, such a threat was huge, since without trade, they'd have to steal things like salt and other items they couldn't make themselves. But neither the guards nor Ijon even blinked. Jubal looked around, realizing his brother wasn't with him any more. "Where's Rann?"

"Please, have a seat. We'll be questioning you separately." Ijon moved around a large, sturdy table and settled into a bright blue chair.

Jubal noticed a matching chair on his side of the table but didn't sit. Through the wall, he could see the field beyond, but he had a feeling the glass wouldn't break easily. He longed for a gulp of fresh air. *Smile, Jubal. They want something. Be a trader.* Without his staff, he felt naked. At least he kept his voice steady as he said, "Traders have amnesty. What is your toll?"

"I assure you, we mean you no harm. Your goods will be returned once you've told us all you know."

"Traders cannot bother themselves with squabbles between tribes." The same words spoken not so long ago by Pops tasted sour on Jubal's tongue.

A beep came from the table, and Ijon tapped the surface. Jubal reeled back as a green face appeared within the desktop. "Ijon, I hear you have news."

"We're interrogating the cannibals now, Councilman. I'll be in touch."

"Thank you." The table went dark again.

Jubal licked his lips. Flying like birds, magical kisses, and... whatever that floating face was. What other magic might the Flame Runnas possess? Could they discern lies? He intended to remain close lipped and hoped Rann would, too, but his insides roiled with doubt.

"Jubal," Ijon leaned forward, one elbow on the table. "I know it doesn't look like it, but the Protectorate wants peace. We've suffered invasions from the tribes, and like you, we fight hunters when they attack. We even offer conversion—green skin—to people so they no longer have to suffer the Hunger. That's how I became a Flame Runna."

Jubal narrowed his eyes. Ijon chose to take the magic? Sefe claimed Ana had been captured by Flame Runnas and changed against her will. He wondered if Eily had chosen or been forced. Ana had run away to find her tribe, but Eily was still here, so it stood to reason she'd taken the path of acceptance.

Ijon continued speaking. "When I was a cannibal, long ago, traders were not forbidden from sharing news. That's all we're asking for. Have the tribes been hunting our dusters?"

Traders dealt in news as often as goods, but there was no price that would make Jubal betray his people. Still, he had to give Ijon something if he wanted to get out of here alive.

He shrugged. "On the Tox, hunters hunt, and Flame Runnas would be as fine a prize as any."

"Have you heard of new weapons among the tribes? Guns? The ability to shoot farther than the best arrows? Where are your people getting them?"

Jubal laughed. "Oh, there are always tales of heroes who can send an arrow into the sun or outrun a windstorm. But I would never tell these tales as news."

Ijon raised a brow. "Humor me."

Jubal closed his eyes and sighed.

Several well-known legends later, Ijon released him, and the guards escorted him outside. Apparently, Rann had held his tongue, for he was sitting at a wooden table beneath the largest tree Jubal had ever seen. The leaf canopy shaded the area from the afternoon sun, and their goods lay spread across the tabletop. "Is it all here?"

Rann shrugged. "I just arrived. What did you tell them?"

Jubal lowered his brows and tilted his head to indicate the nearby guards. Ijon had released Jubal from the building but made it very clear he and Rann would not have freedom while they were here. "He asked for stories, so I told him the ballad of 'Hugh on High."

"Brilliant!" Rann chortled, then hiccoughed. "I just kept telling them I didn't know anything."

Picking up a bag of bitters, Jubal jostled the contents. Should he blame Rann or the Flame Runnas for the decreased weight?

Rann rolled his eyes. "I needed a drink to calm down."

Jubal laid the bota on the table next to some pouches of salt and brushed his hands across the other items, cataloguing what had been in the packs. Nothing appeared to be missing. Satisfied, he raised his gaze to the surrounding fields, taking a deep breath. This place not only looked different, it smelled different, too, with a new scent hitting him every time the breeze shifted. The fields were strangely free of amarantox and verdant with unfamiliar plants. Animals that looked like fat deer wandered inside a fenced area in the distance. Overhead, small birds twittered among the tree branches.

"Think they'll let us take the woman?" Rann asked.

Jubal scowled at him. "Hush."

His brother rolled his eyes again and looked straight at the guards. "They're too far away to hear."

"How much did you drink?"

Rann bolted to his feet and planted his hands on the table with a thud. "Stop bossing me around, little brother."

"You already screwed things up with the One Tree."

Rann glowered at him in silence, breathing hard. After a moment he settled himself back onto the bench. "Sefe would love a matching Flame Runna woman. Maybe she would be enough to free Pops."

Jubal sat next to him and lowered his head as if looking at his merchandise. "One Flame Runna's not enough."

From the south, where several brick dwellings clustered, a man approached on foot. He wore dark clothing nearly identical to that worn by Gid, his black leggings pale with dust at the hems and held up by straps over his shoulders. He stopped at their table and nodded, his gray beard brushing the front of his long-sleeved blue tunic. "My name is Brother John."

Jubal nodded in greeting, his smile firmly in place. "I'm Jubal, and this is my brother Rann. My father traded here many seasons ago."

"Good, you know our way, then?"

Jubal raised his brows and glanced at Rann. "Pops never mentioned anything unusual."

"We ask you always for peace. And modesty. Please not talk to women. They will not trade."

Jubal kept his face neutral. He'd visited tribes where women were kept tightly controlled, and he never liked them. But this explained Gid's attempts to command Eily—not that she'd heeded him. Perhaps Flame Runnas were new here and still learning the ways. "Do you have any slaves for trade?"

John remained expressionless, but Jubal's years of trading helped him catch the tiny twitch of distaste around the man's mouth and the flare of his nostrils. "We have no need of such oppression here."

Jubal grimaced and bowed his head. "My apologies. I didn't

know if your ways had changed since the Flame Runnas arrived. They weren't here when my father traded with you."

"Only six winters past the *Blattvolk* came."

"Blattvolk. That's what you call the green people?"

"Yes. But they call themselves the Haldanian Protectorate."

Flame Runnas, Blattvolk, Haldanian—how many names could one people have? Granted, they were a powerful group... "Out on the Tox, they burn everything. You're lucky they let you live."

John crossed his arms. "We raised our hands in surrender. Now they keep cannibals away. Is Gotte's Wille. Talk no more of Haldanian Protectorate." A huge wagon pulled by equally huge four-legged creatures taller than a man arrived. Three men hopped from their perches atop the wheeled structure and began unloading planks of wood.

Rann pointed to the animals, mouth agape. "What are those?"

Brother John smiled. "Horses."

"They would feed a tribe for an entire moon!"

"We do not eat our horses. But we will have much food tonight." John walked away to help the men at the wagon. He spoke over his shoulder as he left. "The salt trader already came here this year. Not much trade now. But stay tonight as our guests."

Jubal looked from the goods spread across the table to the men who now erected long tables using the planks. Did etiquette require him and Rann to help? He wasn't sure. The nearby Flame Runna guards remained impassive. Rann bent close enough for his breath to tickle Jubal's ear. "No slaves? Now what do we do?"

Jubal chewed his bottom lip. "Let's see if that Flame Runna, Eily, still wants to find her sister."

"She's nowhere in sight. What if they don't let her talk to us again?" Rann looked around, settling on the tall posts near the gate they'd come through. "We could look for a way to get Sefe inside the lightning wall."

The idea might be their only hope. Jubal nodded once and began to organize the goods on their table. "Maybe we can look after dark. Until then, smile."

Chapter Seven

Haldanian Protectorate

Rael leaned forward to look at the seven other Board members sitting around the conference table. Sunlight poured into the room through the transparent ceiling, and the low, persistent hum of the air exchangers as they struggled to keep the building cool niggled on the edge of annoyance. Using his most paternal voice, Rael began his presentation. "I hope you all had time to read the outline I sent."

Several faces looked down at their gamma pads, and he knew most people had barely skimmed the missive, as usual. Fine by him. There were still some kinks in the Doomseeds plan, and this would allow him to focus attention on the most positive aspects.

He forged ahead. "The Doomseeds program will solve two problems at once. First, reversions who cannot be remediated will be allowed to return to the Reaches instead of being euthanized. Second, with the new neurotoxic fungi implanted, they will serve the Protectorate as a deterrent against Fosselite harvesting."

Councilwoman Arnica studied the gamma pad in her hands and furrowed her brow. "You intend to give Eily Kraybill the Doomseeds neurotoxin?"

"Not unless she wishes to stay in the Reaches. We do not consider her a reversion at this time." Rael shook his head. As a native-born Haldanian, conceived in a test tube and raised within the UV-protected walls of the Garden, he—and most of the Board—didn't understand why some converts refused to embrace life within the Protectorate.

Another councilman leaned back in his chair. "Wild as they are, reversions are still too domesticated to survive on their own. We'll only be feeding the cannibals if we allow them to leave."

Rael smiled indulgently. "That's why Eily's part in this is so important. One of the tribes has adopted her sister, and Eily wishes to rescue her. But the tribe may be open to adopting others in her place. The reversions will be safe."

A change in air pressure accompanied one of the main doors opening, and Dr. Tula Macoby, staunch supporter of convert rights, waddled in, her belly huge in the late stages of pregnancy. Rael gestured *welcome*. Tula mumbled apologies and slid into a seat.

Rael continued, "New policies on convert rights and reversions have opened many doors. Once upon a time the only thing we *could* do with reversions was euthanize them. Some reversions will never acclimate, even with the diverse living situations we offer. They want to go back to the Reaches."

Tula, still catching her breath, said, "Councilman, I've reviewed your notes. Your plan will result in their deaths."

He kept his hands relaxed on the table instead of squeezing his fists like he wanted to. He'd assumed that Dr. Macoby would approve of giving reversions their freedom. "I thought you supported the rights of new converts."

"Research on the neurotoxic fungi is not yet complete. Testing has—"

"We can't afford to miss this opportunity to safely reintroduce reversions into their natural habitat. We will of course continue testing in the field."

Councilman Gentian said, "You speak of them like they're lab rats, Rael."

Rael merely cocked an eyebrow. Several council members chuckled.

Tula scowled. "You propose we use them as bait for the Fosselites."

Rael scowled. Six years ago, Tula had borne the brunt of a Fosselite experiment to increase the endurance of harvest subjects under deadly levels of UV radiation; the longer the Fosselites kept their subjects alive, the more neural fluid they could tap. When she'd escaped, she'd brought the Protectorate not only samples of a proprietary telomerase fungus, but also news of the Fosselites' insidious harvest of smuggled Haldanian reversions. "Dr. Macoby, we're trying to prevent anyone from going through what you experienced ever again."

"Your plan hinges on the hope that these reversions will be captured."

This was a subject he'd hoped to avoid talking about directly. "Unfortunately, one or two will need to be harvested for the Fosselites to learn to keep their hands off. But then the rest of our people—reversions included—should be safe from Fosselite hunting."

She rose from her seat and leaned forward to tap the center console, her ponderous belly brushing the table. A chart appeared on the surface, drawing everyone's eye. She pointed to one of the lines. "And what about those who *aren't* captured?

The fungi thrive in the alkaloids our bodies produce under UV exposure. Once they reach critical levels, the victim has only ten days before stroke-like symptoms appear. By the time that happens, the damage is done, and death is certain."

Gentian's eyes widened, and he turned to Rael. "So the reversions only have ten days?"

He waved off the concern. "The fungi won't reach toxic concentrations unless subjected to high levels of ultraviolet light, such as the UV lamps used by the Fosselites."

Tula crossed her arms. "What if these reversions are caught in a UV storm? That much radiation would surely induce neurotoxic fungal bloom."

"Assuming their alkaloid levels don't destroy their organs first?" Rael rolled his eyes. "Everyone knows to get out of a UV storm. Even cannibals."

Another councilman tapped the screen of his gamma pad and asked, "Isn't the toxin detectable within the bloodstream?"

"The beauty of this fungus is that it is completely contained within the spinal column, and the toxin it creates is poorly absorbed through the bloodstream. Standard blood tests are useless."

Tula slapped a hand on the table. "This isn't about how undetectable the toxin is."

Rael took a deep breath and leveled a stony gaze at her. "The reversions should exhibit no symptoms while living on the Reaches." He turned to the rest of the Board members. "We all agree that conversion is a good thing, do we not? A way to eliminate hunger and violence? Yet the conversion process itself has a certain fatality rate when a host's body refuses the chloroplasts. We accept those statistics because photosynthetic skin is the only sure way to end cannibalism. If we attempt a full-on frontal assault with the Fosselites, or even continue to allow them to arm the cannibals as they are now, we would experience far greater losses than my proposal estimates. Eradicating the Fosselite threat is worth the possible loss of a few lives."

"After the Fosselites are no longer a threat, what happens to the released reversions?" Councilwoman Arnica asked. "Do we offer them medical services to remove the fungi?"

Rael cleared his throat. He hadn't anticipated the question. "That would mean alerting them to the plan, which risks the Fosselites finding out. We can't let the information leave this room. But I assure you we are including the very best safety protocols we can offer. The released reversions will undergo the same preventative telomerase treatments Burn Operatives receive for long-term UV exposure. In fact, the neurotoxic fungi are related to the telomerase fungi—the same fungi the Fosselites introduced into Dr. Macoby's bloodstream six years ago, I might add. As you can see, she's fine."

He'd hoped for a chuckle or at least a few smiles from the Board, but their faces remained serious. He licked his lips and continued. "Lab results indicate a healthy organism will be capable of naturally flushing the neurotoxins under normal UV exposure. There should be no long-term effects. Also consider that by placing reversions among the cannibals, we might gain interest in conversion and convince many to give up their violent, cannibalistic ways. We'll be continuing our mission to make the world safe again."

Gentian let out a disparaging breath. "Pfft. I think you're overly optimistic, Councilman. We've seen how difficult it is to convince the people at the Holdout to convert."

"The cannibals may prove more willing than the religious zealots. We must try."

"Is there a way to track the reversions? To collect data on their survival rate?" Arnica asked.

The idea had not occurred to Rael, but he liked it. "I will look into planting a GPS chip during the fungal insertion."

Gentian closed down his gamma pad. "These reversions are on the verge of termination due to noncompliance, anyway. Let's allow them to go."

Arnica nodded. "How many do you propose to trial with this first project?"

"We have a short list of three or four."

Tula slumped back in her chair. "Sending them out there is a death sentence."

Rael nodded. "Perhaps, for a few. This project will take time, I don't deny it. But this program is our best option to nullify the Fosselite threat, and it may be the only long-term hope for reversions who don't want to stay within the Protectorate. If we allow them to leave, we have to protect them. The best way will be to make them poisonous to the Fosselites."

Gentian said, "I vote to give provisional approval."

Arnica heaved a sigh. "We'll consider this a test run. All in favor?"

Rael smiled as seven hands lifted into the air.

Chapter Eight

The Holdout

Eily stuffed a paper-wrapped wedge of cheese into the quilted bag she normally used to carry her knitting. Yarn and needles lay scattered across the kitchen table. She'd already packed a blanket and donned her church shoes, since her regular shoes were old and might not last the journey.

Gid stood with his back to the screen door, blocking the exit. She refused to meet his eyes. He could have at least argued with Ijon on her behalf. For Ana. Violence wasn't allowed among the Order, but words were. Gid hadn't even offered those, only watched as Ijon's goons took Jubal and Rann prisoner.

Gid's mother, Beth, was at the kitchen sink, hands on her hips. "Eily, this is insanity." Her voice had the firm but loving edge Eily had grown familiar with in the six years she'd lived with the family.

Gid crossed his arms. His face was still darkened by grime

from the Burn, making his pale blue eyes appear intense. "I forbid you."

Eily stared at him, her gut twisting. The Order taught that wives were subject to their husbands, and Eily wanted to be a good wife. She wanted to please him. But her sister was alive. "You're not my husband yet, Gid."

He ran his hands through his hair, releasing a cloud of dust. "Do you want to live with the cannibals?"

"No!" Eily took a step back. The Order had a hard time accepting her green skin, but the tribes would outright kill her. Of that she was sure. How Ana had survived this long was a miracle. "But I want to save her. Even if it means disobeying you."

His mouth hardened, and he turned to look out the screen door.

Beth said, "Your wedding is in less than a week."

"This is my sister. I can't leave her out there."

Gid spoke softly, without turning around. "You don't even know where she is."

"The traders said they'll show me the way." The hollowness in Eily's heart made her voice echo in her ears.

Beth asked, "Will Ijon set them free?"

"He has to. They're traders." She hoped he'd honor the code that ruled the Tox. She lifted her bag to one shoulder, swallowing hard at her own defiance.

Gid turned his head to meet her gaze over his shoulder. "In their eyes, you're a Blattvolk."

She hesitated. They'd almost grown up together. From the moment she'd arrived at the Holdout, Gid had been her staunchest supporter, in spite of pressure from the other children to reject a green abomination. He'd never called her a Blattvolk. Was he hinting at his feelings now? Unshed tears pricked her eyes. "They're my only hope. Ana's only hope."

No one spoke for a few heartbeats. Finally, Gid's eyes narrowed. "Then we go save her."

Gratitude warmed Eily from scalp to toes, and a hot tear escaped over her lashes.

"Gid—" Beth began.

He raised a hand, palm out. "Mama, don't argue. She's to be my wife, and I won't let her go alone. We'll take the mini and try to be back in time for the wedding."

"It's not proper for you two to be unchaperoned."

"Would it be more proper for me to allow her to go alone with two strange men?"

Eily licked her lips. "The traders said no dusters. We'll have to walk like they do."

Beth sucked in a deep breath, her brows pinched. "Gid's leg—"

He stopped her. "I pushed the mini all the way back to the Holdout. I'll manage."

Eily wasn't so sure, but she waited until they left the house to speak. "Gid, meeting the traders on the Burn was... not normal. Out on the Tox, if you can't run, you fight back. If you can't fight back, you die."

"If I die it will be Gotte's Will."

She grabbed his sleeve, pulling him to a stop in the center of the dusty lane. "You can't think that way. I don't want to lose you."

"Don't you think I feel the same about you?"

It felt good to hear him say so, but he didn't understand the danger. She took a breath. "When Ana and I fled the Fosselite mountain with Levi and Tula, we encountered hunters. Your Uncle Levi fought back, or we'd all four be dead. God didn't strike him down. Levi lives—isn't that God's will, too?"

Gid chewed his lip. "I suppose..."

"All I'm saying is you must be ready to act in the moment. If dying doesn't serve God's purpose, you must fight back."

He blinked.

A skimmer pulled up, fat wheels kicking up a cloud of dust. Behind the transparent siding, Ijon leaned over and unlatched the passenger door, allowing it to wing upward. "Get in. The Board wants to speak with you."

Eily's throat constricted. She'd been before the Board twice in her life. Once when she'd first arrived, and they'd wanted to meet the reversion who'd lived through Fosselite testing. Then a second time when Tula had petitioned for the Reversion Remediation program. "Are the traders okay?"

"You don't need to worry about them. Now get in. Councilman Rael is awaiting my call."

Gid pushed forward. "I go with her."

Ijon bobbed his head in acquiescence.

They rode toward the Liaison Building in silence. Daylight had faded, but the tall fence lights had yet to come on. They reached the parking bay, and Ijon led the way to his office with quick strides. Eily walked more slowly to accommodate Gid as well as to gather her wits. What if the Board forbade her going? They could lock her up as a reversion. Or what if the traders had changed their minds about showing her the way? As Ijon dialed up his com screen, he indicated Eily and Gid should take seats.

Councilman Rael's kindly face appeared on the desktop, and Ijon tapped the controls to bring up the vertical interactive. "I've brought Eily in, as you asked, Councilman. And her soon-to-be-husband, Gideon."

"Hello, Eily. I hear you want to retrieve your sister from the cannibals."

"I thought she'd sacrificed herself to save me. But she's alive. I owe her."

"The traders seem to think she's happy where she's at."

Eily shook her head. "She's pregnant, and every passing day she's exposed to sunlight means her baby has less chance of survival when it's born. We have to move her into a Garden and wean her off the UV chemicals."

"But what if she wants to stay there?"

Something about his tone made Eily pause. Tula had warned Eily to be cautious when dealing with Board members. The Protectorate fought to keep those they converted—fought to the death. Was Rael worried Ana would be one of those reversions who never fit in? "I'll convince her how good life is here."

The councilman relaxed into his chair. His naked chest looked scrawny under his loops of beads. "The Board has decided to allow a few reversions to return to the Reaches. Since your sister's tribe appears to have accepted her, we want you to take some reversions with you and attempt to integrate them."

A few heartbeats passed as Eily processed his request. Was he saying she was a failure? That she hadn't convinced the reversions, so she couldn't convince her sister? "But... what if the tribe won't take them?"

Rael smiled again. "If these traders introduce them to people who've already accepted a reversion into the fold, that tribe may welcome them. But if not, our experts assure us that a group of three or more reversions can be viable together."

"The cannibals may kill them outright."

"That's a risk these reversions are willing to take. They want to go back to life in the Reaches." His brow descended into a concerned frown.

Eily licked her lips. What he proposed was possible, if not plausible. "Reversions are no longer cannibals, sir. They're too different."

His frown eased. “These reversions will be a first step in peaceful interactions with the cannibals. They’ll show by example that conversion reduces the need for food and the violence required to obtain it.” He nodded toward Gid. “Members of the Holdout have seen that while they suffer and starve during lean winters, you remain robust and healthy. They’ve come to accept you and some have accepted conversion.”

A flush heated Eily’s face. Endorsing conversion among the Order had never been her intent, but what he said was true.

Rael continued, “We’re tired of fighting reversions. It’s time to allow them to make their own choices.”

Unable to argue with this new policy, Eily could only shake her head. The Protectorate had never allowed converts—let alone reversions—much in the way of free will. Why did the Board suddenly think freeing reversions was a good idea? Granted, it seemed more humane than euthanasia, but only to those who didn’t understand cannibal customs. Without the support of a tribe, any reversion caught alone out on the Tox would *wish* for a quick, clean death.

A thought occurred to Eily. “Councilman, have the traders agreed to this?”

“That’s what we’re relying on you for—to convince them to aid you.”

She smoothed her dress over her knees. “The traders said they would lead me to my sister. They may not agree to take the reversions. They can only provide so much safety under their trader’s staff.”

“I go, too,” Gid said. She wasn’t sure how much of the conversation he’d been able to follow, but he obviously wouldn’t allow her to go alone. Part of her was grateful, but part of her felt smothered.

Rael said, “That’s up to the Order. Just know that if the

reversions don't go with you and the traders, we'll release them into the Reaches on their own. It's up to you."

Prickles broke out across Eily's skin. Either way, the reversions were likely to die. The traders could offer moderate safety, but once the reversions left their care, she didn't think they would last long. Perhaps during the journey she could change their minds about the Protectorate. "How many reversions have signed up to leave?"

"I believe you have worked with two of them." He leaned forward and input something on the com screen. Three names appeared along with their conversion data.

She scanned the list. Lisius didn't surprise her. But she was surprised to see Wint. She'd never met the third man. This whole thing was a bad idea. She felt it in her gut.

Ijon produced a small, black nuvoplast box and handed it to Eily. "This is a GPS locator. In case you get into trouble. Just push the button, and it will send out an emergency signal."

The box was surprisingly light. She flipped open the hinged lid. The inside of the lid was a dark glass interface panel, but the box itself held a single black button.

"Don't worry about the gamma screen. All you need to know how to do is push the button."

"You want to track us?"

Rael answered for Ijon. "You may appreciate the signal if the cannibals turn on you. What do you know about these traders, anyway?"

She placed the box on the desk and folded her hands in her lap. "Contrary to what the Protectorate believes, the tribes have some very specific codes they follow. The diplomacy of traders is one. I trust these men to do as they say."

"We will not show ourselves unless you press the button," Rael said.

She looked at Rael's video image and then to Ijon. "How do

I know dusters won't swoop in after I rescue Ana? You'll destroy the tribe."

Rael answered in a grandfatherly voice, like he was talking to a child. "The Haldanian mission is to offer conversion to the cannibals, Eily. For peace."

"Right," she said, remembering her childhood capture. "Tell that to my dead mother."

Ijon lowered his gaze to his lap.

Rael acted like she hadn't spoken. "We won't let you leave without it."

"You can't keep me here!"

Ijon raised a brow. "You may belong to the Order, but there are no religious rules about allowing you to leave. That much I'm sure of. You are a member of the Holdout and under my care. I won't allow you to die if I can help it."

Eily stared wide-eyed at Ijon then at Councilman Rael. *The Board will lock you up and you'll never find Ana.* She glanced at the beacon. It was so small. But it would be a huge betrayal to the traders if she took it. Grabbing the box, she shoved it into her apron pocket. She'd take it now, but they couldn't make her pack it. "When can I leave?"

Chapter Nine

Darkness had fallen, but inside the lightning wall, posts topped with white fire bathed the area with an artificial glow. Around the clearing, pale-skinned men in clothing like Gid's set up tables, and women snapped long sheets of impossibly white cloth to cover the surfaces. The cloth alone would be worth a fortune on the trade route, and Jubal tried not to gape from his spot at their small table, displaying what he now considered a meager show of merchandise. Why hadn't Pops ever mentioned how wealthy these people were?

Rann leaned to whisper in his ear. "Do you think he was serious about not talking to the women? I like how light their skin is."

"Don't." Jubal gritted between his teeth as he maintained a smile. Although no women approached the traders, many glanced in their direction beneath lowered lashes, groups of younger ones often giggling and speaking in their foreign tongue.

Rann said, "I don't see that Flame Runna female anywhere."

Jubal was thinking the same thing. Hope was decaying into panic as he realized they were going to have to sneak away and explore the lightning wall. He nodded cordially at a passing man. The older men all had facial hair except for their upper lips, and no ornamentation whatsoever, which seemed an odd affectation to Jubal, especially in a group so obviously rich. The women also wore no ornaments except the white or black caps covering their hair. Where were the other Flame Runnas? Other than those inside the dome and a handful of what were obviously warriors, they'd seen none among these strangely dressed people. Eily had been the only one. "She might still show up," he said doubtfully.

"I'll go scout the gate. Find a way to get Sefe in."

"You can't. They're always watching us." Jubal smiled at a couple strolling by, but they barely looked at his table. The Flame Runna guards were no longer in sight now that this crowd had gathered, but he had no doubt someone would be set to watch them through the night. And they were expected to finish trade tomorrow. They couldn't return to Sefe with nothing.

Brother John appeared. He gestured toward a table. "Please. You come share food."

The scent of cooked meat made Jubal's stomach growl. He looked at his trade goods then at Rann. "We'd rather not leave our items untended."

"All is safe." Brother John nodded once. "No one steal here."

Rann wiggled his fingertips in a shooing motion and flicked a meaningful gaze down the road to the lightning wall. "Why don't you go? I can handle things."

Brother John's face remained placid, unaware of Rann's silent intent. Jubal hesitated. Most feasts involved entertainment, which would hopefully draw attention away from the trade table at the outskirts of the crowd. The opportunity was less than ideal, and letting Rann go on his own could end in disaster. But this might also be their only chance. He looked directly into Rann's eyes. "Remember. Don't talk to them."

"I promise."

Brother John led the way to one of the long tables and took a seat among the men, patting the bench next to him for Jubal. An empty plate and cup awaited him, and down the center of the table larger dishes sat piled high with food.

Jubal took the offered spot. As one, the men dropped their chins to their chests and began a chant. "Unser Vader..."

The rest of the tables joined in, eyes closed, and Jubal couldn't believe his luck. He checked to be sure Rann had taken the opportunity to slink off, then dropped his chin, emulating the men around him for the final verses. The men raised their heads and began passing the dishes of food.

He recognized sliced meat as the plate reached him and took a piece, but much of the food was unknown. A white pulp might have been cattail but tasted less earthy. Brown lumps resembling mushrooms smelled like the flat cakes the rice tribes served. He passed on the green vegetable matter; would these people dare serve amarantox? Large golden seed kernels seemed safe enough, so he scooped some onto his plate. The man across from him used a utensil with several points to stab the morsels and raise them to his mouth. Jubal attempted to do the same, only to end up with precious food across his lap. He plucked up the spilled kernels with his fingers and popped them into his mouth, hoping he hadn't missed any.

Brother John chuckled, and the others pretended not to notice. An old man with a thinning beard and milky blue eyes spoke over the sound of utensils scraping against plates. "You are new to our Holdout. From which direction have you traveled, son?"

The Flame Runnas had been so interested in the Taguan, Jubal wondered if perhaps these men were sent to gather information he hadn't volunteered to Ijon. He took a measured breath before speaking. "We bring salt from the Great Salt Lake tribes, but before that we had been all the way to the Sunset Shore."

"Have you encountered any other people like ours? Those behind fences, or perhaps who speak as we do?"

Using a bite of food to delay his answer, Jubal considered how much to say. The Fosselites were the only technological rivals he had seen, but they were obvious enemies, hunting the Flame Runnas. He couldn't risk being affiliated with them and taken into custody again, so he shook his head. "Most tribes travel to gather food throughout the year. Far to the north and west, the rice tribes build homes near lakes and harvest rice seeds to keep them through the winters. They make a potent drink called bitters, of which we have a few flasks to trade. On the Sunset Shore, some men live on boats and dredge up huge fish which they come to trade for rice and leather, but they move their boats with the seasons."

Nodding, the old man said, "I fear we are—"

The lights flickered, and a frightening, high-pitched pulse of noise rose out of nowhere. The crowded tables erupted into action. Dishes clattered and crashed; women clutched young children and dashed into the night. Barking dogs joined the earsplitting noise. Tablemates took the old man's elbows and helped him join the flow. Jubal rose, looking around in bewilderment. Brother John clutched his arm. "Where is your brother?"

Jubal's heart galloped. "What's happening?"

"The fence. Cannibals."

Hunters had breached the lightning wall? He'd thought that impossible, but obviously these people had been attacked before. Did Rann have anything to do with what was happening? "Where's everyone going?"

Brother John's gaze followed the last of the people, his jaw trembling. "They will hide."

"Okay." Jubal ran to his goods, grabbed his staff with one hand, and wrapped his arms around as much of his merchandise as he could gather. He took a few steps toward the darkness where the last stragglers had disappeared.

"No." Brother John remained rooted in place. He drew a square of white cloth from his rear pocket. "You are not of us. I will remain with you. The Lord must be our protection."

The man lowered himself to his knees and began waving his cloth overhead as he chanted the same chant the men had made over the meal.

Jubal's heart fell into his stomach. Here in the open, he was vulnerable. A packet of salt tipped from his loaded arms, hitting the earth and breaking open. Ignoring the waste, he dropped the rest of the items back onto the table and settled his staff's butt end at his feet. His trembling hands did the work of jangling the bells, although nothing could be heard over the rhythmic wail of the siren. A Flame Runna machine zipped overhead, completely silent, whirling clouds of dust and leaves behind it. From the craft, beams of light played over the fields. Groups of people dodged toward the distant houses. Every group held small white flags above their heads.

Then the sirens stopped.

Dogs continued to yowl, and Brother John kept up his chant. Jubal swallowed and peered down the road toward the lightning wall. Did the light that direction seem brighter? Three short horn blasts clipped the air. Brother John heaved a sigh, pressing his face into his hands. "Danke Vader, danke..."

"Rann!" Jubal called as he scoured the darkness, hating the tremor in his voice but unable to control it. A light in the sky drew closer until it resolved into the Flame Runna craft. Jubal squinted in the light and dust as the machine lowered toward the earth. The sleek silence reminded him of a predator. All his instincts directed him to flee. On the Tox he would have. Flame Runnas didn't respect the Peace, the Knowing, or trader law. But here there was nowhere to hide.

Brother John clambered to his feet with slow, deliberate ease. Out of the machine hopped several Flame Runnas, their green skin even more brilliant in the artificial light from the posts overhead. Between them they bore a man. They trotted toward Jubal to drop the unconscious figure at his feet.

"Rann!" Jubal dropped to his knees beside his brother. The stink of cooked flesh wafted toward him, but Rann's eyelids fluttered at the sound of his name.

The Flame Runnas chuckled, and one spoke, slowly, as if Jubal might not understand. "Found him near the Gate. Looks like he tried to piss on the fence."

Jubal scanned his brother's body. The front of his leather pants was wet, and the waist-tie was loose. "Will he be all right?"

No one answered. Brother John spoke to the Flame Runnas. "Is power back up?"

"Yes. Tell your guests to stay away from the perimeter. And you might mention the white flag. We nearly flashed him." The Flame Runnas trotted back to their machine, joking among themselves.

Jubal crouched next to Rann and put a tentative hand over his brother's heart. Rann's chest rose and fell. The scent of urine mingled with singed hair. "Rann, wake up."

Rann groaned and flung a hand into the air, but his arm fell back to the ground like a flopping fish. "Brrrrrrns," he slurred.

Brother John joined them, looking down at the prone man.

"You must see to his..." He fumbled for a word, then instead pointed to his crotch.

With a grimace, Jubal tugged at the flap of Rann's pants. Inside, his groin was red, and his genitals were covered in small blisters. Jubal flinched, averting his eyes, his own parts shriveling in sympathy. Pops had warned them that the wall would burn them, so why would Rann touch it, especially with that part of his body? It made no sense.

From the Flame Runna building, Ijon approached on foot. Eily and Gid followed close behind him. When they saw Rann lying there, parts exposed, Gid made a grunting noise in his throat and put an arm out as if to shield Eily. Jubal eased the leather flap back into place.

"What happened?" Ijon's face puckered in tight lines of disapproval. "Never mind. You want our medic—our healer? Or theirs?"

Jubal swallowed past the lump in his throat. "Will he be able to... use it again?"

Brother John shrugged. "Sometimes boys do these things. We'll take him to the Ward and see."

Gid helped lift Rann's legs while Jubal scooped him up by his shoulders. They lumbered past numerous buildings until they reached a tall brick structure with many windows. Inside, a woman greeted them with downcast eyes. She and Brother John spoke a moment then she showed them to a room with a small bed.

"Der Arzt kommt," she said, and exited with Brother John.

Ijon turned to leave, saying, "Let me know if you need anything."

Eily watched the men depart, but she and Gid remained. Rann groaned, and his eyes fluttered open. His hand slithered toward his crotch and he flinched. "By the Knife!"

"Don't touch, Rann." Jubal searched his brother's face. "Why would you put... that part... on the wall?"

Rann cleared his throat, but his voice still came out crackly. "I didn't. I thought it would be fun to piss on it. Then the lightning jumped at me, and that's all I remember."

Eily spoke up. "The fence is electric. Like invisible fire, but a kind of fire that burns water instead of wood. It traveled up his stream."

Rann cracked open his eyes and focused on her. "You." He grinned. "Like what you see?"

Eily took a step back and lowered her eyes. Gid clasped her arm, speaking in their strange tongue.

Jubal rose and turned his back to his brother to block their view of him. "Forgive him. He's in pain from the burns."

A bearded man entered and said something to Gid, and Gid ushered Eily out ahead of him. He looked over his shoulder at Jubal, his face hard. "Healer says go. He will look to brother."

Jubal squeezed Rann's hand. "You be okay?"

"Can't get much worse."

Following Gid out, Jubal stopped in the hall where Eily waited, gripping the edges of her overskirt. She darted a look at Gid and bit her lips together.

The man must not want his woman to interact with the traders. Jubal hid his disapproval; it wasn't his place to counter these people's ways. Instead, he dipped his head at Gid. "I apologize for Rann. He will not act so again."

To his surprise, Eily spoke. "This tribe who has Ana—they've accepted her as their own?"

Ana was a part of the tribe but in a very special, and separate, way. She wasn't quite a slave, he thought, but he doubted Sefe would allow her to leave. "Yes."

"Would they accept other Flame Runnas? Some who used to be of the tribes?"

What was she asking? "You want to go live with her?"

She shook her head. "No. But there are three Flame Runnas who wish to leave the Protectorate. They ask to travel with us."

Jubal's breath quickened. A whole group of Flame Runnas wanted to surrender themselves to Sefe? And she'd said "us," so she wanted to come, too. He couldn't believe his luck. *Too good to be true.* The old trader's saying floated through his mind in Pops's voice: when something came easy, there was a steep price later. But right now, the spirits were with him.

"This tribe calls itself the One Tree, made up of several tribes who have banded together." He almost added *after Flame Runna attacks* but caught himself. "They are very open to new members."

She licked her lips. "Will you—can you—escort us all there, under your trader's staff? I'll understand if you say no. Traveling with Flame Runnas is probably a horrible thought."

Don't give in too easily, or she might get suspicious. He widened his lips in his best trader's smile and winked. "What do you offer in trade?"

Eily's eyes widened. "I'm to be married."

Gid muttered something and shook his head, his gaze fierce on Jubal.

Heat flooded Jubal's face. After Rann's comment a moment ago, of course they'd think that. "I meant goods. Food, cloth, utensils."

Gid's face didn't clear, but Eily's tension eased. "We could trade some food. Maybe blankets? And we'll help carry your trade goods."

Stomach still queasy from his near slip-up, Jubal pretended to consider. After a couple of heartbeats, he held out a hand to seal the agreement. "Done."

She took it.

With a doubtful tightening of his lips, Gid offered a hand clasp as well.

Jubal had to fight to keep his trader's smile from becoming a triumphant grin. Her deal didn't include an escort back. Now all he had to do was escort them across the Tox safely. Keeping them would be Sefe's problem.

Chapter Ten

When Eily and Gid returned home, Levi was sitting at Beth's kitchen table holding a mug of tea. He must have heard the news about Ana and come all the way from his new home with Tula in the city. His beard had grown since Eily'd last seen him, and although he wore modest clothing, the fabric was of obvious Haldanian origin rather than the traditional homespun cloth made at the Holdout. He rose, and she gave him a tight hug. "I'm glad to see you, Uncle Levi. How's Josef? Where's Aunt Tula?"

"Josef's fine." He hugged her back. His embrace was a comfort she'd missed since he'd moved to the city to be near his son, Josef, who had to remain in the UV-protected Garden a few more years. "Tula sends her love. With the pregnancy in the final stages, your aunt can't risk too much sun."

He and Gid shook hands. Then Levi held a tiny box toward Eily. "She wanted to be sure you had these."

Eily took it, glancing at the label. "Allelopathic suppression pills? Uncle Levi, with the telomerase fungi, nobody uses these anymore."

He shrugged. “She said it was important. And wanted me to remind you to watch the yuvee trees for incoming sunstorms—”

Eily laughed. “I know, I know. Don’t touch the leaves. Watch for UV flares after a storm. Be cautious of unknown plants—”

“Don’t take this trip lightly.” Levi’s tone was sharp. Eily stopped laughing and frowned at him. The little lines around his mouth were deeper, his lips pale and tight. “Tula wanted me to convince you not to go.”

Eily stiffened. “Why would she do that? She knows I can’t leave Ana out there.”

“I think it has less to do with you than the reversions.” He rubbed a hand over his hair and down his nape. “You know how protective she can be about her converts. She says to keep an eye on them. Talk them into coming back with you if you can. And leave any unused pills with them if you can’t.”

Frowning, Eily nodded and put the container in her pocket. She took the dishes from the sideboard and began setting the table. “Did they tell you Ana’s pregnant? Your babies can play together.”

He smiled. “I hope so, Eily.”

Gid added, “And ours. We hope to start a family right away.”

Levi cocked his head and grinned at his nephew. “I hope you’ll wait until you get back and can properly marry.”

Gid flushed, taking a step back from Eily, even though he wasn’t within reach. “Of course.”

Eily kept her smile in place and ignored the empty ache in her chest.

A knock sounded against the kitchen’s screen door, and Eily peeked through her bedroom curtains into the blue light of dawn. Newlyweds Ezra and Ruth Beller stood on the porch holding a basket. From the other side of the wall came the creak of Aunt Beth's footsteps as she moved to the door, muffled voices, then the screen banging shut. The young couple retreated down the dirt lane, heads close as they talked.

All day yesterday, people had come and gone from the Yoder home as news of Gideon's trip spread across the Holdout. New shoes for him. A metal pail with a tight lid for transporting perishables. The doctor's daughter had brought a jar of pain-relieving salve for his scarred back and leg. Gid had sweet-talked the machine shop into contributing two new knives. Eily'd managed to acquire donations of old quilts and dried food. Even Ijon had offered some large backpacks for the reversions to carry gear. The reversions had been unable to gather their own items because they'd spent yesterday in the medical facility undergoing final exams.

Active with preparations, Eily hardly had time to think about the upcoming journey. This morning, though, she'd woken in darkness, her mind spinning with memories of fear and hunger. She hadn't been outside the safety of the fence in six years, not counting the brief debacle with Gid's mini. *Lucky debacle.* Without it, she might never have met the traders face to face, might never have learned of Ana.

How had her sister survived so long among the cannibals? Every living human on the Tox considered Flame Runnas mortal enemies. Yet Ana always had been the adventurous one. Self-reliant. Unhesitating. Unlike Ana, the thought of venturing past the Burn and into the Tox made Eily's stomach churn.

Shoving aside her fear, Eily dressed, made her bed, and fit a few last-minute things into her pack. A soft knock sounded at her door.

"Yes?"

Gid poked his head in first, then entered. He held a long

walking stick in one hand, much like a trader's staff but without the dangling ornamentation. "I'm ready when you are. Ma made us breakfast."

Eily might not need to eat but had grown used to the luxury while living at the Holdout. This morning, she didn't think her stomach would accept food. "Go ahead. I'll be there in a minute."

He reached to the top of her dresser and picked up Ijon's black transponder. "Don't forget the beacon."

"I'm not taking it."

"What? Why?"

She took the box from him and placed it firmly back on the dresser. "I don't trust them."

"But what if we get into trouble? Ijon promised they wouldn't come unless we call."

"The Protectorate's mission is to convert or kill every cannibal. I won't endanger the people who have kept Ana alive all this time."

Gid frowned and seized the beacon again. "It was part of the deal."

Eily huffed and snatched the box from him. "Fine." She dropped the beacon on top of her open pack, then turned to pretend to look for her toothbrush.

"I'll see you downstairs."

She nodded and waited until his footsteps creaked on the staircase. After a generous moment, she plucked the beacon from her pack and dropped it inside the top dresser drawer. Gid didn't understand. People in the Order were honest; if they agreed to do something, they did it. The Protectorate wasn't so trustworthy. Once she'd retrieved Ana, she would never know if the Board secretly sent Burn Operatives to eradicate the tribe. She couldn't risk it. But she didn't want to argue with Gid, either.

Down in the kitchen, Gid shoveled eggs and ham into his mouth. Gid's father, Samuel, sat grimly at the head of the table, his Bible beside him, stabbing chunks of fried potato with his fork. Eily took her seat and helped herself to a single hotcake and raspberry jam but found it difficult to swallow.

Beth brought two cloth-wrapped packages to the table and put one beside Eily's plate and the other next to Gid's. "Lunches." Her voice trembled. "Do you want extras for your reversion friends?"

Eily shook her head. "I don't want to coddle them. Maybe by the time we reach Ana, they'll change their minds and come back home."

Beth nodded, her eyes shining with tears, and turned back to the sink to wash dishes.

Eily looked around the warm kitchen, memorizing every sight and smell. Even Samuel's ruddy face, downturned toward his Bible, made her heart ache. She forced down a few bites in silence, then rose and hugged Beth. "I love you. Goodbye."

Chest shuddering, Beth dabbed at her eyes with her apron. "Auf Wiedersehen."

Samuel nodded his goodbye, ever as stiff as his son, and said, "Be careful."

"I'll wait outside for you, Gid." Eily exited to give him a few moments alone with his family. Anything could happen on the Tox, and this might be the last time Beth would see her son. Eily was prepared to die for her sister, and grateful Gid wanted to help, but the thought of him being slaughtered by cannibals was almost enough to make her forget the whole thing.

The sun crested the horizon, sending long shadows across the yard and promising a hot day. Eily fiddled with her pack and water bottle until Gid emerged from the house. Beth and Samuel stood on the porch steps as she and Gid began the trek toward the Gate where they would meet the rest of the party.

On other porches, families stood watching them pass, and when Eily and Gid reached the fence, a small crowd waited. A handful of Old Order stood on one side, murmuring about evil leading the way. A larger bunch of New Order well-wishers, some with final parting gifts, surrounded them. A few handed her tokens—a stubby wax candle, a nub of maple candy—but most gifts were for Gid. One girl handed him a packet of jerky. Miss Blythe, the schoolteacher, offered him a miniature New Testament Bible.

The two traders waited with their packs near the Gate. Rann's features were pinched in discomfort, but according to the doctor, he would heal. Jubal, his smile as dazzling as ever, spoke to Brother John. The trader laughed at something and clapped John on the shoulder. Eily looked away, an undefined longing rising in her. Above the hinged portal, a sign read *The Gate is Narrow* to remind the faithful to keep their hearts on God.

Jubal rose to greet them. "We're ready."

The crackle of tires on gravel announced Ijon's arrival with the reversions. The men climbed out of the skimmer. Pulo's muscles bunched as he shrugged into his pack. He helped Wint into his, Wint's pudgy gut bulging as he fastened the waist harness. The two of them entwined fingers and smiled into each other's eyes, and Eily suddenly understood why they wanted to leave the Holdout.

Eily caught Lisius's eye, and he grinned, eyes twinkling. "We're going home."

She bit back her reply—no need to start the trip on a sour note, especially if she hoped to talk him out of remaining on the Tox.

Ijon looked everyone over. "Good luck."

Eily said firmly, "We'll be back soon."

"Ready?" Gid asked, looking at her.

She nodded. He faced the gatehouse and raised a hand high

to signal the gatekeeper waiting at the low door. The man dipped his chin at them before disappearing inside. When the faint hum from the fence ceased, Gid opened the latch. He pushed the Gate outward and gestured to Jubal to lead the way. Rann followed with the reversions, then Eily and Gid, who closed the Gate with a metallic clunk.

For a moment, they all stood gazing toward the green line of the Tox. Eily swiveled to take a last, long look at the crowd behind the fence. Then they set off to find the cannibals.

They reached the edge of the amarantox within the hour, and soon the large, ribbed leaves blocked out the sun. Gid, taller than the others by several inches, stretched to touch the ceiling of vegetation every now and again as they walked, exposing a glimpse of blue sky. An ever-present breeze rustled the canopy but couldn't reach them down on the narrow dirt path between the stalks.

Eily found herself walking differently, lighter on her toes, more careful of where she placed each step, her limbs loose yet primed for action. Her senses, muted so long, seemed to explode like the breath a swimmer releases after surfacing from a lake. Every rustle of leaves drew her attention, every shadow her gaze. *Friend, foe, food?* A short distance ahead, the reversions followed close behind Jubal, pointing and chattering between themselves. They wanted to return to their former lives, but they seemed to have forgotten the terror of the Tox.

Or maybe her days spent fleeing the Fosselite mountain with Tula and Levi had scarred her far more deeply than growing up in a tribe ever could.

At least on this journey they were not fleeing Fosselite night vision or Protectorate Burn Operatives. Ijon had assured her that Burn Ops flight crews had been instructed to stand down for the next two days, so they needn't worry about being mistaken for cannibals. But she still scanned the skies whenever Gid opened a line of sight upward.

At a small creek crossing, Jubal paused and told everyone to top off their water bottles. The bank sloped gently to the water, and the amarantox gave way to tamarisk thickets and cattail reeds. The breeze could reach them here, offering welcome relief from the stagnant tunnel through the weeds, and everyone dropped their packs for a break.

Gid reclined on a flat spot to stretch the kinks out of his leg. He'd been keeping up well, but she wasn't sure how long he could maintain this pace. Lisius had his head together with Wint and Pulo. They'd captured a beetle and passed it between them, arguing over who got to eat it. Jubal stood at the edge of the water and gazed across the creek, his trader's staff in hand. She joined him, searching the amarantox on the other bank.

He turned his head toward her, his eyes roaming down her skirt. "You'll be able to cross this?"

She glanced into the water for the first time. She knew how to swim but had never tried in a dress. She licked her lips and took a quick peek at Gid, realizing for the first time that she was the only female in the group. The reversions had quickly divested themselves of the Order's modest clothing, and all three now wore only trousers and boots. Lisius retained the wide straw hat worn by men in the order. He and Pulo had rolled their cuffs up around their knees. Wint retained his suspenders; in spite of his photosynthesis, he'd eaten enough at the Holdout to plump out his belly, and his hips would no longer hold up his waistband. *He'd make a fine meal*. She shook her head, horrified at her own thought, as if the Tox was reverting her against her will.

She turned her attention back to the flowing brown water.

It looked calm enough, but that could be deceiving. "How deep is it?"

Jubal moved close enough that their shoulders touched, and a small thrill chased outward from the contact. With one hand he indicated the bottom of his ribcage, about level with her armpit. "And slippery."

Sighing, she sat down on the bank and began unlacing her shoes. Her bare feet would grip the slippery rocks better. Her dress, however, was another problem. Even tucked into her waistband, it provided a lot of fabric for the current to catch hold of. And if she slipped and went under, it would be a lot of weight to struggle with. She rubbed her hands up and down her thighs. The dress had to come off. Gid would be horrified. *He'll be more horrified if you drown.*

She loosed the first hook and eye at her collar. Then the next. Underneath, she wore a white sleeveless chemise and panties. As she lowered the dress around her shoulders, Gid lurched to his feet and rushed to her side in such haste that his foot splashed into the edge of the stream and he nearly tumbled in. He gripped the dress and yanked it up to cover her. "Eily! What are you doing?"

"I can't swim in a dress, Gid."

He glanced in horror at the others, his face twitching. Bending close to Eily, he whispered, "But we'll see you."

She tried not to smile as his eyes flicked toward her breasts. *I want him to see me.* Taking a step back, she kept her gaze locked on his and dropped the dress around her feet. "Then don't look."

Gid spun to face upstream, his shoulders heaving with his rapid breath. A tiny nudge of disappointment made her chest ache. Then she caught Jubal's eye on her. He didn't look away as she met his gaze. The ache inside her exploded into trembling butterflies. Flushing, she bent and gathered her dress, folding it neatly and placing it inside her pack.

She lifted the load to the top of her head. "I'm ready."

"We'll go together." Jubal swung his pack over his head with practiced ease and settled it onto his shoulders. He stepped into the water, unconcerned for his wet leggings, and waited for her to join him.

She followed, edging out into the current carefully. The rocks scraped against her bare feet, jagged and slippery at the same time; her soles had grown soft at the Holdout. The chill water stiffened her joints, but she kept her focus on the other side.

"Eily, wait!" Gid called behind her.

She didn't stop moving. About two thirds of the way across, her foot slipped sideways, but Jubal caught her elbow and kept her upright. He kept a supporting grip on her as they finished crossing. When they reached the far bank, he helped her lower her pack.

A cry from the water drew her attention, and she spun just in time to see Gideon's head go under. She lunged forward. Jubal's grip around her arm jerked her backward and she stumbled against his chest. "Gideon!"

Gid surfaced, arms flailing, and went under again. Loose items from his pack swirled into the current. On the other side of the bank, Lisius shrugged out of his pack and dove into the muddy river. Eily struggled against Jubal's grip. "Let me go!"

"You'd only be another body to save. Stay put."

Lisius reached the churning water where Gid struggled and grabbed hold. With strong strokes, he moved toward shore. Jubal released Eily's arm, and she fled down the bank to where the drenched men crawled onto the rock.

"Gideon, are you all right?"

He coughed and nodded, weakly attempting to push the

shoulder straps of his pack off. She squatted to help. The pack's top hadn't been cinched closed, and most of the contents were missing, including all their food.

Lisius pushed onto his hands and knees and then to his feet, breathing hard. "That was close."

She stood and threw her arms around him. "Thank you."

He rubbed a hand up and down her back and nodded. She let go and held a hand down to Gid to help him up. He'd lost his staff, and a tear in the shin of his trousers dripped watery blood onto the rock. He looked up at her and his brows drew together. "Put your clothes back on."

His admonition made her drop her chin in shame. Her dark nipples showed clearly through her chemise. Crossing one arm over her chest, she shuffled to her pack. Jubal waited where they'd left the water, his dark eyes on her. Her skin tingled under his gaze, and she averted her eyes while she pulled her dress over her head and fastened the hooks.

Gid joined her as she finished the final clasp. "You should have waited."

She met his blue eyes. "I didn't want to lose my nerve."

Jubal leaned close to her and asked, "Why is he angry with you?"

She'd forgotten he couldn't understand Gid's language. "He worries."

"I can see that."

Gid scowled but didn't respond. The others forded the creek without incident. The reversions had removed every stitch of clothing, and Pulo dropped his pack once he reached their side and dove back into the water. He surfaced and shook water from his hair like a dog. "We're free!" he crowed. Wint joined him and they embraced and locked lips in a joyful kiss.

Gid stared at the naked men and hissed, "Avert your eyes!"

Rann, who had remained clothed, emerged from the water

cradling his crotch. "By the Knife! That stings!" He peeled out of his leggings as soon as he was clear of the water.

Gid let out a strangled, choking sound and grabbed Eily's arm to twist her away from the sight. Eily sighed. "Gid, nakedness is natural. It's the way God created us."

"The Prophet directed, 'Cover your flesh that you do not inspire lustful thoughts among your brethren."

She wanted to ask if he had lustful thoughts but decided against it. When the group resumed walking. Gid kept close to her side, muttering about godless cannibals.

Chapter Eleven

Jubal stepped from beneath the foliage canopy into the afternoon glare. A ribbon of cracked pavement intersected the trail through the amarantox. In either direction, the sun beat down on the hulks of ancient vehicles, anything of value looted long ago. He checked back as the three Flame Runna men emerged on his heels. Eily and Gid followed not far behind. Lagging farther back, Rann limped along in a bow-legged gait, his face pale.

Jubal frowned and sighed. *It isn't Rann's fault he's hurt.* But they had moved more slowly than usual so his brother could keep up. Retreating to the shade of the amarantox, Jubal jabbed the butt of his staff into the earth, kicking some rocks up around the base so it remained upright. "We'll stop here tonight."

Lisius remained on the pavement. "Still have plenty of light. We could make good time on this path."

"We will tomorrow."

A few steps away, Eily spoke to her group. Gid gazed at his feet and nodded. The male Flame Runnas argued among themselves, gesturing into the surrounding amarantox. The tallest one said, “We can gather enough for him.”

Jubal approached the party. “Is there a problem?”

Eily answered, “All of our food is gone.”

The fat Flame Runna chimed in. “Pulo says we can find beetles in the tamarisk.”

“There’s enough light left to hunt a bit,” added the one called Lisius.

Jubal shook his head. He couldn’t chance losing a single Flame Runna to the dangers of the Tox, even if it meant he went hungry on the journey. “You don’t know the area well enough to go out on your own. And there could be hunters. I have enough food to share.”

Jubal untied the bundle from his pack. The people at the Holdout had been generous in their parting gifts—not only in food but in other goods. In return for three salt packets, one woman had traded him a precious swath of pure white fabric like the kind Eily wore on her head. The color would fetch an outrageous price. Too bad he’d never be able to trade with the Holdout again.

He opened the bundle. “I have some ‘bis-kits.’”

“They should trade us for food,” Rann interjected. He raised his eyebrows at Eily. “How ’bout some spirit healing for my pain?”

Eily took a step back, and Gid cocked his head in question.

Jubal interceded before Rann caused any trouble. “Let me have your staff, Rann.” He drilled a look of warning into his brother. “Go use the salve the healer gave you.”

He held the biscuits out to Eily. He’d have to find a secluded moment to talk to his brother. If they weren’t careful, Eily and the others could get suspicious and turn back to Flame Runna territory.

She took the food without smiling, and the image of her

sleek green limbs flashed through his mind for the tenth time. He'd seen plenty of naked women, and her skin color should put him off, but somehow her modesty made her more alluring. He brushed away the thought. She was a Flame Runna. Not a travel companion.

Eily said, "Spirit healing. Is that what my sister is doing?"

Jubal met her eyes, considering his words before speaking. What did Eily want to hear? "She's very powerful."

Eily's dark eyes were so intense he worried she might see his soul. Was this a part of the spirit healing he didn't know about? His skin prickled, but he didn't look away.

She asked, "Have you used her?"

"No! No." He was glad he could say this so quickly and genuinely. "The king, her man, is very proud of her."

Tears sheened her eyes, and she broke eye contact. "She always wanted to be powerful."

Gid limped into the space between them, stepping on the blanket and blocking Jubal's view in order to speak to Eily. He'd been doing this kind of posturing all day. "Kann ich helfen?"

Jubal rose, his chin only at the level of Gid's shoulder. He could smell the sweat of travel and the slightly sweet scent of Gid's straw hat. His pulse raced as he shifted his weight to the balls of his feet. A fight with Gid would be interesting.

Gid didn't turn to face him.

Eily straightened and spoke in slow, deliberate Cannibal, frowning at Gid. "Please, eat."

Gid bent and swept up a biscuit. He took a bite and stared into the amarantox as he chewed, jaw muscles bulging.

Why did the man keep offering a confrontation, then pointedly ignoring Jubal's return challenge? Was Eily his woman or not? *Do you really want a fight?*

Taking a biscuit for himself, Jubal contemplated the situation. Gid was worth nothing in trade, yet Jubal wished the man no harm. *If only I could turn Gid around and keep the rest.* He'd hoped nature would resolve the issue when the man had slipped in the river. Eily's determination to save Gid had impressed him, but he couldn't risk losing her; Ana's twin would be their most prized bargaining chip.

If Rann was well, they might be able to outpace Gid. The river had proven what a liability he was. But even if they could sway Eily to abandon him, Jubal doubted Gid would let his woman go without a fight; Jubal wouldn't, if he had a woman like Eily. Jubal shook his head. She was a Flame Runna. Best to bury thoughts like that.

He picked up another biscuit and stared at it to avoid looking at Gid. Now wasn't the time for violence. He had to focus on getting these Flame Runnas to the Taguan. He'd never dealt in human cargo. Pops had always avoided slaving. He said slavers ended up slaves themselves in the end.

He settled to the ground across from Gid, studying the man's scars. The art was even but not finely executed. A jagged pucker at the bottom of the longest scar looked like the tattooer had slipped and hit the muscle. "Gid, tell me about your marks."

Gid met Jubal's gaze. "Marks?"

Jubal ran his fingers across his face, mirroring Gid's lines. "The pattern is unfamiliar."

"I was in..." Gid began, then stopped. He frowned at Eily. "Wie sage ich Unfall?"

She ignored Gid, instead nodding her head rapidly at Jubal. "Yes. Of course Gid is a Knowing. He keeps the secrets of the flying machines. He's one of the few who can make them fly."

Gid scowled at her. "Das ist nicht wahr."

"Ich lüge, um Sie sicher." Her words, directed at Gid, were frustrated. When she turned back to Jubal, she smiled again, the kind of smile a trader used when he was about to lose a deal. "He's a very important man among our people."

Jubal rubbed his chin. "Not so useful on the Tox."

She lifted her chin, shoulders back. "He is Knowing."

With a noncommittal grunt, Jubal snagged some jerky and rose to join Rann at the other side of the clearing. The most sacred law on the Tox made the Knowing untouchable even by hunters; to kill one meant shunning and death for the entire tribe. Only Flame Runnas killed without discretion. But Gid's knowledge was a Flame Runna skill. Did he qualify? Jubal didn't want to break any more laws.

A whiff of smoke caught his attention, and he spotted the three green men squatted around a pile of kindling. Wint was fanning a small lick of flame.

Lisius sat with his arms crossed, his face twisted with derision. "Wint, you pussy. You brought a lighter?"

Pulo grinned. "It *is* easier to start a fire with one."

"Stop standing up for him." Lisius punched Pulo in the shoulder. "He's gotta go back to the old ways if he wants to stay alive."

Jubal strode over and kicked aside the pile of sticks. "No fire."

The Flame Runnas hushed, twisting to glare up at him.

Disconcerted by the green faces, Jubal drew himself taller. "You want to attract hunters?"

Lisius glanced down at the scattered sticks then scanned the amarantox suspiciously.

"No fire." Pulo nodded.

Wint groaned and flopped back to sprawl against the ground.

"Hush," Jubal said. "You've chattered all day. No one could hear my trader staff over you even if they tried. We're leaving

Flame Runna territory, so you'd better learn to be quiet, or I can't promise you'll reach the Taguan."

Behind him, Eily said, "The Taguan? I remember trading there as a child! Is that where we're going?"

He nodded without turning to look at her, his chest tight. She'd been a child among the tribes. She knew the Taguan. *They're not like us,* he reminded himself. *They're Flame Runnas.* Yet betraying her felt so wrong. She'd never done anything to harm him. Plus he was betraying the trade laws that had kept him alive for much of his life. Even the Flame Runna Ijon, who'd pushed hard at the boundaries of the Peace by questioning him, had honored the law and let them leave. Jubal's stomach churned.

"Will my sister still be there when we arrive?" Eily asked.

"Yes. The One Tree has remained there many seasons." He spread his blanket on the ground next to Rann. "Now everyone get some rest. We move at dawn."

Easing onto the blanket, he lay on his back and stared at the dusky sky. If he found a way to spare Eily from the trade, would Gid fight to protect the other Flame Runnas? Jubal didn't think so. But Eily would. She was a protector. She wanted to save her sister. She'd stood up for Jubal and Rann at the lightning wall. Betraying her violated the very spirit of the Peace.

You only promised to take them there, not that they'd be safe and accepted upon arrival. He could send Eily back, now, before she realized what he'd done. The three Flame Runna men would be enough to buy Pops's freedom. But Eily would never give up without her sister. And once Sefe saw her, he'd want the twin to his beloved Ana.

Rann sighed loudly. "Some bitters would go down easy right now since the Flame Runna won't give me spirit healing."

At the mention of spirit healing, Eily's naked body came to mind, and Jubal's groin stirred. Would she and her man make love tonight? He shook off the thought and said in a low voice, "You need to watch your mouth or they might turn around and go back to the lightning wall."

"Would a kiss kill her?"

"Their people don't share their women. And there are more of them than us, so you need to behave."

Rann sighed again. "Right."

Jubal lay back against his blanket, listening to the camp settle as darkness filled the sky. The Flame Runnas whispered among themselves as they settled in to sleep, then the camp fell quiet. He told himself he was listening for hunters, but he kept turning his face toward Eily and Gid's blankets. All he could think about was her lying next to Gid. Beneath Gid. He waited and listened for the inevitable sounds of sexing from their blankets. If Jubal had such a woman, he'd make love to her every night. But the sounds never came. Wint's snores were as obnoxious as his chattering. Jubal squinted into the darkness, his eyes struggling to see in the meager light from the stars.

Eventually, he gave up and rose. If he couldn't sleep, he'd patrol the perimeter.

Chapter Twelve

Eily stared at the night sky and inhaled the lush scent of the crushed amarantox. She didn't even try to close her eyes. It wasn't fear that haunted her but something else. Anticipation, yes, and more. Perhaps this feeling was what drove reversions to flee the Protectorate. *The Holdout is your home. Your safety.* But the air out here energized her.

The camp rumbled with Wint's snores. How had the boy survived the Tox before being taken by the Protectorate? All that noise would alert every hunter within range. She hoped the trader staves would be enough to protect the group as they moved deeper into cannibal territory. From the opposite edge of the camp came rustling, then soft footsteps passed her and Gid's sleeping spot toward the open expanse of the old road.

She turned her head to look at Gid, flat on his back. During the long hospital stay after his accident, he'd learned to sleep through anything. At least he didn't snore. Slowly, she lifted her blanket aside and crept toward the road, eyes wide in search of the other wakeful party member. Maybe she'd get a chance to talk to Lisius or Pulo and begin convincing them to return to the Holdout with her.

In the feeble light of a crescent moon, at the edge of the clearing, Jubal's trade beads caught the moonlight. Maybe she could learn more about Ana from him. She tiptoed over. "You can't sleep either?"

Jubal jerked, his voice a little too loud. "Eily!"

"I didn't mean to startle you." She settled next to him amid last year's fallen amarantox leaves and wrapped her arms around her knees.

Starlight picked up the white of his eyes. The rest of him remained part of the darkness. He said, "Don't know how anyone can sleep through that snoring. I couldn't even hear you approach."

She looked out across the dark road—shadows on top of shadows, the remains of a world long gone. "I don't remember anyone snoring when I was a child."

The night wind sighed through the leaves at their backs. After a few heartbeats, Jubal said, "Which tribe were you from?"

"Under Stone. Ana and I tried to help Mama run when the Flame Runnas came. She was heavy into pregnancy." The memory was so old, it felt like someone else's. "But they killed her."

"I heard tales of them taking children. But no one ever thought it was to... make them into Flame Runnas. How do they do it?"

She shuddered. "The best way to describe it is like tattoos. They poke needles into you, and then you have green skin. It hurts. But now I never dread the hunger. Do you see how only Gid needs to eat? I can survive on nothing but sunlight and water, like the amarantox."

"That is truly a gift worth having. Why doesn't your man have green skin?"

"His people say that God's work should not be altered. They would rather face the hunger."

"That's just plain stupid. If the Flame Runnas weren't so hated on the Tox, I'd take green skin."

"There's more, though. The sun makes me feel... 'drunk' is the best word. What you call spirit healing."

"I heard sexing with a Flame Runna makes men feel drunk for a while. Didn't realize Flame Runnas felt it all the time."

Eily tightened her grip around her knees, sickness washing over her. Did Ana's man force her to share herself? The tribes cared less about monogamy than they did about status and survival; men often encouraged their women to lie with the other men of the tribe. If there was a chance a woman bore the leader's child, she and all her children might be spared the Knife during future hunger times.

Jubal cleared his throat and leaned slightly toward her. "Your man is smart not to indulge while on a journey."

A strange sensation fluttered low in her stomach, and she was suddenly all too aware of the man beside her. Not afraid, as she'd been with Rann's request for spirit healing earlier. Just... startled. What would kissing Jubal be like? She trembled. She'd kissed Gid once, and only once. He'd flinched, then admonished her never to do it again. But the worst part was when he'd confessed to the Elders. For an entire winter, she'd had to endure weekly lectures about propriety and modesty from the village matrons. "We're not married. It would be improper for us to... indulge."

"But he is your man?" Jubal's voice seemed deeper and more hushed. His eyes caught the moonlight again, causing her heart to rise to her throat.

The air seemed too thick to breathe. She wanted her

betrothed to look at her the way Jubal did now. Like he had at the creek crossing. With desire. *Gid's always been there for you.* She whispered, "He's my man." *Focus on Ana.* She swallowed and took a deep breath. "Tell me about my sister. Has she been with her man long?"

The dry amarantox leaves crackled as Jubal reclined to face the sky. "I was only at the Taguan a couple of days. The tribe seemed well. The manna beetles grow thick in the area, and Sefe said they've not called a Hunger in four years. It would be a pleasant place to live."

"I remember there being hundreds of people at the Autumn trade. By the time it ended, there was nothing left to eat nearby."

"The One Tree posts watchers to hunt the pecker-birds and voles that eat the beetle larvae. And they've constructed supports to keep the amarantox from collapsing in the wind as the beetles grow in the stalks, so the beetles are easy to harvest. They collect so much, they store the dried meal and eat from it all winter. They even have enough to spare for trade."

She let go of her knees and turned to face him, resting her palms against the dirt. "They're farming?"

"What's 'farming'?"

"Like they do in the Holdout. Intentionally growing food in a given area. Enough food to sustain them without needing to migrate. Do you know what this means?"

He let out a puff of air. "That they're vulnerable to Flame Runna attacks if they're discovered."

Eily's heart flip-flopped. She was now doubly glad she'd left the beacon behind. "I suppose. But that won't be a concern once the Protectorate knows the One Tree isn't a threat. If they're farming, they aren't hunting. They can negotiate a Peace like we have at the Holdout. Maybe the reversions *can* be safe there!"

Chest heaving with excitement, she rose to her feet. This new information gave her such hope, she wanted to resume travel now, in the dead of night. But that would be silly. She took a few paces toward the road and lifted her face to the sliver of moon. The way it hung in the sky reminded her of a sideways smile, and she smiled back.

Behind her, Jubal's beads clicked together as he rose. "Peace is a lot to hope for."

Jubal sat up from his nap and glanced out past the amarantox canopy. The faint odor of burned amarantox had reached him, but he saw no sign of smoke from this vantage. No one else seemed to notice the scent. Sweat tickled its way down his spine. The heat pressed against the earth like a suffocating shroud, so he'd given in to the group's request for a brief rest at the edge of the pavement where the amarantox provided better shade.

He glanced around. Rann sprawled in the dirt, mouth slightly open in sleep. Eily talked softly to the other Flame Runnas. They'd travelled the first half of the day in near silence, the Flame Runnas having taken his advice about their chatter seriously. Now he heard the words *peace* and *farming* as Eily waved her delicate hands excitedly. She reminded him of a bird approaching a snare. His gut ached. He rose and turned away. Let her talk to them of peace—all the easier to get them there, rescue Pops, and leave all this behind.

Walking cautiously upwind, he butted his staff on the ground with each step, making the ornaments clank. About a hundred paces ahead, the road curved right. At the turn, wilted leaves drooped from the amarantox stalks: bright green, as though they'd been cooked. Farther off the road, the stalks turned black and flattened into a huge, ashy clearing. Three charred corpses lay curled amid the cinders. He sucked in a breath. His gaze flicked skyward and he took a step back. He collided with someone and spun. Gid stood close on his heels.

"Jubal. What is?" The Holdout man pinched his nose shut and looked over Jubal's head at the clearing, brows furrowed.

"Nothing. Go back. We must keep moving." He pushed at Gid's chest with the edge of his staff, as if herding goats.

The man teetered and grabbed Jubal's shoulder for support. Jubal braced himself until Gid stabilized. The big man's blue eyes widened and he pointed to the clearing. "Was ist das?"

Jubal didn't look. He'd hoped to bypass the burned area without alerting his party. He didn't want to chance them turning back in fear. And there was a lot to fear, from both Flame Runnas and any remaining tribesmen. "Go back. This has nothing to do with us."

Gid ignored him and hobbled past Jubal to enter the clearing without a single glance at the sky. He dropped to a knee beside one of the corpses. His hands fluttered above the body as if unsure what to do.

Horrified, Jubal could only watch. Was the man an idiot? Survivors would be back to recover the bodies. And if they found his group in the area—a party of Flame Runnas—they'd be certain to exact justice, trader's staff or not. Gid moved to the next body, still oblivious. *You wanted to be rid of the man. Let him stay.*

Flaring his nostrils against the stink of burned hair and flesh, Jubal spun and raced back to his group. "We move. Now."

Rann groaned. "It's too hot."

"Rann!" Jubal barked in his best imitation of Pops.

His brother scrunched up his face and gathered his legs beneath him to rise. He lifted his pack partway, and it bumped the front of his thighs. "By the Knife!" He let the load sag back to the ground.

The others languidly stretched, searching for water bottles and other items. Wint opened his pack and began to dig for something. Eily brushed off her skirt and looked around. "Where's Gid?"

Jubal's heart raced, but he kept his voice low and firm. "We must move quickly. Flame Runnas have been here."

Rann jerked his head up to look at his brother, taking only an eyeblink before heaving his pack to his back. As he settled the straps in place, he scanned the sky above the road. "Ready."

Eily stood immobile, mouth hanging open. "Ijon told me they'd hold Burn Ops back until we were out of the area."

The others had donned their gear. Jubal hoisted his pack into place. "Flame Runna lie. We must leave the area."

Eily lifted her bag and began calling for Gid. Jubal's throat tightened. He grabbed her arm. "Hush. Do you want to tell the whole Tox where we are?"

"But we have to find Gid."

"We have to get moving. Now." He pushed her toward Rann, who took her arm. She winced and struggled to free herself. Jubal glowered at her. "I'll get him."

Eily's shoulders relaxed. "Thank God. There he is."

Gid limped their way. A small white scrap of cloth fluttered from one upraised fist. Jubal turned to his brother and pointed into the amarantox. "Start moving north, off trail. Watch for hunters. They'd love to take revenge on a Flame Runna right now."

Rann nodded and ducked into the foliage, Lisius and his friends at his heels. Eily stubbornly remained behind.

Gid reached them, out of breath. He said something. Eily turned to Jubal, eyes wide. "Why didn't you say there were casualties?"

"Their tribe will come back for them. No wasting. Now let's go!"

Eily shook her head. "He says there's a survivor. A child."

He held aside a broad leaf for her to follow Rann and the others. "The tribe will find him."

"But what if they don't? We have to save him." She turned and pelted down the road, the folds of her skirt ballooning behind her. Gid followed, holding the white cloth in the air and limping.

Jubal shot a glance at the trail Rann had taken. He could leave Eily and Gid here, to the mercy of the tribe. He had three Flame Runnas. Plenty to buy Pops. He should go.

Instead, he dashed after Eily, his heavy pack cutting into his shoulders with every jarring step.

At the burned area, Eily crouched with her head nearly touching the ground, peering beneath a small stone outcrop. "Come out. Here, that's it."

She eased a naked, battered body from the depression. A girl, no more than three, her blistered eyes sealed shut. Oozing skin covered where the little one's hair should have been. One shoulder glinted white bone at the upper curve.

The child whimpered as breath whistled rapidly in and out of her open mouth. She wheezed and began coughing wet, shuddering spasms. Eily eased the little one to the ground.

Jubal clenched his jaw. "She breathed the fire. There's no hope for her."

Eily looked up, her eyes shiny with tears. "We can't leave her here."

Gid babbled something and thrust his cloth into Eily's hands before limping back the way they'd come. Eily lurched upright to stare after him open-mouthed. The usually healthy cast in her green cheeks had drained away.

Jubal swallowed, pulled his shoulders back and yanked his

knife from his belt. Gid was right. They had to go. "May the Mother guide my Knife."

Before he could think about it more, he sliced the blade deep into the child's throat until blood pulsed from the wound. At least her death would be swift.

Eily screamed and fell to her knees, pressing her apron to the gaping wound. "No! No, no no!"

"Her tribe will be back, and they'd be glad to have a Flame Runna pay for their loss. It was mercy to end her suffering." Jubal shuddered but didn't pause for regret. Eyes could be on them even now. On Eily. He grabbed her arm and yanked her to her feet.

Chapter Thirteen

Eily stumbled along in Jubal's grasp, a silent scream still ringing through her head. He was right; with lungs burned beyond even Protectorate technology, the child was as good as dead. But Eily had forgotten how cruel cannibal mercy could be. *Would it have been better to allow the child to suffer while waiting for God to take her?* It was a question she didn't want to answer.

At the bend in the road they met Gid coming back. In his hand he carried a small, black box. *The beacon. He'd brought the damned beacon.* She winced, awash in guilt and dismay. Had the Protectorate been tracking them and sent a duster ahead to clear the way? Gid had no idea what he'd done. She wasn't positive, either, but her mind reeled with probabilities. Was the child's death on their hands?

Jubal pushed past the larger man, still tugging Eily beside him.

Gid looked at her bloody hands and apron, his scars drawn tight. "The child?"

She shook her head, not trusting her voice.

"We should bury them," he said to her retreating back.

"Hunters are coming," was all she could manage past a throat tight with emotions. After a moment, Gid's footsteps sounded behind her.

They paused only long enough to pick up her pack. Jubal pulled her into the amarantox on the north side of the road, following a trail only he could see. Gid kept pace behind them, his footsteps heavy and uneven with his limp. When Jubal finally released his hold on her, she bent to scoop up a handful of dirt and abrade the blood from her palms as she walked.

The light beneath the canopy grew dim as the sun approached the end of its arc. Jubal checked over his shoulder to be sure she still followed, but he didn't slow. A pecker bird tat-tat-tatted against the canes in the distance. Eily flinched at the sudden noise. By the time they reached Lisius and the others at a gangly stand of tamarisk, the horizon glowed orange with sunset. Jubal planted his staff upright and dropped his pack. "Everyone stays close tonight."

She took out her blanket and spread it, unwilling to look up and face either Gid or Jubal. The blood on her apron made her stomach roil. She removed it and tossed it to the edge of camp. Today's events had brought back emotions she'd thought never to encounter again. Jubal had done something no one at the Holdout would have had the courage to do. Gid would be beside himself if he knew. Yet she understood the strength in Jubal's mercy. More than that, she appreciated it. The realization scared her.

Gid slumped to the ground opposite her. "Here." He held out the small black box. "You left it in your dresser."

She batted the beacon out of his hand, sending it skittering into the debris of twigs and dry leaves beneath the tamarisk. "They killed those people!"

"Everything happens by Gotte's Wille." His placid blue eyes seemed foreign.

She scowled. "How can you say that—excuse what they do so easily?"

"I'm not excusing them. But Ijon sent the beacon to aid us."

"They have no interest in helping a dying cannibal child." Eily fought the weakness of tears, but her voice betrayed her with a sob. "There *was* no helping her. This is the Tox. Better she die quickly."

"We did what we could to save her."

Eily bunched her fists in her skirt, tears running hot and free. "I left that beacon behind for a reason."

"You promised you'd bring it." His voice remained calm, but his gaze was full of censure.

Heat crept over her face and she twisted her head away. She'd hoped they'd never have cause to use the beacon. That he'd never know she'd left it. Now she couldn't even claim to have lost it. "You don't understand."

"No, I don't. At home, you work for the Protectorate. You further their interests with not only the reversions you counsel but also the Order, in spite of our Elders' misgivings. Now you claim the Blattvolk are not to be trusted. Which is it?"

She hung her head and wrapped her arms around herself. In the cooling night air, heat radiated upwards from the sunbaked earth. "It depends on who you are."

Gid stretched out his legs and lay back, tipping his hat down over his eyes to sleep. "Let me know when you figure that out."

Her skin tingled, as if every chloroplast was trying to jump out. She was whoever she needed to be to survive. Protectorate citizen, member of the Order... child of cannibals. Playing so many sides had become exhausting.

Gid only wanted to keep her safe. *How's he going to do that without fighting back?* At least he'd kept quiet when she'd lied to

Jubal about Gid's scars. Her empty stomach ached. She was the one protecting him. Trembling, she realized for the first time how alone she was out here.

She closed her eyes and let the tears fall. Had she ever truly belonged anywhere? Only with Ana. She missed her sister like a lost limb. If Jubal was right and the dead child's tribe attacked them, the beacon might save their lives. And to reach Ana, she had to stay alive. Taking a breath, she opened her eyes again and stared into the gray tamarisk branches that twined about each other. She couldn't tell where one tree started and another began. Together, she and Ana would be whole. They'd be on each other's side. They would settle in at the Holdout. Ana would have her baby, and Eily would marry Gid and become a proper wife. Maybe they could even find a husband for Ana. Life would be fine and peaceful.

She rose and dusted off her skirt. Walking to the spot where the beacon had landed, she crouched and dug through the debris. The box was thankfully undamaged. She opened it to be sure, then snapped the lid shut and slid the box into her skirt pocket. *The cannibals wouldn't hesitate to use it if the roles were reversed.*

"What's that?" Jubal spoke from over her left shoulder.

She turned and looked him in the eye with a tight smile. "Something to trade. If I need to."

Haldanian Protectorate

Rael walked toward the back of the duster hangar, careful to avoid the techs scurrying among the assorted parts and tools. They were too busy to notice an old man, even a councilman. There was no privacy screening on the hangar walls, and the surrounding buildings reflected the city back at them. Beyond the duster pad on the eastern side stretched the red, barren sweep of the Burn.

"Councilman Rael!" Panone, the Burn Ops Supervisor, darted through the hangar to shake his hand. He had a smudge of grime under one eye and wore a single nuvoplast neck torque that wouldn't get in the way of his mechanical work. "What can we do for you? Need a ride somewhere?"

"Let's go to your office." Rael didn't smile but kept his voice civil in spite of the seething frustration he felt.

Panone's eyes narrowed. "Of course. This way."

They walked together through the teeming activity, techs clearing the way at Panone's nod. The hangar grew quieter as they passed. Rael followed the supervisor into a small room with a desk and three chairs. Panone said, "Privacy." The walls from the inside didn't change, but they could no longer be seen by the crews in the hangar. The supervisor indicated a chair and walked around the desk to take his own.

Rael put a hand on the back of the offered seat but remained standing. "You were told to keep your teams away from our tracking signal."

Panone raised his brows. "And we have."

"A flashing took place less than half a kilometer from the signal late yesterday."

"We were within distance specifications."

Rael pressed his lips together. Eily's beacon signal had moved to nearly on top of the location of the flashing within an hour of the occurrence. If she and her reversions encountered a bunch of angry, fleeing cannibals... He needed those reversions to reach the Fosselites alive. "Then we need to extend the specifications."

Panone leaned back in his chair and folded his hands across

his belly. "Your team was in no danger of being flashed. My men are under control."

Rael lowered himself into the chair. Offending the head of Burn Operations would get him nowhere. Panone hadn't been informed about the details of the operation; no one knew except for those techs directly involved, and the Board. They couldn't afford to have a stampede of reversions asking for freedom. "I know you have full control of your men," Rael said. "But you don't have control of the cannibals they flash. The ones who escape will be out for blood."

"Cannibals are always out for blood."

"True, but vengeance makes a man reckless, less cautious about his own survival. That could mean casualties on our end. Understand? Pull back from the area. Give the signal a wider berth. A kilometer at least. More, if you can."

"Your team is walking a well-known trail, one we keep an eye on. I have quotas to fill." Panone tucked his chin, nostrils flaring.

"If this is a matter of quotas, I'll have them relaxed for the duration of our operation."

The supervisor raised his brows and sat forward. "Can I get that in writing?"

Rael stood and held out a hand to shake. "I'll have it to you within the hour."

The Tox

Jubal organized a watch, assigning Rann and Wint first. He hoped to rest a little before taking the second shift. Instead of sleeping, however, he lay listening to the sighing of the wind, the quiet step of the watchmen as they moved about, and the creak of tamarisk branches. He couldn't stop thinking about the burned girl. As the moon's scythe cleared the trees, he gave up on sleep and rose.

Lisius joined him, stretching. "Second watch is the worst." He spoke around a yawn and ambled toward the opposite end of camp.

Jubal took a drink from his water skin and began a walk of the perimeter, stepping carefully to be sure of his footing. When he reached his staff, a scuff against the earth caught his ear. Probably a party member, but to be sure he said, "Keep the Peace."

Eily's voice floated back, "Keep the Peace."

He relaxed, making out the movement of her white hat. "You should get some rest."

"I don't want to close my eyes."

A strange sensation spread through his chest and down his arms, making his fingers tingle. He wanted to protect her. And not just because she was the surest way to gain Pops's freedom. When he thought of the other tribe catching them and hurting her, his insides trembled. *Why do you care? She's a Flame Runna.* He hardened his voice and said, "Don't expect us to slow for you tomorrow."

She choked on a sob. "My mother was caught in Flame Runna fire. When they captured me and my sister, they left her to suffer."

His own mother flashed to mind. He'd been only nine when the Hunger came, and Rann got sick. Momma had taken the Knife rather than give her son over to it, allowing him time to get well. Rann had never been the same, the playfulness of childhood transforming into more precarious diversions. When Pops had returned from trade that spring, Jubal had been glad to join him on the trail, leaving the Red Hand and the ghosts of their hollow-eyed faces celebrating her flesh-feast.

He hung his head a moment. At least he'd been there to tell his mother goodbye. The Flame Runnas had taken that from Eily. Her skin was green, but inside, she was just a woman in need of comfort. He swung around to sit cross-legged next to her, one shoulder barely touching hers. In the colorless light of the moon, she didn't look like a Flame Runna at all. "Death comes to everyone. Some find it more peacefully than others."

Against his shoulder, he felt a shudder roll though her. "Gid can never know."

"About your mother?"

"The child. Let him think she died on her own."

Jubal squinted in her direction, but she turned away. Why would she want to lie to Gid? Easing the child into death had been risky, but Jubal couldn't leave her there like that. Perhaps Eily considered his mercy weak. Gid had been strong. He'd walked away. Or perhaps she begrudged Jubal his action because he wasn't a Shaman. Should he have left the deed to Gid? He spoke through tight lips. "It wasn't a proper Knife, but I ended her pain."

Eily took a deep breath. "Do you ever wish it could be different?"

"Of course. I dread the day I must share my father's flesh-feast."

"Your father's alive?"

Jubal stiffened. He'd said too much.

She shifted to face him. "Is he a trader, too?"

He considered his words. "He was. But he woke one day unable to walk. We spent an entire summer at a fish camp on the Sunset Shore while he recovered."

"But he didn't take the Knife."

"Many wanted him to. But we had enough merchandise to keep us."

"Where is he now?"

"I'm looking for a place for him to settle," he evaded.

"You should have brought him. He might have stayed at the Holdout."

Jubal straightened, surprised by the offer. Pops was old, close to the Knife. A burden and expense most tribes would not bear. Yet behind the lightning wall, there had been more elderly people than Jubal had ever seen in one place. So many wrinkles and bent backs, and even one man with milky-white eyes who seemed to be blind—something never seen among the tribes. When the alarm had sounded, several young people had taken time to help the elders flee. *Elder relatives.* Strangers would be different. "He's an outsider."

Her white hat caught the moonlight as she tilted her head. "They took me in. And you'd have to stay and work to support him. Respect the Holdout's laws. Help with the crops and animals. A different kind of life."

He sucked in his cheeks, staring into the dark. If he hadn't seen the people behind the lightning wall, he'd never have considered such a thing possible. What would it be like to live without fear of the Knife? Could he give up his trade to care for his father? His trade was his life—all he knew. "Then why do Lisius and the others want to leave?"

She slowly let out a breath that fanned over his skin with the scent of evergreen. Pulling her knees to her chest, she said, "There are some rules not everyone agrees with. Wint and Pulo's relationship, for one thing."

Jubal shot a glance toward the men's blankets. Homosexuality wasn't an issue on the Tox; not everyone wanted to bring children to life out here. "What about Lisius?"

"He's not as docile as the Holdout requires. No one fights there, ever."

Jubal scrunched up his face, trying to digest this information. "How do they decide who is their Big Man, then?"

A small laugh came from her. "It's kind of like everyone's a Big Man. Everyone has a say. They agree to abide by consensus and compromise."

"What if someone doesn't agree?"

"Oh, they always agree eventually."

He shook his head. "But what if they don't?"

She hesitated. "Not long after I arrived, the Order split into Old and New. The Old Order refused to accept conversion—green skin—under any circumstances, and the New Order decided to accept the procedure in return for lifesaving medical treatments. But the disagreement was peaceful. We still live side by side."

"And you trust this Old Order not to harm you? What if they were to disagree about that?"

"Both Orders believe violence is a sin. Even those at the Holdout with green skin. They would never harm me or anyone."

He pushed to his feet, shaking his head. Peaceful Flame Runnas? And yet, he and Rann had been there and lived to tell.

As he walked away, she said, "Your father would be safe there."

Jubal's pulse pounded in his ears. Even if he could find a way to spare Eily, once she found out about his betrayal, he'd never be welcome beyond the lightning wall again. He could never be anything but her enemy.

Chapter Fourteen

Dawn spread across the sky, and Eily shielded her eyes with her arm in one last attempt to sleep. Too many thoughts had kept her awake. But at the coming light, the men roused and began packing. With a sigh, she tossed aside her blanket. Most of the food was gone, but she made sure Gid ate a couple of bites of jerky before handing the packet back to Jubal.

Jubal donned his pack, took out his machete, and began carving a thin trail into the amarantox. The foliage had become shorter here, and the stalks grew close together. The trader moved quickly, barely making enough room to pass. Lisius ducked through the leaves after him, with Pulo and Wint close behind. Eily followed with Gid right on her heels. Rann brought up the rear.

"Why we going so fast?" Gid called out, his face pale and thin lipped, but he kept up his swaying gait.

Eily was proud he spoke Cannibal but embarrassed he didn't have the sense to keep his voice low. "There could be survivors from the fire. Cannibals eager to take revenge on a group of Flame Runnas."

Pulo bellowed back, "Let them come."

Farther ahead, Lisius added, "The group would be smaller after a Flame Runna attack. Easy to take out."

Jubal scowled over his shoulder and stopped long enough for the group to catch up. In a low, firm voice, he said, "We're traders, not hunters. Be quiet, and keep moving."

Then he continued cutting trail without a backward glance. The reversions lowered their gazes and followed without complaint. Eily breathed a sigh of relief, once again grateful for Jubal's intervention. Her legs and feet burned from so many days of travel, and she longed for Gid's mini more than she ever thought possible. At least she had her natural alkaloids to dull the pain. She considered offering Gid a kiss to ease his suffering but knew he'd refuse.

As the sun reached its zenith, the heat became stifling. Even the plants seemed to feel it, leaves drooping in utter stillness. The shorter stalks sometimes lowered below eye level, allowing her a view of the rolling miles of plants around them, but unfortunately there was no breeze to be had. Sweat coated her legs, sticking her skirt to them as she walked. She longed to ruck up the hem and expose her legs to the air, but one glance at Gid quelled the impulse. Instead, she lowered her head and concentrated on putting one foot in front of the other. Wiping sweat from her eyes for the tenth time, she blinked. Had the light faded? Her head rose above the canopy again, and she saw the horizon had turned deep gray. Far in the distance, a low rumble echoed across the sky. In response, the limp foliage rustled as a breath of wind sighed across the top.

Jubal's machete strokes increased pace, his staff rattling in his other hand. "Lightning storm," he grumbled. "We need to find shelter."

Soon, the stalks were bending their heads low to the east, thrashing as the wind flung loose debris against the travelers. Clouds blackened the sky. Eily squinted against the grit as her dress tugged against her legs. Her bonnet strings slapped her face. She jerked the hat free and stowed it in a pocket with the beacon before the wind took it. Ahead, Gid trudged on, head down, holding his hat firmly in place with one hand.

Just ahead, Jubal and Rann had stopped and put their faces close together to shout over the storm. Rann pointed north, but Jubal shook his head and gestured east. Rann shrugged, and they changed course so their backs were to the wind.

"What are we doing?" Gid asked.

"I think they're trying to find the trail," Eily yelled into his ear. "The cannibals have common shelters along most trade routes."

Lightning flashed overhead, then a peal of thunder shook Eily clear to her feet. They passed a stand of tamarisk, trunks holding against the wind while thinner branches whipped about in frenzy. Past that, the amarantox thinned, and Jubal halted. He shielded his eyes with one hand, looking left and right. Leaning over, he put his mouth near Rann's ear again.

Lisius ventured further east to the top of a small rise. He turned to shout at them, swinging one arm in a broad "come on" gesture. Eily couldn't hear over the wind, but his mouth seemed to form the word, "cave." He disappeared down the other side of the hill.

Jubal shouted, "Lisius, wait!"

Lightning flashed again, followed almost immediately by the crack of thunder. Jubal raced after Lisius with Rann right behind him. Wint and Pulo followed but stopped at the top of the hill. Wint dropped to a crouch.

Eily grasped Gid's hand, tripping over stalks to reach the others. Fat drops of rain began hissing around them. Eily could barely keep her eyes open against the deluge. Her dress ballooned and then slapped against her thighs, drenched within seconds. She had a rain poncho in her pack, but it was too late to keep herself dry now. At least the pack was waterproof.

She stopped next to Wint and tried to shield her eyes from the downpour. A ragged path of broken amarantox led the way to a flat rock jutting from the opposite rise. "What is it?"

Pulo said, "I think they killed Lisius."

"What?" Eily squinted harder. Rain cascaded off the rock and flowed past, churning with mud. Jubal and Rann shook their staves at a dark hole beneath the stone. Behind the curtain of water, Eily could just make out the shapes of men. The tips of their spears broke through the sluicing water to menace the traders. Lisius's prone figure lay curled just outside the entry.

"We have to help!" she cried, lunging down the hill. Her foot went out from under her in the mud, and she fell, sliding feet first toward the cave. Halfway down she regained control and rose to stumble the rest of the way.

Jubal was arguing with the men in the cave. "I said keep the Peace!"

Gid reached Lisius just behind her, waving his sodden hanky as a peace flag. Cannibals didn't honor peace flags, but she'd never gotten around to telling Gid that fact. He waved it at the spearmen like he was washing a window, shouting, "Geep de Peace!"

She dropped to her knees next to the fallen reversion. The water flowing around Lisius's body ran red. He clutched his ribs, bright crimson bubbling between his fingers.

A stocky warrior clothed only in short leather leggings redirected his weapon Eily's way. A fire from within the cave turned his silhouette into a shadow. "More Flame Runnas!"

"Keep the Peace!" Eily put her hands in front of her, palm out. She blinked rain out of her eyes, torn between Lisius and the threat from the cave.

"The Peace doesn't count for Flame Runnas," the man said, his stance wide. The rain pouring from the overhang sluiced over his shoulders and trickled from his beaded beard.

Jubal edged sideways to place himself between her and the cannibals. "They're under my staff. My property."

"No toll you can pay to let Flame Runnas live." Another burst of lightning brightened the sky.

Rann plunked his staff against the ground and stepped forward. "We're taking them to the One Tree. To trade with King Sefe. That's where we're going."

The man facing Jubal hesitated, then looked to his comrades. "Hold."

Eily's racing heart squeezed tight. She cleared a wet strand of hair from her eyes. All three spears swung her direction. She could barely breathe.

The man's attention shifted past her to the hill. "How many you got?"

She twisted her head to see Wint and Pulo descending. Jubal crouched next to her, one hand hovering over Lisius's mouth and nose. "One less, I think."

The cannibal seemed to consider, then jerked his head sideways and backed into the cave.

Pressing her fingertips to Lisius's neck, Eily found a weak pulse. He didn't move, and his skin felt cold. Something stung the back of her neck, and then her hand. A ball of hail bounced off Lisius's cheek. She looked up at Jubal. "Get him inside."

Jubal grabbed Lisius under the shoulders, and Gid carried his feet, hauling the wounded man inside the overhang. Rann passed them, removing his pack to sit by the fire as if he owned it. Wint and Pulo edged inside, barely past the deluge of water. About ten paces in, three more men crouched against the far wall, armed with knives. *Hunters.* But even hunters would honor the Peace in a storm.

"How is he?" asked Gid.

Blood trickled from a wound just below the center of Lisius's ribs, creating a dark puddle on the dirt floor. She pressed both hands against the seepage. "I don't know what to do, Gid."

She ran through her minimal first aid training from the Ward. The bumps and scrapes of children were no comparison. When a serious injury had occurred, the doctor had handled it. Gid slipped off his pack and dug inside to produce the small first aid kit. He opened it so Eily could peer inside. The bandages and analgesic pills would do Lisius little good. He needed a surgeon. "The beacon! Gid, it's in my pocket. Call for help."

Gid fished in the folds of her skirt and found her pocket. "Where?" He switched to the other side. "Are you sure you have it?"

Her brows pinched with worry. She'd felt the box banging against her thigh as the wind had picked up. She couldn't remember the last time she'd been aware of it. "Yes. I picked it up before we left camp. Here, keep pressure on this." She transferred his hands to Lisius and stood to search her pockets. Empty. She trembled. "I must have dropped it outside."

She scrambled toward the opening. Gid called over his shoulder, "Eily, let me."

Jubal caught her arm. "What are you doing?"

"I dropped something!"

"You can't go out there."

She tried to elbow past him. "It's the only thing that can save him."

Gid raised his voice. "Eily, take care of Lisius. I'll search for the beacon."

Jubal tightened his grip. "Unless you have some Flame Runna magic, nothing can save him."

Eily stopped struggling against him and swallowed. The sky flashed and shook, sending a gust of wet air against their faces. *Tell him the truth.* She squared her shoulders. "The black box you saw last night—I can use it to call the Protectorate and bring them here. I had it in my pocket a few minutes ago."

Jubal blinked at her a few times, mouth hanging open. "The flying machines will come here?"

Eily swallowed. "I have to push the button—but yes, we were to use it if we got into trouble."

His teeth clicked shut and eyes narrowed. But there was no time to make him understand that she hadn't intended to betray him. She yanked her arm from his grip and darted into the storm. The tracks they'd left in the mud had already washed away in the pounding rain and hail. The wind tangled her wet dress against her legs, and she fell. She blinked back dirty water.

Chunks of ice the size of her fingernail pummeled her. She flinched, instinct telling her to run for cover, but the desire to find the beacon drove her outward. They'd come over the rise from the west, so she put her face to the wind and stumbled up the hill, trying not to slip again. Wind and rain sucked her breath away until her chest ached, but she didn't stop. The box could be anywhere out here, carried away in the runnels of water. She reached the top of the incline and shielded her eyes against the onslaught, trying to decide how to proceed.

A firm hand drew her back. "Come inside," Jubal shouted. "He's gone."

For a moment she couldn't process what he'd said. Then she stiffened. Lisius was dead? Had Jubal killed him like he had the child? "No. He can't be."

"It's not safe out here."

She jerked from his grasp. "Did you kill him?"

His mouth turned into a deeper frown, lines appearing between his brows. "No one could save him. I didn't need to wield the Knife. Now come."

She tried to look into his eyes, to see if he was lying, but the rain made it difficult. His hand gripped her arm again, drawing her toward the cave. She pushed her dripping hair out of her face and allowed him to guide her.

Her foot slipped on the hill, and she caught herself on her other knee. An arms-length away, she spotted the sharp edge of the beacon poking out of the mud. She surged forward to scoop up the box, limbs weak with relief. She'd found it. Then she remembered it was too late for Lisius, and her stomach soured.

Jubal helped her up, then held out a hand. "You must never use that. Give it to me."

She clutched the box against her chest. Would he refuse to continue his escort if she didn't comply? *He promised to take you. Promised you she's safe.* If he lied to her, his word as a trader would be compromised. He'd never be welcome at the Holdout again. A trader's life depended on his integrity.

But the beacon changed things. He'd be within his rights to surrender everyone to the hunters in the cave. Even if she pushed the button, she and the others would be dead before the Protectorate could arrive. Was he really asking too much? He was risking his life to guide them across the Tox. All for a few blankets and other odds and ends. Why?

Blinking rain out of her eyes, she asked, "Why did Rann say Sefe is trading for Flame Runnas?"

Lightning flashed overhead, and Jubal flinched, eyes on the sky. "He was trying to get us into the shelter, that's all."

The storm *was* a great danger. And Jubal had never done

anything to treat her or the others like prisoners. He'd even asked them to take part in night watch after they'd stumbled onto the duster attack. She had to trust him. Taking a deep breath, she placed it on his outstretched palm.

He responded by urging her ahead of him toward the cave.

Chapter Fifteen

Jubal skittered down the incline, legs braced against the slippery mud, one hand tight around Eily's arm to keep her from falling. His other hand clutched the small black rectangle she'd given him so hard the edges cut into his palm. If he hadn't been to the lightning wall and seen the magic the Flame Runnas possessed, he'd never have believed such a small thing could summon the flying machines. Could summon death. Had she planned to summon Flame Runnas to the Taguan all along?

They entered the cave, and Eily stumbled to a halt next to Wint and Pulo where they crouched at the entrance. Wint's eyes showed white as he watched the hunters clustered against the cave wall. The cannibal leader remained standing, spear in hand. Next to Lisius, hat removed and head bowed, Gid knelt, chanting.

Without a word, Jubal joined Rann where he sat drinking from a bota beside the fire. He showed his brother the box and bent close. "Flame Runna magic to summon the flying machines."

Rann's eyes widened. "Should we destroy it?"

Jubal considered. Stranger things had been of use during his travels. Like the goats the rice tribes raised for food ending up carrying extra goods on the trade route. "She says there's a button." He found the hinge and opened the lid. Inside, a raised circle made it very plain how to use it. Snapping it shut, he said, "Never know when we might find a use. Let's carry it awhile."

His brother tipped his head to one side, lips pursed, then shrugged. "I guess it could be a valuable trade."

While Rann took another swig of bitters, Jubal surveyed the six hunters. They kept their hands on their weapons, watching the newcomers with stony gazes. Other than the crackle of logs, the cave remained silent.

After a time, Pulo spoke. "We must honor his flesh-feast."

Jubal looked over a shoulder. Pulo stood gazing down at Lisius's body. Wint remained crouched as if to flee, his body nearly touching the spray from the rock overhang.

The hunter leader said, "We demand the flesh as a toll."

"You broke the Peace!" Pulo's voice rang against the walls of the small cave.

All three spears lifted in his direction, and the other three hunters took wide stances to brandish their knives. The leader's lip curled up in a snarl. "How do you keep your slaves without binding?"

"We're not slaves!" Pulo said.

Jubal stroked the metal bits hanging from his staff so they tinkled against each other. His entire plan was about to come apart at the seams. He had to convince the hunters the Flame Runnas weren't a threat. "Without their flying machines, the Flame Runnas are helpless. Where else can they go on the Tox?"

The knuckles on the hunter's spear-hand whitened, and he rocked back on his heels slightly.

Jubal continued, "Your toll is too much. If I paid such a price to every tribe along the trail, I'd have no goods left to trade."

"Not our problem."

Jubal had encountered this threat before. Smiling, he raised his brows. "It will be when you reach the Taguan, and every trader there turns you away."

The cannibal didn't lower his spear. "What do you counter?"

They'd used up nearly all the food they carried feeding Gid. "Salt, cloth—"

A shake of the cannibal's head cut Jubal off. "We've already traded this season. A man dealing in Flame Runnas must offer something more worthy."

Jubal reached over and lifted the bota from Rann's grasp. "Bitters from the Rice Tribes. A luxury."

"Three botas. Full."

Rann jerked the bota back. "Maybe they'd like an even rarer luxury. Flame Runna spirit healing."

Jubal's throat tightened. What was his brother doing? Did he think these hunters would let them leave with three Flame Runnas once they experienced the spirit healing? Rann could barely keep his own hands off the merchandise, and he understood Pops's life depended on them. These hunters wouldn't hesitate to kill traders to take such valuable stock. Jubal jumped to his feet. "Two botas, plus the one my brother holds—all we have."

The hunter raised a hand, his men gathering behind him, their eyes hungry with curiosity. "The spirit healing is true, then?"

Jubal untied a bota from his pack and shook his head. "No spirit healing. These slaves are Sefe's, and I won't risk harming them before we reach the One Tree."

Rann snorted and took another drink. “Sefe will never know, brother.”

Jubal bared his teeth in a smile and prodded Rann with a toe until his brother clambered to his feet. “Excuse us a moment.”

Rann followed a few steps toward the cave’s entrance where Eily and the others waited. Jubal rounded on him. He kept his voice low so the hunters wouldn’t hear him. “What are you doing?”

“We’re out of food, and at least the bitters fill my belly. Why give away our supplies when the spirit healing costs nothing?”

“It’s not ours to give.” Jubal glanced behind him to where Eily stood listening. “They don’t share their women.”

“You’re always going on about using up the merchandise. I’m trying to help.”

His brother had a point. The old Jubal would have agreed. But he couldn’t see Eily used like that. “We made a promise to get them to the Taguan safely.”

His brother stared over Jubal’s shoulder at Eily. “I think you want her yourself, first. Take her. Sefe won’t care as long as we get them there alive.”

Jubal hissed through a clenched jaw. He wanted to break every one of Rann’s teeth.

“What?” Pulo asked.

Gid asked Eily something, and she responded, her voice trembling. Gid sucked in a breath.

Jubal clenched his fists. Lisius was already dead. Eily and the rest wouldn’t come peacefully if they found out they really were destined to become slaves. He was losing control. “Rann, you promised to let me handle things. Remember why we’re here.”

Eily put a hand on his shoulder and pulled him around to face her. “You *are* slave traders.”

He refused to meet her eyes as he shook his head. “No. I’ve never traded in slaves in my life.”

"But you mean to trade us."

Rann grinned and stepped closer to her. "I wonder if you're as potent as your sister?"

With both hands, Jubal shoved Rann's chest, knocking him away. He raised his voice to reach every cranny of the earthen walls. "My brother doesn't speak for us."

The hunters murmured to each other. Rann regained his balance, balling his fists and glaring at Jubal beneath his brows—but he kept silent.

Eily whispered, "Are you saying he's lying?"

Jubal let out his breath, still avoiding her eyes. She was one to talk. She'd intended to call the Flame Runnas upon them. He was surrounded by double-crossers.

I'm no better.

He shook off the thought. He didn't have a choice. Pops's life was at stake. He shot his brother a warning look before whispering to Eily, "If you're not my property, I can't protect you."

Pulo said, "Like you protected Lisius?"

Jubal thrust his chest out and glared at Pulo. "You're a Flame Runna. Your kind doesn't keep the Peace. Lisius should have waited to approach."

The hunter leader called across the fire, "You!"

Jubal stayed focused on Pulo. "You can be my slave, or I can hand you to the hunters." Without waiting for an answer, he spun to face the cannibals. "These slaves are already paid for. They're not ours to share. You've taken the life of one. Have him, and I will find a way to explain to Sefe."

He wished he'd agreed to their exorbitant price from the start. The flesh-feast would keep the hunters from pursuing them when they left, and his group already had enough to carry without Lisius's body.

The leader tilted his head to look over Jubal's group once more. "We want to experience the spirit healing."

For the first time, Gid said something, his voice firm and surprisingly calm. "Please you let us go in Peace."

Narrowing his eyes, the leader seemed to see Gid for the first time. "This is your Shaman?"

Gid stood with his palms pressed together and his shoulders squared. The man's scars did look a little like a Shaman's, plus he was tending to the dead at this very moment. Jubal swallowed, mind jumping through solutions. He had to keep the hunters away from the Flame Runnas, or his whole party was doomed. Hunters would ignore trade law if the reward was big enough. He would be slaughtered and Eily and the other Flame Runnas tortured.

But everyone respected the Knowing.

The Knowing couldn't be killed. But they could be slaves. Maybe he could take care of two problems; save the Flame Runnas and divest himself of Gid.

He cocked his head at the hunter leader and raised his brows. "You need a Shaman?"

Eily grabbed Jubal's arm, digging her nails into his bicep. Did he really mean to trade Gid? Her betrothed barely spoke Cannibal. "He's not a Shaman."

"He prays for the dead, yes?"

She caught Gid's solemn gaze across Jubal's shoulder. Did he comprehend what was happening? She had to protect him. "Jubal, you promised to take us to my sister. All of us."

Across the fire, the hunter seemed to be gaining courage. He took a step toward her group, his gaze on Gid.

Jubal leaned close to speak so the hunter couldn't hear. "Gid is a Knowing. He'll be safe with them and perhaps eventually escape back to the lightning wall. If the hunters taste your spirit healing, they'll kill us to keep you for themselves."

The hunter eased closer to them. "A Knowing slave is not easy to keep. Would he come willingly?"

"No!" Eily stumbled forward to block the hunter from her party. All she could think about was Gid in the hands of cannibals. He would practically throw himself onto the cook-fire for them.

The man jerked to a stop, his bearded cheeks twitching. Then he bared his teeth and grabbed her. She squealed as his bruising grip pulled her against him. "Then I will have you."

His spear shaft dug into her shoulder blade as he wrapped his weapon arm around her. His breath smelled of bitter-root. The heat of his naked chest seemed to burn through the fabric of her bodice. She squeezed her eyes shut and tried to rear back, but his hold was too strong. Straining her neck to keep her face away, she said, "Promise you'll leave them alone first! Then I give myself freely."

"Stop," Gid said from beside her.

She opened her eyes.

Gid stood with his shoulders back and jaw set, his pale lips the only indication of fear. He spoke in German. "I came on this journey to protect you, Eily. Trust in Gotte's Wille." Then he spoke Cannibal. "I give myself for Peace."

The hunter's grip on her relaxed. She clutched the man's shoulders, pressing her chest to his in a vain attempt to keep his attention. "No! Take me! Gid, I can't let you!"

Gid put a hand on her shoulder and pulled her away from the cannibal. "You must save your sister."

"There has to be another way."

From behind, Jubal's hands clasped her arms and pulled her backward, away from Gid and the hunter. She struggled, kicking backward, scratching his hands, but he was too strong.

To the cannibals, he said, "The spirit healing only lasts a short while. A Shaman is yours to keep."

"No!" Eily strained forward but couldn't break free. "Gid, help me!"

He looked over his shoulder. "I am."

Eily collapsed on the damp cave floor at Jubal's feet, unable to tear her eyes from Gid's broad back.

The hunter looked Gid up and down. "And he will not run?"

Gid put a hand on his chest and shook his head. "I come for Peace."

Twisting to peer at his comrades, the hunter shrugged one shoulder. The others murmured together, then nodded. He turned back to Gid and held out a hand.

Gid accepted.

Eily's limbs were numb. The edges of her vision grew dark, and she leaned forward onto the dirt floor with both palms. This couldn't be happening. Gid would never be able to convince them that he was a Shaman.

Outside, the rain hissed and splattered while distant thunder rolled against the clouds.

"Gid—" she croaked.

He was at her side. Taking her hand, he drew her to her feet. "We don't have much time."

She could barely feel his palm against hers. Her vision still threatened darkness. "Run away. Now. Just go."

With a thin-lipped smile he shook his head and squeezed her fingers. The hunter had retreated to his side of the fire. Jubal and Rann sat on this side again, drinking as if nothing had happened.

Her eyes burned, and she fought to keep her face from crumpling. "I can't let you go."

"You must. You have to find Ana."

"They think you're a Shaman."

"Tell me what that is."

"A..." she struggled to find a word. "A religious leader. Sort of."

He brightened, raising his brows. "Perhaps I've been sent to teach them the path to God."

"Don't be stupid! Their religion is nothing like yours. A Shaman helps guide the deceased spirit to the Mother. Wields the Knife during Hunger times. Can you do that? Put your hand to a killing blade?"

His scarred face drained of color. He shook his head. "I will show them a better way. God wouldn't put me here without a purpose."

"God didn't put you here." She lowered her forehead to press it against their clasped hands, closing her eyes. She whispered, "You have to escape from these hunters as soon as you can."

He pulled his hands from hers. "I promised to go with them."

"To hell with promises!" She grabbed his hands again, crushing his fingers. He seemed determined to die. Time and again, she'd dreaded seeing Gid killed on the Tox but never the terrible reality of separation—of not knowing when his end came. How long could he last alone among cannibals? How long until they discovered he was a fraud? "Your scars make killing you taboo only as long as they believe you're a Shaman. If you see an opportunity to get away, you take it. Before they ask you to wield the Knife."

He frowned but didn't argue. "What about you and the others? The traders betrayed us."

The space behind her eyes throbbed. She blinked it away. "Jubal says they're just pretending we're slaves. The trade laws protect us as goods." But inside she had her doubts. Jubal had a quick answer for everything, yet Rann looked at her like a dog contemplating its neighbor's bone. And what was this business about Sefe? She didn't fully understand, but Sefe had her sister, so that was where she must go. "Plus I found the beacon."

"Good!" He closed his eyes and nodded vigorously. "As soon as you reach Ana, use it."

Pulo's voice drew Eily's attention. "So the flesh is ours?"

He squatted by Lisius's body. Nausea roiled inside her. "Pulo, no."

His face was hard. "No wasting."

She checked on Wint, who hunkered by the entrance, biting his lip. How could she argue with them? They'd come back to the Tox to live this way. And she'd facilitated it. The horror left her paralyzed.

Gid released her hands and approached Pulo. "I will pray for him."

On unsteady legs, she followed behind him to murmur in his ear, "They mean to eat him."

Pulo pulled out a knife, looking down into Lisius's face. "You honor us with your flesh, brother."

"Wait," she whimpered, knowing it was pointless. At the fire, Jubal and the others had shifted to watch, their faces unreadable in the dancing firelight. She scrambled for an excuse, anything to stop Pulo from making this final regression. But she came up blank.

Gid knelt, holding a gentle hand toward Pulo's knife. "Flame Runna meat is... toxic."

Pulo's knife halted. He cocked his head. "I was never told this."

All the air left Eily's lungs. Gid's lie was brilliant, yet she could hardly believe he'd just told it. The Tox must be affecting him—first he'd allowed Jubal to think he was a Knowing, now this. She continued quickly, before Pulo doubted. "That's because we're not cannibals. You're not a cannibal. Flame Runnas don't need to eat. Why would you need to know such a thing?"

At the fire, the tribe leader bared his teeth. "You would have traded us poisonous food?"

Lifting his hands, palms out, Jubal said, "We didn't know."

Rann bumped Jubal's shoulder with the half-empty bota. "That's not right. Didn't Sefe say the flesh-feast was glorious when they shot down that flying machine?"

Time seemed to halt as Eily processed Rann's words. Flesh-feast? Flying machine? Scattered puzzle pieces slid into place. She wanted to say something, but the air was too thick to force her words out.

Across the fire, the hunter with the bone labret in his upper lip pointed his knife at Gid. "The Shaman lies to us?"

Chapter Sixteen

Jubal's pulse roared in his ears as he groped for an explanation.

The hunter with the labret rose from his squat and tossed his knife from hand to hand. Although the other hunters remained sitting, they all slid their hands to their weapons. The cave echoed with the sound of rain pounding the earth outside.

Why would Gid claim Flame Runna flesh was poisonous? And worse, why would Rann deny the claim? Marking Gid a liar would negate the deal they'd made. The Knowing didn't lie. Their immunity relied upon knowledge, and knowledge required truth.

Rann capped the bota and slid a glance Jubal's way, scrunching his lips with one eye squeezed half shut in regret.

Jubal eased his face into a soothing smile. "Who knows the ways of the Knowing?"

Footsteps came from his left, hard shoes against the packed dirt floor. He felt Eily's gaze prickle the back of his neck before she spoke.

"Sefe shot down a flying machine?"

The leader stood. "Your slaves don't know?"

The hunters followed the leader's example, weapons in hand, and began to sidle slowly around either side of the fire.

Jubal scrambled upright, Rann at his side. *This is how it will end.* He edged the toes of his right foot beneath his staff, hooking it into his hand. The baubles jangled, heightening the tension in the air.

"Tell me the truth," Eily persisted.

The woman didn't know when to keep her mouth shut. If Jubal didn't show these hunters he was in control, they'd take everything. He spun and grabbed Eily by the throat, propelling her backward to the wall. In a loud voice, he said, "Sit down."

She wrapped both hands around his wrist, eyes wide as she gasped for breath, even though he didn't squeeze nearly as hard as he should have. He shoved her down. Gid and the other Flame Runnas remained crouched, mouths agape, too shocked to defend her. *Good.* Breathing hard, Jubal pointed his staff at them. "The first one who speaks will regret it."

The hunters stopped their advance and now argued with each other across the fire. "The Shaman lied about the flesh. What's to stop him from lying to us?"

"He's Mambabarang. In league with the Flame Runnas. We should kill him."

"The traders knew. They lied, too."

"Maybe he hexed them."

"But why waste good meat?"

The leader held a hand up to his men. "Perhaps Flame Runna flesh is more valuable than we thought. He's keeping us from it."

Jubal thrust out his chest. "You agreed to take the Shaman as your toll."

"He's Mambabarang. You tricked us."

"He's not evil. His ways are different, but he's loyal to those he serves."

Rann added, "He's a Flame Runna Shaman. They waste everything. Even their own."

The leader took another step forward. Jubal widened his stance, one foot toward the entrance. He could run. Leave the Flame Runnas to their end. Find another way to rescue Pops. But Eily's terrified face stopped him. Her fate with these hunters would be worse than with Sefe. At least Sefe honored Ana. There was a good chance he'd take care of Eily, too.

Jubal shook his staff so the noise echoed around the cavern. "We will renegotiate the toll."

Rann spoke up, "Sefe says there's spirit healing in Flame Runna flesh. To eat it makes a man drunk."

The leader's eyes flashed with interest. Jubal pounced on the advantage, pointing to Lisius's body and infusing his words with exaggerated frustration. "Sefe wants these Flame Runnas alive, but he'll pay for the flesh, too. Take..." he pretended to consider, "half the flesh in payment and let us be."

Drawing himself taller, the leader said, "We will take it all."

Relief flooded through Jubal, but he was careful not to show it. He'd go hungry a few more days on the trail, but he'd have enough Flame Runnas to free Pops.

"And the Shaman," the leader added, shoulders back, chin high.

Pulo lurched to his feet. "You can't take both!"

Jubal used the butt of his staff to punch Pulo in the gut. He felt as if he'd taken the blow himself. He'd been ready to lose Gid; eager, even. But none of this trade exchange had been smooth. He didn't want to give these hunters anything. *You have no choice. Get out of here so you can save Pops.* "Bah! Trading in Flame Runnas is proving to be more hazard than profit. Take your toll and be done with it."

He stalked past the nearest hunter, limbs stiff, and jerked up both his and Rann's packs. "Rann, tie the slaves. We're going. Now."

A keening rose from Eily, and she wrapped her arms around Gid. Rann stowed his bota with a grin and started straight for the woman.

"Pulo first," Jubal commanded, hoping to give Eily a chance to say goodbye.

Rann's grin became a grimace, but he did as he was told. Eily continued to moan. Gid, his face pale as ashes, remained exactly as he'd been, crouched over Lisius's body. He murmured foreign words of comfort to Eily. Wint had backed completely out of the cave, but his shadow remained visible on the other side of the falling water—there was nowhere for a lone man to escape to on the Tox.

Jubal held a hand out to Eily. Gid looked up at him, his blue eyes burning. "Take her to her sister."

A guilty pang lanced Jubal's heart. Eily wanted to save her sister, just like he wanted to save Pops. Gid had been caught in the middle. But Jubal couldn't change that now.

Gid rose, drawing Eily upright before prying her hands from him and guiding her toward Jubal. Her face glistened with tears, her shoulders trembling violently as she clutched at Gid's arms and hands.

"Eily, nicht. Don't." Gid's voice was soft, coaxing.

She lifted her chin to look at her man, then twisted to Jubal. "Please. We can't leave him with them. He doesn't speak Cannibal."

Jubal swallowed past a lump in his throat, shaking his head. "The deal is done."

At the entrance, Rann was ushering a bound Pulo, loaded with both his own and Eily's packs, through the curtain of water. The hunters remained vigilant near the fire, gazes hungry.

On impulse, Jubal unstrapped a full bota of bitters from his pack and thrust it toward Gid. He looked square at the leader. "This belongs to the Shaman."

The hunter scowled but dropped his chin sharply in acquiescence.

Jubal turned back to Gid, unsure what to say.

The man wrapped his fist around the bota's carry-strap, knuckles white. "You keep Eily safe. Please."

A shiver chased up Jubal's spine and down his limbs. He stepped back, light headed, and found himself nodding.

Gid took Eily's face between his hands and kissed her forehead. "Geh mit Gott."

Then he guided her into Jubal's grasp. As Jubal pushed her toward the exit, she covered the spot of Gid's kiss with one hand, as if to keep it from washing away in the deluge.

Haldanian Protectorate

The Com Ops building sat on a dome of earth at the northern edge of the city, its unobscured view of the Burn infused with the orange light of the setting sun. Rael stood with his back to the communication specialist and gazed at the radiant clouds to the northwest, savoring the hint of fresh rain brought in on the air circulation system. The storm had disrupted several feeds, including the GPS implants on the reversions.

"I still can't get a lock on the third transmitter," said the specialist. His computers made soft pipping noises as he adjusted the tracking systems. "They probably took shelter during the storm. If they're in a cave, the signal may be blocked."

Rael turned to watch the multicolored lights from the monitors dance across the tech's features. The nanotransmitters they'd installed in the three reversions were kinetically powered, fueled by the flow of blood. Once blood flow stopped, they could transmit for about twenty-four hours on power reserves. But extreme heat—like cooking—would completely disable all systems. "Or he could be in a cannibal's stomach."

The specialist nodded, tapping a finger against his lips as he scanned the screens. "Impossible to tell, since the storm scrambled the signals. Once they start moving in the morning, we'll have a better guess."

Rael paced to the eastern view, watching the first stars materialize on the horizon. If the group had reached its destination and the cannibals were killing and eating the reversions rather than taking them to the Fosselites, his plan would have been for nothing. The Fosselites needed the reversions alive. "I want to send an all-frequency alert."

"Sir, all Burn Ops teams have reported back to base for the night. There's no one in the Reaches." The specialist furrowed his brow, his eyes leaving his screens for the first time all night.

"Just do it." The emergency com system was intended to reach all dusters on duty to warn of incoming blow-outs or to alert them to escaped reversions. It was how the Protectorate had made first contact with the Fosselites. With night coming on, the Fosselites might be tempted to leave their mountain, given the right bait.

The specialist input some commands and handed Rael a mike. "You want it live?"

Rael nodded. He held the unit up and waited for the specialist to nod before speaking. "All units, emergency Romeo Echo Victor One. Three convicted reversions located at following coordinates." He twitched his fingers at the specialist to code in the data. "Lethal force authorized. Proceed with base camp procedures and move at first light. Priority one."

He set the mike down. "Set that on repeat for the next hour. And send hourly updates on the transmitter locations to my personal gamma pad."

The specialist scratched his head. "Yes, sir. You do realize the Fosselites are the only ones likely to pick up on our signal?"

Rael didn't turn around as he passed through the door. "I'm counting on it."

Chapter Seventeen

The Tox

The ache of loss threatened to double Eily over, and she could hardly lift her feet out of the mud to take another step. Ahead of her, Wint and Pulo struggled to keep their balance with bound wrists and loaded packs. Gid's name rolled across her thoughts over and over, echoed by the deep-throated thunder rolling farther and farther west. How could she have been so wrong about everything? As the heavens exchanged the dark of the storm for the blackness of night, rain continued to wash away her tears.

They halted at a swollen creek, and she collapsed to the wet earth. Pulo and Wint crouched on either side of her. Eily flinched away from the heat of their bodies. She'd brought them to this end. If she hadn't agreed to Ijon's plan, they might at least be free together on the Tox. It was all her fault for trusting the traders. Was this what Tula had feared all along, wishing her not to go?

Rann's voice cut through the murky darkness. "Tie them together?"

Jubal's voice sounded hoarse and tired. "I suppose we have to. I'll do it."

She felt as much as saw him as he reached for her wrists. His touch was gentle, but the rough cattail fibers of the rope stung her rain-soaked skin. From deep inside, she found her voice. "You broke the trade laws, Jubal. Why betray us?"

His hands trembled as he tied her. "You were going to call the Flame Runnas."

Her insides knotted. She jerked against the rope, forcing Jubal to catch her hands again. "I didn't betray you. I gave you the beacon. *You* dishonored the trade. The Holdout will never buy or sell with you again."

"I have no need to trade with Flame Runnas," he said through gritted teeth.

She set her jaw. She'd believed Jubal held her in some esteem, even if his brother didn't. Obviously she was nothing more than another Flame Runna. But she couldn't allow his scorn to hurt her. "Other traders will spread word of your treachery to the tribes. You'll be discredited everywhere."

He twisted the rope into a knot and looped it through the tethers on Pulo and Wint. "I have no choice. I have to save my father."

Where she'd detected scorn before, his words now seemed to hold regret. The rain slackened, and a sliver of moonlight poked through the wispy clouds. Maybe he really wasn't a slaver. Maybe she could still talk him out of this course of action. "I told you the Holdout would shelter your father. Take him there."

"Sefe's holding him ransom until we replace the escaped Flame Runna," Jubal said. "We need you to get him back."

"If he's not already dead," Rann added.

Jubal dropped her hands and squelched through the mud back toward his brother. "If he is, it's your fault. This whole rotting thing is your fault. First you free Sefe's Flame Runna, then run your big mouth in front of hunters."

Eily tried to sort out what they were talking about. "Wait, did Rann try to free Ana?"

Jubal answered, "Another prisoner. One from the flying machine."

Rann yelled, "I didn't free her! I keep telling you that!"

As the brothers continued to argue, a plan took shape in her mind. The cannibals were hunting dusters. Hunting Flame Runnas. All deals were off. She had to do whatever it took to free her sister. The fastest way was to get the beacon back. She only needed it long enough to push the button and could probably even do it without the traders realizing what she'd done. All she needed was a kiss. Rann had been asking for one since before they'd left the holdout, but she knew he wouldn't stop there. She shuddered. What did it matter? Gid was gone. Who was she saving herself for? If she could, she'd seduce Jubal. But that left Rann. She'd have to kiss them both. Probably more. Her skin crawled at the thought of Rann's touch. *Ana would do it for you.*

She let out a steadying breath. She'd need to begin slow, as if she were getting used to the idea of being a slave. Give them time to let their guard down. How close to the Taguan were they? It wouldn't do to use the beacon too soon. She had to make sure she was close enough to rescue Ana before alerting the Protectorate.

Jubal cut off his brother's argument with a warning that they were still within range of the hunters. Rann's huffing breath filled the humid air with the weight of his anger.

Eily ventured a quiet question. "How long until we reach the Taguan?"

"You can't escape," Rann answered sharply.

She swallowed, and allowed her voice to tremble a little. "Does Sefe really treat Ana as well as you said?"

Jubal answered this time. "He might keep you as a pair, if that's what you're asking. But he does need some Flame Runnas to trade to the Blood Eye."

His words slammed into her. Unexpected memories kept her reeling. Men's faces assessing her through helmet visors, the whites of their eyes red as blood. Needles and tubes and excruciating concentrations of light. She stuttered, "B-blood Eye? You mean the Fosselites?"

Wint whispered next to her, words choked with dread, "They've found a new way to harvest Haldanians."

Eily wriggled upright to her knees. Pulo and Wint's rope drew tight as they struggled to sit beside her. She wouldn't go back to the Fosselites. Couldn't. She'd kill herself first.

But this was bigger than her personal safety. The Fosselites would use the cannibal tribes to destroy the Holdout without a single regret. The people there would die, and the converts would endure unthinkable torture at Fosselite hands. Most converts at the holdout were little more than children. "We have to warn the Protectorate!"

Rann laughed in the darkness. "They already know."

She twisted her wrists as if she might free herself but only succeeded in causing more pain. "Ijon wouldn't send us out here if they knew."

Jubal answered. "He's the one who told us. You didn't know?"

She froze, her thoughts spinning. "But why would he..." She covered her mouth with her bound hands, the scent of mud filling her nose. "Oh, God. The beacon."

"What?" Pulo said.

"You have a beacon?" Wint said. "Why didn't you call for help?"

"Shhh," she said, trying to think. Just as she'd feared, the Protectorate was tracking the beacon. But why had they insisted she bring the reversions? She could have carried the beacon alone, and she would have done so gladly if she'd known the Fosselites were involved. *The reversions are bait.*

The Protectorate didn't just want the armed cannibals. They wanted the Fosselites to come out of hiding. A huge weight settled into her gut. The bottle of allelopathic suppression pills Tula had sent made sense now. The pills were old technology, once used by Burn Operatives during UV exposure in order to limit the effects of alkaloids in the bloodstream. The discovery of the telomerase fungi had all but eliminated the need for the pills. Unless someone expected to undergo unusually intense UV radiation.

Like Fosselite lights.

Eily choked on all these realizations. Tula had known. The Council had likely forbidden her to say anything. So she'd tried to warn Eily with the pills.

The moon, nearly half full, broke free of the clouds, cutting shadows across the camp. "Wint, what did Councilman Rael ask you to do once you reached the cannibals?"

"Nothing. He pulled me out of jail, sent me for a conversion treatment, and then delivered me to the Gate."

Jubal interrupted, "Time to sleep. Everyone quiet."

Pulo lowered his voice but only a little. "You were in jail?"

"Stole a skimmer," Wint whispered.

"Nice."

Rann spoke up, "We said no talking."

Eily ignored him. If she activated the beacon before reaching the Taguan, would the Protectorate even come? Or would they wait until the Fosselites arrived? She needed some answers before she did anything stupid. "I think the Protectorate is using us as bait. When the Fosselites arrive to collect us, they'll attack. Are you sure no one back home asked you to do anything? Or you, Pulo?"

Pulo shrugged. "Nope, just said I'd had one too many fights."

Rann said, "We should separate them."

"But the Fosselites never leave their cave," Wint whispered.

More memories flooded Eily's mind, of searchlights and the beat of Fosselite copter rotors. Of fleeing blind through darkness and hiding in holes. Her words strained against her throat. "They will at night."

The sound of footsteps hushed them. Eily stiffened as a man's shadow blocked the moon and rough hands found her bonds. Rann's voice tickled her ear, "I think you'd better keep me company tonight."

Chapter Eighteen

Jubal jumped to his feet as the scuffle broke out. The night hid everyone from view, and it took a moment to orient himself.

"Don't touch her," Pulo said. A grunt, and then the ground vibrated as someone fell.

Bodies writhed on the muddy bank to the left. Jubal charged over, trying not to get knocked down as arms and legs thrashed out of the swarming mass.

"Kill him!" Pulo's naked chest caught the moonlight as he rose up before dropping again into the chaos.

Rann shouted, then his voice choked off. Eily's distressed cries intensified from somewhere among the tangle. Rann let out a feral string of curses.

"Enough!" Jubal bellowed, heedless of nearby hunters. He bent and grabbed the first body part he could latch onto—an ankle. Both hands around the appendage, he dragged the person free.

His brother yelped, kicking at Jubal before rolling to his

feet. Once upright, he darted back in to kick Pulo's gut. "I'll kill you, by the Knife!"

Jubal snatched his brother's tunic, pulling him back. "He's no use to us dead."

Rann shrugged off Jubal's hold but didn't advance again. "He tried to kill me."

"You got too close. He's a slave. Of course he's going to try to escape."

Taking a single step forward, Rann said, "Help me get her loose."

Eily had pulled Pulo's head onto her lap, her shoulders heaving in small, shuddering gasps. Jubal faced his brother, blocking the slaves from view. "You're not taking advantage of her."

The creases of Rann's scowl deepened in the moonlight. "You want her, too. I've seen the way you look at her."

Jubal's face turned hot, and he was glad for the darkness. He thought he'd hidden his desire better. "She's been the only woman around for days. We've all looked at her. But I need force myself on no woman, slave or otherwise. And neither do you."

Huffing, Rann said, "It's not about the sexing, I told you that." He lowered his voice. "We could hide her and only give Sefe the other two. Once we get Pops back, we retrieve her from hiding and move on. Imagine never needing to buy bitters again. We could even sell use of her, like Sefe does."

The thought sickened Jubal. But Rann's plan had a kernel of possibility. Could he save Eily? They only needed two Flame Runnas. He stared at the huddled slaves. The whites of Wint's eyes gleamed as he stared in Jubal's direction.

Rann continued, "If you want her first, go ahead. Sharing won't diminish her magic. I want you to try it. Then you'll see."

Jubal's heart was racing, desire stirring in spite of his distaste. He wanted her, but not like this. He didn't want to share her with Rann. He didn't want to share her with anybody. "No. She's our most valuable merchandise. What if Sefe says these two men aren't enough? I won't risk harming her before we reach the Taguan."

"Pfft. We won't harm her. She might even enjoy it. And if we have to trade her for Pops, we should make use of her while we can."

"No."

"You act like she's your woman. What if I decided to use one of the men? Would you have issue then? I bet not. Sefe says the magic is the same. But I'd prefer a woman."

"I thought you'd changed after what happened with Pops, but you swilled yourself into nearly getting us killed by those hunters. Now you want to use up our other goods." Jubal crossed his arms, shaking his head. "You've used up your share. The slaves are off limits. All of them."

Rann balled his fists, chin high. "She's mine as much as yours. I've let you boss me around too long. I'm the elder. I make the decisions."

"Your decisions only result in trouble. Pops put me in charge."

"Really? I didn't hear him say that."

"You were out cold!"

"You can't prove he did."

Jubal gritted his teeth, his chest heaving. "Leave the woman alone."

Rann crossed his arms and widened his stance the way he had as a boy, daring his younger brother to try to tackle him. "Make me."

While the traders fought over Eily's chastity, she squeezed her eyes shut and tried to think like a Haldanian. The Protectorate was undoubtedly tracking the beacon, and the reversions were intended as decoys or maybe bodyguards. Once she reached the Taguan and started back, the dusters would know to look for the camp at the endpoint. The help button was intended for exactly the situation she was in, to summon aid if the cannibals tried to keep her as a slave.

And she'd given the beacon to Jubal.

Why had she trusted him? Why hadn't she pushed the button before Gid was taken from her? Despair threatened to overwhelm her, but she clamped down on it and pushed it aside. She could no longer help Gid. But she could try to save the Holdout. She had to get her hands on the beacon, even if it cost her virginity. Whatever it took.

Straightening her spine, she prayed her alkaloids would be strong enough to knock the traders out. But she shuddered to think of Rann's body against hers. Jubal first, then. She lifted her chin and tried to make her voice strong. "I would lie with Jubal."

The brothers' argument fell silent.

After a few heartbeats, Rann chuckled. "She wants you, brother. Now what?"

Jubal's muscular shoulders blocked out the stars as he approached where she sat. Her pulse thundered through her ears and her insides trembled. At home, she'd never been able to tempt Gideon into more than a peck on the lips. There'd been safety in that, knowing he'd be the strong one, the one to put on the brakes. This wouldn't stop with a kiss. She clenched her jaw and lifted her bound hands toward Jubal.

He untied the end of her lead rope before drawing her upright by her cinched wrists. Her legs threatened to collapse as she walked with him to his bedroll.

Rann called after them, "Don't take too long."

Jubal didn't answer.

At his blankets, they halted. Then Jubal just stood there. Her heart raced. He stood close enough for her to sense the warmth from his body. Her skin tingled as she waited for him to touch her—wanted him to touch her. Was she supposed to do something? Swallowing, she said, "Should I... what would you like me to do?"

He took a step closer, so their chests touched, and looked down into her face. His breath fanned her skin like a caress. "Why?"

She couldn't stop trembling. She was about to give away something she could never get back—the only thing still pure about her in the eyes of the Order. But some part of her was excited. Yearning. Her voice emerged as a husky whisper. "This is my first time."

He stiffened and stepped back. "I meant why are you agreeing? And how can this be your first time?"

"Women at the Holdout wait until marriage." She swallowed, trying to keep her voice from shaking. "We only ever lie with one man."

He rubbed his hands over his hair and half turned away.

She furrowed her brows. Would he refuse to lie with her because she was a virgin? Perhaps it had been a mistake to mention it. Sweat prickled her skin. She had to convince Jubal to take her. If he didn't, Rann surely would, and while the thought of Jubal's touch made her blood race, the thought of Rann's made her want to vomit. "But I'm yours, now."

"You and Gid never sexed?"

She shook her head, muscles tense, then realized he might not be able to see her. "No," she croaked. She needed to be more seductive, but she was paralyzed with doubt.

He let out a short puff of breath.

Panting, she took a hesitant step toward him and whispered, "I don't want Rann to be my first."

He wrapped his hands around her biceps, not pushing her away, but not drawing her close. "I can't keep you for myself."

He sounded like he wanted to. Her heart ached, and tears pricked her vision. "I know."

He turned his head slightly and dipped down to her mouth. The contact sent a wave of heat plummeting toward her navel. As his lips moved against hers, the sensation plunged deeper. One of his hands crept from her bicep to cradle the back of her neck as she opened her mouth to him. His other arm wrapped around her waist to pull her close. Her bound hands were trapped between them, but he didn't seem to notice. He spent a long time brushing his lips against hers, trailing his tongue along her teeth, caressing her neck and hair.

When he finally pulled back he sucked in a long breath. "Beautiful."

Flushed and breathing hard, she tilted her face up for more. He took her wrists and looped her hands around the back of his head, then scooped her up to lower her to his blankets. Nuzzling against her neck, he ran a hand along her side, fitting her against him. She could feel his arousal pressing her hip. The sensation both excited and frightened her. She lay very still.

After a moment, he lifted his head to look into her face. His features were shrouded in darkness, backlit by the moon and feeble stars. "Are you afraid?"

She contemplated lying. Wouldn't a seductress be encouraging? But she found she couldn't speak. She shook her head instead, so stiff the movement was more like a tremor.

He chuckled and stroked a finger down her cheek. "You're a liar. I knew it from the moment you crossed that first river."

His words eased her a fraction. "I've been told it hurts."

"I'll be gentle." He nibbled her lower lip, sending jolts of pleasure through her.

Running a hand down her side to the hem of her skirt, he slid his palm up her leg, drawing the fabric with it. When he reached the edge of her underpants, he paused, rubbing a thumb over the soft cotton fabric covering her hipbone. Unconsciously, she arched toward him. He sneaked his thumb beneath the edge to stroke her skin. She whimpered, her fingers tangling in his hair. How she wanted to be unbound—to run her hands against his skin in return.

His hand drifted upward to caress her through the bodice of her dress. "Does this come off?"

She nodded and raised her hands from behind his head. The closures on the front of the dress were hooks and eyes, and difficult to separate with her wrists tied together.

"Here," he said, and with deft fingers, loosed the knotted rope. As he removed it, he circled one of her wrists with his fingers. "I wish you weren't a..." He halted, dropping his forehead to press against hers, his breath hot on her neck. "You won't try to escape?"

Her heartbeat thundered with such need... She could barely remember her real purpose, but she knew it wasn't escape. She pressed her fingertips lightly to his cheek. "I won't try to escape."

He swooped in with a kiss that took her breath away. Alternating between forceful and gentle, his hands and his mouth covered her body with shivers of pleasure. At the actual instant of their joining, she cried out in pain, yet writhed against him in a subliminal request for more.

When he finally heaved a panting sigh and rolled onto his back, he pulled her with him, his right arm under and around her in a loose embrace. Eily felt as if he'd coaxed her soul to the surface and breathed it to life. Every one of her bones had melted. She'd never expected sex to be like that. She rested her head on his chest. He smelled warm and earthy with a hint of fresh rain. She wanted the moment to last, to sleep in his arms, and wake in his arms, and do it all again.

Would her wedding night have been like this? Her heart constricted at the thought. She'd never have a wedding night. Even if she did manage to reach her sister and the Protectorate rescued them, Gid was gone. Life as she knew it was over. Sex was nothing more than a tool now. She had to get the beacon.

It was so difficult to want to move. His beating heart tried to lure her to sleep like a lullaby. She'd kissed Jubal to incapacitate him, but she felt drunk herself. Did he feel it, too? Of course he did. He was drugged with her kisses.

She twisted her head and looked up at his profile. The scant light limned his eyelashes in silver, his face relaxed and beautiful. Maybe she could talk to him. The Protectorate could rescue not only Ana but his father, as well.

She trembled at the idea. "Jubal?"

He stroked his fingers against her bare shoulder, a slight smile lifting the corners of his lips.

The moment was broken by Rann's voice. "I was right, wasn't I? Magic."

Jubal's eyelids fluttered as he rolled his face toward the sound. "Hmmmm."

Rann's calloused hand gripped her wrist to pull her toward him. "My turn."

Jubal tightened his grip around her shoulder, eyes popping open. "No."

Rann planted a booted foot against Jubal's hip and pulled harder. "I let you go first!"

Eily yelped as her shoulder joint strained, and Jubal released his hold. Rann fell backward, dragging her across the rocky earth so she landed across his legs. She scrambled away on hands and knees, tangled skirt slowing her progress. Her heart raced, and all previous euphoria was gone. She'd known she'd have to incapacitate both traders if she wanted the beacon, but the reality of it hadn't hit home until this very moment.

Rann pounced on her. He straddled her and attempted to turn her to face him.

Jubal rolled to his knees, the influence of her kisses obviously affecting his reflexes. "Stop."

Hope flooded Eily. But Jubal was moving so slowly. How could he defend her?

Rann grabbed her hands to hold them above her head. He laughed, his sour breath filling her nostrils. "I've been waiting for this too long."

His weight twisted off her as Jubal's body slammed against him. She scuttled backward with her hands and feet as the men wrestled.

"I demand my share!" Rann bucked, sending Jubal off him. He jumped to his feet.

Jubal swiped at Rann's ankle, tripping him. "Your share came out of all the bitters you drank."

"By the Knife!" Rann kicked at him. "How are you going to give her to Sefe if you can't even share her with your own brother?"

Jubal halted his forward crawl. Rann kicked out again and got to his feet without taking his eyes off him.

Sitting back on his haunches, Jubal hung his head. "We can't both be drunk at the same time."

"Already thought of that, big brother. I trussed the others up so tight they can't blink."

"Oh."

Rann stalked toward her, dropping to his knees and pushing her shoulders back to the ground. He yanked a rope from his belt and bound her hands.

"Wait," she whimpered.

Rann crushed his mouth against hers. His hands groped at the hem of her skirt, yanking the fabric up around her hips. She twisted her face, but his teeth clamped onto her upper lip, almost hard enough to break skin.

"Be gentle," Jubal's voice was thick.

She fought sobs and stared up at the fathomless stars, praying it would end soon.

Chapter Nineteen

Swaying on his feet from the euphoria of Eily's magic, Jubal clenched his hands at his sides. *Be gentle? That was the best you could do?* The stars spun out of alignment, righted themselves, shifted again. He tensed as Rann rucked up Eily's dress.

You warned her you couldn't keep her for yourself. He wanted to turn away, but he couldn't leave Eily to his brother's mercy. Two people warred inside his head—a logical trader who acknowledged his brother had a right to a share, and a jealous lover who wanted to beat Rann to a bloody pulp. In the fog from the spirit healing, Jubal stood immobile.

He managed to move his lips enough to say, "You're hurting her."

Rann didn't answer, mouth still fastened against Eily's. She whimpered, the whites of her eyes reflecting the moonlight.

Rann shoved a knee up between Eily's legs.

Think of her as merchandise. But with her kisses a lingering memory across his lips and face, he couldn't. He'd been with other women, but in the moments of intimacy with Eily, he'd been closer to her than to any other human being in his entire life. He wanted to save her. To keep her. To protect her... but he couldn't see how. He couldn't see a way out without choosing between her and Pops.

As his brother rose on his knees to release a knot on his breech cord, Eily twisted her head to the side, eyes squeezed closed.

A dam inside Jubal broke. In two strides he had his hands on Rann's shoulders. "Get off."

Rann shrugged him away, pulling aside his breech flap.

"I said stop."

Rann batted at Jubal's hand and lowered himself against Eily.

How could he end this? He doubted he could win a fist fight when his reflexes were weakened from her magic. And Rann wouldn't give up even if Jubal did win. He was justified in his demands; she was a slave, and her flesh was to be shared equally between owners.

In a wisp of clarity, Jubal said, "I claim her children as mine."

Rann jerked to a stop and twisted his head to look at his brother. "What did you say?"

Claiming a woman's children promised her a man's protection. It freed her from slavery. It made him her man. Confidence infused Jubal as he said it again. "I claim her children."

"She's a Flame Runna! And a slave!"

"Sefe claimed one. It's been done."

"But I own half of her."

"I've never taken my share of our goods. I'm doing so now."

Rann lurched upright with a roar. He stood straddling Eily, glaring down at her with his hands outstretched as if to strangle her, his shoulders heaving. Eily lay still, covering her breasts with her hands, eyes still shut tight. Rann spun and stalked to his bedroll. Over his shoulder, he said, “You’re a rotting hypocrite.”

Eily sat up and tugged her skirt over her exposed legs. Her hands trembled as she pulled her blouse across her breasts and refastened the hooks.

Jubal held his breath until his brother had flung himself onto his blankets with his back to them. At least Rann had the sense not to force one of the other Flame Runnas. Pulo had already rebelled once. Collapsing to his knees, Jubal gulped air. He’d just bound himself to a Flame Runna. He tilted his chin toward the sky. The stars seemed to dim and brighten again.

He blinked, seeking focus, and realized Eily was on her hands and knees in front of him. “Thank you,” she whispered.

“What have you done to me?” He gasped. Maybe this was why Rann had freed Sefe’s Flame Runna. He reached out to touch her face. His woman’s face. He’d sworn to never claim a woman on the trail—never create a family he had to abandon for months at a time to ply his trade. And now he’d just taken the most dangerous woman of all, one who would need constant protection.

He dropped his hand to his lap. And what about Pops? How could he save his father now? Would the other two Flame Runnas be enough in trade? If Sefe saw Eily, he was sure to demand her as his due.

She clasped her fingers over his fist. “We shouldn’t be fighting each other. Sefe holds people dear to each of us. We need to save the fight for him.”

“There’s no way to fight him. He has too many warriors.”

“The Protectorate can fight him. If we use the beacon.”

Rann started laughing from his bedroll. “Of course she wants to call her Flame Runnas. You’re a fool, brother.”

Jubal pulled his hand away from her. “They’d destroy everyone, us included.”

"Not if the Taguan surrenders. Like the Holdout. The Protectorate's looking for peaceful people to convert. It's their mission. If we instruct people not to fight, the Flame Runnas won't burn them."

Did she think he was a fool? "Are you saying that child we found a few days ago fought back?"

Eily opened her mouth, shut it, then opened it again to say, "Her tribe did. Children get caught in the crossfire."

"Sefe will get us all caught in the crossfire."

Rann sat up. "Sefe could shoot them down, easy! Then he'd have lots of Flame Runnas."

She sat back on her heels. "We'll need to get the innocent people into the cave. Sefe'll fight outside. Once the Flame Runnas eliminate Sefe, we can negotiate peace just like the Holdout did."

"There's only one entrance to the Taguan. There'd be no escape," Jubal said.

"As long as the people in the cave don't fight back, the Flame Runnas won't attack them."

A laugh rose from deep in Jubal's chest. "I'm too drunk to listen to this right now."

"I will stand with you. I'm that sure."

"Enough." His head was spinning, like he'd walked for days without sleep, and his hunger gnawed at his gut. He needed to close his eyes. Maybe when he woke, this would all be a bad dream. "We'll talk more in the morning."

"Can I at least untie Wint and Pulo?"

"They stay tied," Jubal said.

"We should tie her, too, Jubal." Rann said. "She'll free them while we sleep."

Jubal rubbed his eyes. Could he trust his own woman? "Do I need to tie you to keep you from freeing them? Nothing's changed for them."

Wint's voice came from the darkness. "We wouldn't try to escape."

Eily dropped her chin and stared at the ground. Then she eased herself back onto Jubal's blanket. "I'm sorry, Wint," she called out. "You and Pulo need to be tied just a little longer."

Eily woke with the humid air chill against her back. After a moment, she realized she was lying on Jubal's chest. She sat upright with a start. The sky was colorless and pale, undecided if it should dawn clear or cloudy.

Jubal breathed deep and stretched, ending in a yawn. Opening his eyes, he met her gaze. He raked a look down her torso. "You're still here."

Her face heated. "Good morning."

He gave her a lazy smile, and her entire body flushed and tingled. She was his woman. And he was going to help her save Ana. She bent down and brushed her lips against his.

Nearby, the two reversions sat up. Wint scrubbed his hair with his tied hands. Pulo's face was dark with bruises, and a huge purple stain spread across his naked ribs from Rann's thrashing. Rann's bedroll was empty.

Jubal stood up, scanning the rain-beaten amarantox. "Rann?"

Eily crawled over to check on Pulo. "Are you all right?"

"Need to piss," he said.

Jubal nodded at Eily. "Untie him. We'll let them go one at a time."

"Can't we free them? You don't need them to save your father."

"No. I can't risk them running. They remain prisoners."

Eily opened her mouth to argue, but the stern expression on Jubal's face stopped her. At the Holdout, she'd be expected to obey him... but this was the Tox. Cannibal women had just as much say as their men. Still, her position was tenuous, and she'd better tread carefully if she expected him to cooperate at all. She whispered, "I'm sorry, Pulo."

"Not your fault," he grumbled and ambled to the nearest clump of amarantox. When he finished, Jubal tied him again and released Wint's bindings.

From the trail upstream, Rann appeared. "Looks like we can cross a short way up."

"Good," Jubal said, pointing toward the southern horizon. "The moon is nearly half. Sefe will give Pops to the Knife soon."

Rann grunted. Without looking Eily's direction, he rolled his blankets to stow them. She was grateful he took Jubal's claim so seriously. Her stomach fluttered as she remembered Jubal's body against hers. She bent to gather her own load, hoping no one noticed her heated skin.

Jubal took the lead and Rann the rear as they began the day's march. As the morning light grew stronger, the scent of wet earth rose on tendrils of mist. The down-beaten amarantox slowly perked up, but much of it was broken, and the canopy remained ragged.

Eily kept her eyes on the ground, stepping over broken stalks and skirting sloppy puddles along the trail. Sunlight glared off standing water, and heat shimmered in humid waves from the drenched soil, making her dizzy. By midafternoon, sweat trickled down her sides, and her skirt stuck to her legs.

Behind her, Pulo stumbled and fell, bringing Wint down with him. Rann swore, urging them to their feet.

"I need water," Wint said.

"You can drink the next time we stop. Move."

She looked over her shoulder. Wint's posture matched the beaten amarantox. Pulo seemed hardly able to lift his feet, let alone place them squarely ahead of him. Had he suffered a concussion in the fight? She slowed until he caught up with her. "Let me see your eyes."

He looked at her, pupils fully dilated in spite of the sun.

"Keep moving," Rann prodded Pulo.

"Wait!" Eily put her hands on Pulo's arm.

Rann shoved him. "Pops can't wait."

"I think he's got a concussion."

"Can I sit down?" Wint asked.

Eily glanced at him. His pupils were full-sized, too.

Her gut tightened. Both of them? She blinked, dizzy herself. From the heat? Or something else? A classic sign of UV poisoning was dilated pupils. And disorientation.

Jubal called from the trail ahead. "No stopping! We have to move if we're to make the Taguan in time."

She faced Rann, blinking sweat out of her eyes. "Are my pupils big?"

He refused to look at her. "Go ask your man."

Clenching her teeth, she stumbled down the trail. Jubal started walking again when he saw her start to move. She shouted, "Jubal! Wait!"

He looked over his shoulder. "What?"

"I need you to look at me."

He hadn't shaved this morning, and the stubble on his jaw was attractive. She longed to run her fingers over it. *Stay focused.* The high she could normally ignore was making her mind wander. "How big are my pupils?"

"I don't have time to gaze into your eyes." He scowled and continued walking.

For a moment, she stood transfixed by the broadness of his retreating back.

"Go," Rann prodded Pulo, forcing the prisoners past Eily.

UV storms were most common after a blowout or heavy thundershower. *You should have remembered that.* But there had been a lot going on. She scoured the horizon through rents in the canopy for the domed top of a yuvee tree. The genetically altered plant was the one type of vegetation the Protectorate would allow to grow within the city itself, in spite of the toxic interaction it had with Haldanian skin. The leaves would turn almost white when they received large amounts of UV rays.

Through a gap, she thought she could see a pale, umbrella-like shape. She ran up the trail, nearly tripping over windblown debris as she passed the prisoners. "Jubal! Jubal, we have to get under shelter! Look at the yuvee tree!"

He stopped, shading his eyes until he spotted the domed top she pointed toward. Shaking his head, he said, "They're not fully white. We press on."

"You don't understand. Flame Runna skin is more sensitive."

Wint tottered, catching himself against some thick stalks of amarantox. He slid down onto his backside, dragging Pulo with him. Pulo giggled and rolled over on top of him. Wint asked, "Can I have water now?"

Jubal examined the two prisoners. Jaw muscles bulging, he swung the water flask from his shoulder and offered it to Wint.

"We could die," she said.

Rann sneered. "She's stalling."

"Look at my eyes." She thrust her face toward Jubal, pointing to her eyes. "This is not normal. You'll kill all three of us if we go on. We need shade."

"By the Knife." He ran a hand through his hair and faced Rann. "Set up the blankets."

"The moon is—" Rann began.

"It'll do no good to arrive without Flame Runnas."

Casting a disgusted look at the reversions, Rann dropped his pack and tugged his blankets loose. Jubal and Eily did the same. Using his machete, Jubal cut some amarantox stalks. He propped them into tripods, and draped a blanket over the top to create a canopy. "That'll hold one person."

Eily untied Wint and disentangled him from Pulo's embrace, helping him stand. He smiled at her with one side of his mouth, wavered, and sat back down again. Pulo sprawled on his back, arched over his pack. "At least I'll die happy," he said.

"You're not going to die," she snapped.

With Jubal's help, she dragged Wint upright and into the shelter.

They made a connecting shelter for Pulo and carried him inside. A ray of sunlight still sloped beneath the overhang, so Eily walled him in with a third blanket.

Jubal wiped sweat from his forehead. "Why aren't you as drunk as they are?"

She shook her head, bringing on a wave of dizziness. She wasn't sure. The reversions were acting like they'd just escaped a Fosselite lab. "I've been a convert longer. I guess I'm more used to it."

By the time she took a shady spot herself, her limbs felt as supportive as jelly. She'd never been caught outside in a sunstorm—there was always a house nearby where everyone retreated if the yuvee turned white. Last autumn, Uncle Samuel had been working the fence crew, and he'd been caught outside. The skin on his neck and hands had blistered the next day.

She beckoned to Jubal. "You'll sunburn if you don't find shade, too."

He sat next to her, shoulder brushing hers. Her skin was prickling in the heat, but she liked that he didn't mind touching her. He splayed his legs out in front of him and leaned back on his hands to look up at the blanket. "Pops doesn't have much time."

"The effects should pass in a few hours, as long as we keep out of the sun." She considered administering the pills Tula had sent but decided not to. They may need them if they were sent to the Fosselites. The telomerase fungi should be adequate to repair the damage from this short exposure. She was feeling better already.

Lowering himself to lie on the ground, Jubal said, "Tell me when they're ready to move."

Eily glanced toward Wint and Pulo's tents. She was more talkative than tired. "We should work out the details of our plan. When we reach the Taguan, you can leave us in a hiding spot with the beacon—"

"I hope you know what you're doing, trusting a Flame Runna, brother," Rann said from where he sprawled with one forearm covering his eyes.

She faced Jubal, hoping he'd see the sincerity in her eyes. "I won't betray you. Betraying you would also betray Ana."

Jubal looked away, rubbing a hand roughly against his stubbled cheek. "Eily, I've been thinking on this. We can't risk the lives of everyone at the Taguan just to save your sister." The muscles in his jaw bulged and he sucked in a deep breath before turning to face her. "I plan to give the beacon to Sefe."

Chapter Twenty

Jubal didn't plan on giving Eily time to argue, so he kept talking as her mouth opened to speak. "If Sefe wants a fight, we'll give him one. I'll suggest he take the beacon far away from the Taguan and use it to call the Flame Runnas into an ambush. Once he's gone, we'll sneak your sister out. And no innocent people at the Taguan are at risk."

He let silence hang for a few heartbeats as she contemplated his idea. To his surprise, she leaned down and kissed his cheek. "You're brilliant."

His heart swelled with relief. Maybe he could save her, Pops, her sister, Wint and Pulo—everyone. Cupping her face in one palm, he basked in the warmth of her gaze. She closed her eyes and nuzzled into his hand. Was this why men took women as their own? He finally understood.

Rann interrupted the moment. "He may win, you know."

Eily opened her eyes and pulled back, breaking contact to look at his brother. "The Protectorate knows if I trigger the beacon, it means trouble. They'll be prepared."

Jubal sat up and crossed his legs, dreading his next words.

Eily hadn't argued about the first part of his plan, but she'd battle him on the second half. "If Sefe sees you, he'll want you. You need to stay behind."

She blinked. Her huge pupils gave her a childlike innocence. "Only me? What about Pulo and Wint?"

"I don't want to be a slave trader, Eily. But I can't return to the Taguan empty-handed. Sefe will kill my brother and me on sight."

"But you'll have the beacon."

"It may not be enough."

"Promise me you'll set them free once Sefe leaves with the beacon."

He took her hand again. "If we can, I'll set them free. But not until after we get Pops."

"Hold on!" Rann burst out. "Those slaves are mine, too."

Jubal winced. "If we were keeping slaves, yes."

"I'm keeping the small one. He'll be valuable on the trade route."

Eily shot Jubal a beseeching look. He scowled at his brother. Rann was within his rights. Jubal couldn't stop him from taking slaves; he could only refuse to travel with him. "Pops won't agree to that."

"I don't care what Pops says." Rann's face was hard. Determined.

A lance of worry pierced Jubal's breast that this time his brother really would defy their father's wishes. The desire for spirit healing was strong. Jubal had never been able to sway Rann in this state, but Pops might still get through to him. Shaking his head, Jubal leaned back to close his eyes for some rest. "We'll see about that."

He waited until the sun dipped below the amarantox before prodding everyone into motion.

Rann yanked the blankets from the canopy, "About time. Pops could be facing the Knife right now."

Eily stretched. Pulo and Wint woke more slowly, faces slack with somnolence. Jubal hoped they'd be able to keep up the pace.

Eily dug into her pack and then approached Wint and Pulo. "Are you feeling any better? I think you'd better take these."

She held out a small object.

Rann flung aside the blanket he'd been rolling and dashed over to snatch the item. "What is it?"

"Pills." She grabbed at Rann's hand, but he jerked away. He shook the container, rattling what sounded like pebbles inside.

Jubal extended a hand to his brother. "Let me see."

Rann ignored him and pried at the box. Small, white beads flew out and scattered across the dirt.

Eily cried out and dropped to her knees, plucking them from the ground. "We can't waste these. They may be our only hope."

"Rotting Flame Runna magic." Rann dropped the container and stomped back to his pack, heedless of his feet crushing some of the white pills to powder.

Eily groaned low in her throat, shaking her head as she searched the ground.

Pulo let his head loll to one side, closing his eyes. "How far do we have to walk?"

Dusk had fallen, making it hard to see. Jubal dropped down to help Eily retrieve the pills. At least Rann was no longer interested in them. He held out his palm with what he'd gathered, and Eily smiled gratefully. He said, "I think we can reach the Taguan by morning if we leave now."

"Good." She handed a pill to each Flame Runna. "You know what these are?"

Wint accepted the pill with a listless hand. Pulo shook his head.

Eily frowned. "Allelopathic suppression. They'll help you recover from UV poisoning."

"K," Pulo said. He put the pill into his mouth.

"They can walk?" Jubal asked. The male Flame Runnas were acting like small children who needed to be carried by their mothers.

"The medicine should start to work soon. They can take another pill in a little while." She tucked the container into Pulo's pocket.

Jubal led the group along the trail in near darkness, the moon not yet risen. He placed his feet carefully to avoid tripping over unseen obstacles. They reached a bend in the river as the moon reached its zenith. He turned to Eily. "Hide near the water here, in the rushes. I hate to leave you alone on the Tox, but I can't allow Sefe to see you."

She nodded, the tendons on her neck showing as she swallowed. "Hurry."

So strange to think of all they'd been through. Only yesterday, they'd been at odds—enemies—and now he was sworn to protect her. A lump filled his throat as he bent to kiss her. He hesitated just shy of the kiss; then she closed the gap, pressing her hands against his cheeks. He savored her lips, breathing in the subtle, spiced scent of her skin. A wash of her spirit magic reached him through the contact. He pulled her closer.

"We're not waiting," Rann said, already several paces down the trail with Wint and Pulo.

Jubal opened his eyes, looking into Eily's moonlit face. A shimmer on her cheeks told him she was crying. He wiped the tears away with one thumb. "Be careful. This is the edge of Taguan territory. People may pass by."

She nodded mutely. He turned to catch up with his brother.

The trail grew wider as they approached the Taguan and the amarantox on either side less ragged. Stakes and woven netting supported the towering stalks in the wind and had protected them from the storm, allowing the manna beetles plenty of time to tunnel and grow before the harvest. Ahead, Jubal spotted a man-shaped shadow and signaled a halt. He held his breath a few moments. When the figure didn't move, he crept forward and realized it was a panakot—a "man" made of bunched bullrushes and dressed in discarded clothing to scare away the pecker birds.

He continued, pushing Wint and Pulo until the Flame Runnas were stumbling. The way Wint shuffled one foot reminded him of Pops. He urged them faster. Near another panakot, Pulo went to one knee, and Rann walloped him with his staff. The bigger man lumbered drunkenly to his feet.

Jubal stepped between his brother and the slaves. "We'll rest here."

"Dawn's coming." Rann pointed to the bruise-colored sky in the east.

Jubal pressed his lips together, not wanting to admit his brother was right. "We'll settle them here and move on. Hopefully Sefe will accept the box, and we won't have to trade them."

"Do you really think Sefe's going to accept that beacon thing for Pops's life?"

Jubal drained the last of his water flask and capped it. His empty stomach churned around the fluid. "We're pretty good traders, Rann. If anyone can convince him, we can."

Rann shrugged. "I'm all for keeping the Flame Runnas for ourselves. I guess we can give it a try."

Without arguing the point, Jubal pushed into the amarantox until they were far enough off trail that only someone tending the staked plants might find the men. Sitting them back to back, he tied their hands and feet. He wasn't happy about leaving them unattended so close to the Taguan, but if Sefe demanded more than the beacon, he wanted to be able to provide a quick alternative.

He pulled out Pulo's flask and gave them each a deep drink of water. "Be still and quiet, or you'll have no hope of freedom."

The men were exhausted. Pulo's head already nodded against his chest.

Rann scowled down at them. "What if the sunstorm hasn't ended? We should put a blanket over them or something."

"They'll get too hot," Jubal said.

"We'll be back soon."

Hesitantly, Jubal draped a blanket over the slaves' heads. He intended to get Pops and be away from the Taguan quickly, maybe even before the sun reached its peak. The slaves shouldn't suffocate in that short time. He and Rann trotted back to the trail. To mark the spot they'd left the slaves, he hung a string of beads around the panakot's neck.

As the first rays of the sun spread fingers up the horizon, the acrid scent of burning wood drifted toward them. The familiar tang of cooked meat thickened the air. His head spun with hunger, but he hadn't the time or the means to deal with it now. Once he had freed Pops, he would retrieve his stashes of goods and flee this place. He picked up his pace, the weight of his pack jarring against his back with every step.

From the crest above the cave, Jubal looked down onto the twist of river and empty beach. A male voice came from a cluster of rocks to their left. "What tribe?"

Startled, Jubal jangled his trader staff. "Traders, Cousin."

A small man armed with one of Sefe's guns emerged from the rocks. "I know you."

"How's my Pops?"

The man shrugged. "Not long from the Knife."

Jubal's heart eased. Pops was alive! "Take us to him."

They followed the guard down the trail. The savory smell of meat lingered in the close air. All Jubal could think was how glad he was it hadn't been Pops. They entered the dark hall toward the cavern where Sefe presided. The quiet sounds of sleeping people mixed with bursts of noise from those who'd begun to stir. A baby cried and was hushed.

The moment they entered the central cave, Jubal's gaze sought the cages near the back. The spaces were empty. Where was Sefe keeping Pops?

Their guard approached the sleeping king. Sefe rose onto an elbow, his movements stiff with sleep. He yawned, face twisting as he stretched. Next to him, Eily's sister struggled upright, her belly larger than before. She propped herself up on one arm and regarded Jubal with cold, dark eyes.

He swallowed, amazed at how like Eily she looked, yet how unlike her at the same time. This woman was all cannibal and queen of her domain. Her exposed breasts were swollen from pregnancy, and her shrewd gaze took in every detail. Where Eily had offered to sacrifice herself again and again—first for Gid, then for Pulo and Wint—he doubted Ana would do the same. How would she react when he told her Eily was waiting for her?

Approaching the dais, he stayed alert for his father in the crowded room. Behind him, he could feel the weight of the guards' gazes. Lowering his pack to the ground, he dug out the beacon. "We've brought you Flame Runna magic."

Sefe gestured to Ana, who rolled onto her hands and knees and languidly shifted forward to kiss him. Jubal's pulse thrummed like a river current against a sweeping branch. Sefe broke the kiss and rose to his feet. "Show me."

Jubal held out the box, realizing how small and insignificant it looked. He squared his shoulders, clutched his staff in his other hand, and spread his lips in his trader smile. "This will summon a flying machine."

Sefe flicked a glance toward the box, one eyebrow raised in disdain. "This trade isn't what I asked for."

"Take it to a place where you can hide in ambush." Jubal opened the lid and held it up so Sefe could see the button. "Push this. When they arrive, you can shoot them down in safety."

Huffing, Sefe rolled his eyes. "Useless magic. I told you the crash kills the Flame Runnas. I want them alive. This is no good."

Jubal swallowed. His heart beat so hard, he thought everyone in the cave must be able to hear it. "The Flame Runnas use this to find their own kind. They won't shoot, they'll land and begin to search on foot. Easy prey." He snapped the box shut. "But if you don't want it, I can get more for it from someone else."

Sefe's eyes glinted. "Then take it to them. Tonight we will feast on your father."

Ice surged through Jubal's veins. Before he could speak, Rann said, "We will give you what you want."

A leer spread across Sefe's face. "You do have Flame Runnas. You thought you could keep them from me?"

Jubal kept his eyes on the king. He'd known it could come to this. He rattled his trader staff. "We want a fair trade."

"What price do you put on your lives? I told you not to come back without payment."

Jubal kept his chin high. "Where's Pops? For all I know, you've already killed him."

Sefe flicked an arm out to point toward the far wall. "The old man should have gone to the Knife long before now. But I would not have had you think I'd broken our deal."

Where Sefe pointed, Jubal spotted his cousin, Rodi, standing with fists clenched at her sides. A prone form lay on the floor next to her. She shook her head, her mouth a thin line.

Without waiting for permission, Jubal strode toward the small woman. Pops lay on a blanket, eyes staring at the ceiling. His gaze shifted toward Jubal, but he remained still and silent.

"Pops?" Jubal whispered.

"He fell the day after you left. Sefe told me to keep him alive," Rodi's voice broke. "But he wants the Knife, Jubal."

Chapter Twenty-One

Haldanian Protectorate

"Councilman Rael!" An aide burst into Rael's sun-streaked office.

Rael jerked his head up from reading his gamma pad. His eyes burned, and his jaw ached from grinding his teeth. The Doomseeds project had taken a turn for the worse in the lab, with one human subject in critical condition and Rael's lead researcher threatening to go to the Board. "What?"

"We've got a Fosselite on the com." The aide's voice squeaked as he wrung his hands. "And he's requesting you."

Rael's throat tightened. Two nights had passed, and the two remaining reversion signals continued to creep across the Reaches along with Eily's beacon, unhindered by Fosselite intervention. In retrospect, he had to admit the after-dark broadcast to the Reaches had been a little crude. The Fosselites must suspect something.

"I'll take it in here," he told his aide. He straightened his nuvoplast necklace and activated the vid-com.

An image appeared on his desktop: a dark room and the sharp planes of a man's face, lit only by the glow of the communication screen he faced. The caller's eyes glistened red where others' eyes were white. Fosselites were extremely sensitive to light, but Rael wondered how much they used it as an excuse to conceal their body language during their dimly lit transmissions.

The man's voice was brusque. "Councilman, I understand you currently oversee reversion policies for your government."

Rael raised an eyebrow. "Our policies aren't your concern, Dr....?"

"What are you doing with your reversions these days?"

Rael sat back in his chair. He rubbed his fingers and thumb together beneath the desk as he considered how to respond. How much did they suspect? "I'd like to know who I am speaking to, if you don't mind."

"The name's Torin. No doctor. I'm the new head of external affairs." The man leaned forward so his face completely filled the screen. "We intercepted your transmission two nights ago."

Heart racing, Rael cleared his throat. The man was going to jump right to it. Of course the Fosselites wouldn't fall for his clumsy attempt to lure them in. And now they'd be watching for anything amiss. The Doomseeds fungi weren't detectable in a blood sample, but if the Fosselites tested further... He had to make them believe the transmission had been valid. "We have things under control now. You need not concern yourselves."

Torin cocked his head, then settled back away from the camera until he became little more than a silhouette. "Are you tagging all your citizens with tracking signals these days? Or only your escaped reversions?"

Rael's body turned cold. They'd discovered the signals? *Of course. You gave them the coordinates.* The muscles in his right cheek twitched. He spread his mouth in a smile to cover his distress. He had to come up with an explanation, fast. A policy change? He let out a breath of relief, his smile becoming more genuine. "We've changed our reversion policy."

"You release them into the Reaches?"

"Not intentionally. But we have certain factions insisting on freedom of choice." Rael pressed his lips together in what he hoped came across as bureaucratic frustration. "We do our best to keep an eye on potential troublemakers. We cannot allow them to negatively affect our citizenry."

"Are these escaped reversions dangerous, then? You did authorize lethal force."

"We've determined they are far enough away at this point that they no longer pose a threat."

Torin steepled his hands in front of him. "So you have no intention of pursuing them?"

Rael had to work hard not to show his glee. *Go ahead and take them!* He hardened his features and said, "As I told you, we have things under control."

Torin's teeth flashed in the darkness. "Good day to you, then, Councilman."

Rael cut the com, then allowed his face to bloom into a wide grin.

The Taguan

Jubal fell to his knees and put a hand on his father's forehead. The skin felt rough and dry, and the old man's pale, chapped lips trembled. A cloying reek of dried sweat and urine hung about him. Pops blinked rapidly, as if trying to use his eyelids for speech.

"I'm sorry, Pops." Jubal bent and kissed his father's head, then got to his feet, his chest tight with grief.

Rann knelt at Pops's side, head bowed, clutching one of his father's limp hands. He still wore his pack. Jubal rolled his shoulders and darted a glance to where he'd left his pack at the dais. His hand ached from gripping his staff.

He'd known this day would come, but somehow it hurt more than he'd imagined. He lifted his chin to face Sefe. "You honored your deal. For that we give you the summoning box." His throat strained around his next words, and he fought the bile that rose in his throat. "Let your Shaman give Pops the Knife. You may celebrate his flesh-feast."

Sefe crossed his arms. "Where are the Flame Runnas?"

Jubal took a deep breath and shook his head. Circumstances had changed. He would do everything he could to keep Wint and Pulo out of Sefe's hands. "You have my Pops. And the box will bring you many Flame Runnas. We give you a fair trade."

"I say no. A stringy old man's flesh-feast is no replacement for a live Flame Runna. And how do I know this magic you offer will do as you say?"

"A trader doesn't lie." Jubal shook his staff, awareness of his recent falsehoods burning through his veins.

"You were to bring me two Flame Runnas to replace my lost one."

Jubal rubbed his forehead. Pops had promised an extravagant trade because he never intended his boys to return. *You're a trader. You can make this work.* "This box will bring more slaves than we could have brought you on foot."

Sefe uncrossed his arms and held his palms out as if calling the Peace. "You can't keep them from me. Tell me where you've hidden them."

"We do not deal in slaves."

Face darkening, Sefe dropped one hand and thrust his other

arm forward to point at Jubal. “I warned you never to show your face here again without proper payment. I’m being generous to allow you to replace my Flame Runna. If you have none, then I claim your brother’s life.”

Rann rose from Pops’s side. “Jubal, we have to give him what he wants.”

Jubal closed his eyes. He’d promised Pops he’d keep Rann safe. He had to resign himself to surrendering Pulo and Wint. He was glad Eily was a good distance from them. “Fine.”

Voice warbling in relief, Rann said, “We’ll go get them.”

“Do you think I’m a fool?” Sefe crossed his arms. “You’re not leaving here.”

“Then come with us,” said Rann. “We stashed them in the fields.”

Sefe showed his teeth in a feral grin. “How many do you have?”

Jubal shook his staff. “Two, according to your terms.”

Purposefully squaring his shoulders toward Rann, Sefe said, “We are trading for his life. He’ll do the dealing, now.”

Clenching his teeth to keep himself in check, Jubal glared at Sefe. At least he’d separated Eily from the others. They’d hand over the two men and be done.

“Leave your goods,” Sefe pointed toward Pops. “My Shaman will see to the Knife while we’re gone.”

Jubal met Rodi’s gaze as he propped his pack against the stone wall. “I’ll be with him,” she said.

He nodded thanks. He didn’t want to think about the dead. He still had to think about the living. After touching his father’s face one last time, Jubal rose and joined the crowd clustering outside the cave mouth.

As they climbed the path out of the Taguan basin, he took a lingering look down. Mothers stood with their arms around their children watching the excited hunters depart. Alone at the cave entrance, Ana stood with her chin high and haughty. What would she do if she knew her sister was near? That Eily could be in danger? If only he'd had a chance to tell her so she could be planning her escape.

He turned away and took the trail in long strides, ready for this ordeal to be over. *Never deal in slaves. For any reason.* Pops's instructions had kept them alive on the trade routes for so many years. But the days of following his father across the Tox were over. He thought of Pops lying back in the cave, awaiting the Shaman's Knife. He wished the old man had gotten a chance to meet Eily. Or at least hear about her.

Rann's voice broke his reverie. "Through here."

At least thirty men, several with guns, had accompanied them to this point, decorated in hunter beads and piercings. Sefe selected four of the largest men who stood close by. "The rest of you stay here."

Jubal ducked through the foliage to where Pulo and Wint sat beneath their blanket. Rann pulled the cloth from them. Pulo squinted up. "Water?"

Jubal knelt to put his bota to the man's lips. Pulo barely took a sip before his chin lolled back toward his chest. Wint hadn't moved.

"What's wrong with them?" Sefe's brows knit with disgust.

"The sunstorm yesterday weakened them. They'll recover," Jubal said. Eily had assured him they would. He prodded Wint. The Flame Runna didn't respond. He pulled out his knife and cut the bonds, freeing the man's limbs. Wint slumped to the ground.

"He's dead," said a warrior whose head had been shaved to imitate his king.

Sefe stood over the prone form. "Check for his breath."

Jubal felt at Wint's nose. The air moved faintly. He let out a whoosh of air, realizing he'd been holding it. "He's alive." He turned to Rann. "The pills Eily gave him. Where are they?"

Rann squatted by Pulo and shoved a hand into the man's pockets. He pulled out the small box and opened it.

Jubal pinched one of the white beads. His hand shook as he shoved the pill between Wint's slack lips. "Swallow, by the Knife."

"What is this?" Sefe had his hands on his hips.

"Flame Runna magic," Jubal replied as he massaged Wint's throat.

Rann jammed a pill into Pulo's mouth. Pulo stuck out his tongue, the white bead sticking to his lips. "More water."

Jubal scrabbled over and held a water bottle against the man's lips. To his relief, Pulo swallowed. But try as they might, they couldn't get Wint to take the water.

"These Flame Runnas are as good as dead. Useless to me," Sefe said.

"We need to get them back to the Taguan. To shade." Grunting, Jubal hoisted Wint over his shoulder, his back protesting the uneven weight. He needed Eily's advice, but that wasn't an option. "Can Ana help them?"

Sefe scratched his scalp. "I don't know."

Rann waved a hand at the larger Pulo. "I can't carry him alone."

Sefe gestured to his warriors. Two stepped forward, one taking Pulo's arms, another his legs. No one offered to help Jubal. The king led the way back to the main trail, where the waiting hunters cheered at the sight of the inert, green-skinned men.

"Back to the Taguan!" called Sefe, nudging a bare-chested warrior out of the way. The rest of the crowd parted like skin from flesh.

As they reached the rise overlooking the cave, Wint's body stiffened and shuddered. Thrown off balance, Jubal nearly fell as his burden began to thrash. He tried to lower Wint to the ground gently, but the Flame Runna threw himself free and lay convulsing on the trail. The rest of the party backed away. Wint's back arched, the green flesh on his chest stretching tight over his ribs. His tongue protruded between his grimacing teeth as he jack-knifed forward again, limbs flailing in an invisible storm. Bloody foam sprayed from his mouth. His legs jerked like he was trying to run.

And just as quickly, his entire body went limp.

A dark stain spread across the front of his pants. The accompanying foul scent told Jubal the Flame Runna's bowels had also released.

For a moment, everyone stood there, staring. A few turned their heads and spit against evil. Wint didn't move.

Jubal's heartbeat felt like it had assumed Wint's convulsions. He bent to cup a hand over Wint's nose, checking for breath. Nothing. Pink, foamy spittle dribbled to the dry earth beneath his cheek.

"No breath?" Sefe asked.

Looking up at the king, Jubal shook his head.

Several people in the crowd slipped away, spitting toward the fallen Flame Runna as they departed. Convulsions were caused by an evil spirit. The flesh of someone who died like this was considered tainted. Jubal glanced toward where the retreating carriers had dumped Pulo. He'd seen enough of the world to know spirits were easy scapegoats. On the Sunset Shore, there had been men who thought Pops's malady was caused by evil spirits and argued for his termination. Fear was a powerful tool.

But Sefe hadn't backed off with the others. He pointed the tip of his spear towards the body. "Listen for his heart."

Jubal lowered to his knees and pressed an ear to Wint's chest.

Silence.

Wint was dead.

Sitting upright, Jubal kept his face a cool mask and shook his head.

"This one is no better," Sefe said, placing a calloused foot against Pulo's chest and shoving. Pulo rocked and settled without opening his eyes.

Jubal slowly got to his feet. He strode to Pulo's side and held a hand over his nose and mouth. "He lives. He needs shade and more Flame Runna magic. Maybe your Ana can help."

He reached into his belt pouch for the pills, intending to give Pulo another. The lid popped open, scattering the white pebbles at his feet. He dropped to retrieve them. Worry for Eily filled his gut. What if she was in trouble, too? She hadn't kept any pills for herself. He had to get this resolved quickly and find her.

Forcing himself to focus, he sifted through the dirt for the pills. "Rann, help me."

Rann darted over and scraped pills and dirt alike into his palm, dumping it into the box. He picked a single one from near Pulo's head and pried the supine man's mouth open to drop it inside. Pulo gagged and curled into a fetal position.

Jubal snapped the box shut, ignoring the few remaining white specks on the ground as he patted Pulo's back.

"Water," Pulo gasped, his mouth chalky with the remains of the pill before he collapsed back into unconsciousness.

Rann glanced toward Sefe. "See, he's alive."

Sefe's cheek muscles twitched. "Unacceptable. He could harbor the same curse as the other."

"He doesn't. I swear."

"You will remain my slave until he is well again." Sefe gestured his warriors forward.

Rann straightened and backed away, but warriors closed in behind him. They pointed their spears.

Jubal clenched his jaw and stood. "Sefe, you treat us unfairly. You have the box. You will get your Flame Runnas."

Sefe rubbed his chin, eyes narrowed as he looked between the brothers. His warriors continued to point their spears. After taking a deep breath, Sefe nodded once, his lips pursed with distaste. "We'll call you and your brother guests, then, until we have completed the ambush."

Rubbing the back of his neck, Jubal made eye contact with Rann. Setting up an ambush could take days, and Eily was alone on the Tox, possibly dying at this very moment. He had to make sure she was all right. "My brother will remain. It was his crime. I have business to attend."

Rann stiffened, his eyes wild as he looked at Jubal. "What? You can't leave me here."

"I'll come straight back." Jubal stared intently into his brother's eyes, and shook the pill box slightly. "I have to check on our other goods. I will come back. I promise."

Sefe crossed his arms and widened his stance. "You fear the summoning will not work."

Rann grabbed Jubal's shoulders. "You'd choose a Flame Runna over your own brother?"

The idea was tempting. But blood was blood. He wouldn't abandon his brother to Sefe's underhanded dealings. "I give you my word on Pops's memory."

"Pops abandoned Momma. You'll abandon me. I won't let you." He shoved Jubal away and turned to Sefe.

"Rann, no!" Jubal grabbed at him, knowing what came next, unable to stop the words falling from Rann's lips.

"We have Ana's twin."

Chapter Twenty-Two

The Tox

Caged by a dense wall of cattail blades rising out of the stagnant water, Eily sat on a rotting log, her back against a stubby limb. The cattails' fat, sausage-like heads bobbed against the blue sky, and her stomach rumbled. She hadn't eaten in nearly a week, and although she didn't require food, life at the Holdout had accustomed her to regular meals. She tilted her face to the afternoon sun and closed her eyes. The still air smelled of sulfur and mold, and insects whined like small warning sirens all around. *Alone on the Tox.* One of a cannibal's greatest fears.

An insect skittered over her hand and she jerked. One foot splashed into the brackish water. At the sound, she froze, heart thundering. The trail was only a few strides from where she hid. She cocked her head to listen. Nothing. Exhaling, she lifted her dripping foot back onto the log.

To take her mind off what she had no control over, she caught a floating twig and scraped at a section of algae-coated wood at her feet. First a circle for a face, then arms and legs. Soon an entire family decorated the surface of her log. She pulled her feet up tight against her to make room for one more little stick figure, added a necklace of trade beads to the tallest one, and blinked as she realized they were all green.

A family. Since losing Ana, she'd longed for a family. It was the main reason she'd agreed to marry Gid. Before they left the Holdout, he'd even told Levi he wanted to start a family right away.

She closed her eyes, throat aching. Gid was gone. Was he still alive? Would she ever see him again? Even if she freed Ana, how could she go back to the Holdout without him? He made living there bearable. She loved Aunt Beth and Uncle Samuel, but she couldn't live with them forever. She wanted children of her own.

Her eyes flew open as another thought flooded her mind; she'd only lain with Jubal once, but there were women at the Holdout who claimed to have gotten pregnant the first time. There were no unwed mothers among the Order. It was unthinkable. Who would marry her, with her green skin and a cannibal's child in her belly? What would become of her?

You have a husband.

Jubal wanted her. He'd claimed her. Her blood tingled at the thought of having his children. She loved Gid like a brother. Her feelings for Jubal were... exciting. Deep. He made her heart flutter and her legs grow weak. Did he want children? She'd need the protection of a Garden during pregnancy; her skin tied her to the Protectorate whether she wanted it or not. Jubal would have to join her. Would he agree to live at the Holdout? He could bring his father. Her chest tightened. Would the Elders allow such a thing? They'd blame her for Gid's loss. They might not even allow her through the Gate. Tears filled her eyes at the thought of the Holdout without Gid.

She could move to the Protectorate city. Aunt Tula would help. But they'd require Jubal to convert, to accept green skin as well as their restrictive ways. And they'd never take his elderly father in. Plus she had a feeling he loved trading too much to settle down in one spot for long. He'd want to venture back out, and green skin would be his death.

The sound of her name brought her out of her thoughts. She bolted upright, grasping the log to steady herself. The sky overhead had drained of color and the clearing in the rushes where she waited was bathed in twilight. She listened. The call came again, "Eily, come out!"

They're back! She swung her legs around and splashed down into the mucky water, careless of the noise.

An unfamiliar voice cried out nearby, "I hear something over here!"

She froze, hand out to part the spiky curtain of rushes. Splooshing footsteps and rustling fronds told her someone searched the water a few steps away.

Rann shouted from the trail. "Eily, it's Rann. Jubal needs you."

Trembling, she pushed through the foliage toward shore. A man with multiple studs up his earlobes and a short spear grinned at her. Another man with a beaded beard loped toward them from downstream, a rifle in his hands. Behind her, a spearman emerged from the water. The pit of her stomach twisted into a tight knot of caution. Rann appeared from the rushes to her right.

The failing light masked his expression, but a bruise surrounded his left eye and his lip had a long gash. He pressed a palm to his chest. "Good. You're all right."

"Where's Jubal?" She searched the trail behind him then turned to look the other direction.

"I'll take you to him," Rann said, holding out a loop of rope. "But you have to play a slave. Give me your hands."

She glanced at the other men and put her hands behind her back. "Is he all right?"

"No. He needs you. If we hurry, we'll reach the Taguan before dark." He grabbed her arm and jerked a loop of rope around her wrist.

She twisted to keep her other arm out of his reach. "Wait. What's wrong with him? Where are Pulo and Wint? Is Ana alive?"

"You just have to trust me." He gave up on her other hand and started pulling the short lead of her rope down the trail. The hunters waited for her to move, then followed a few steps behind.

She skipped to catch up to Rann and whispered in his ear. "Who are they?"

"I can't talk now," he said, quickening his pace.

Something wasn't right. Had Jubal been caught trying to free her sister? Rann's secrecy had to have a reason. Her limbs trembled as she hurried to keep up. Maybe Jubal was dead, and now Rann would sell her into slavery again. Sourness filled her throat.

As night descended, the trail grew wider, exposing a bright swath of stars overhead. The moon rose in a perfect half-circle, reminding her of Jubal's father. "Is your father safe?"

Rann didn't answer. Instead, he jerked the rope. She took that as a bad sign and lowered her gaze to the path. Eventually, the trail jigged left and dropped away. She stumbled to a halt. Rann tugged her rope, urging her to a shelf of rock where the route descended into a basin. Within the darkness below, faint light gleamed from what looked like cracks in the earth.

She followed Rann down the steep slope. Hugging the wall as closely as she could, she kept her eyes on the ground at her feet. As they drew near the bottom, Eily realized the mouth of the great cave she remembered as the Taguan had been enclosed by stone walls. Light from cook-fires inside crept between the stacked rocks in an eerie imitation of banked coals.

Rann strode into the opening, pulling her along without pause. The corridor twisted left, then right, small rooms opening out on either side. Each one had a fire and a few people inside. She craned her neck as they passed each door to look for Jubal or Ana. Talk hushed as people spotted her, but no one seemed inclined to follow.

Smoke and the familiar aroma of cooking meat mingled with the stench of sweat and urine. The anticipation of seeing her sister churned against dread about Jubal's condition. At the end of the hall, the passage opened into a huge cavern lit by a central bonfire. Smoke stung her eyes, but not before she spotted the spit and the human shape tied to it.

For the first time in her life, Eily thought she might faint. The carcass was definitely male, broad-chested and wiry. The genitalia and head had been removed prior to roasting. By tradition, the head would be shaved then boiled, while the genitals were a delicacy reserved for the young male relatives of the dead. *Jubal?* She could barely catch her breath. Her sight clouded. She closed her eyes, bending and planting her hands against her thighs to try to regain her balance.

Rann raised the cord in his hand, drawing her upright. "I have her!"

The bustle of the cavern ceased, leaving only the fire's crackle and the sickening sizzle of cooking meat. She wanted to vomit. Opening her eyes, she encountered what felt like hundreds of faces staring her way. Where was Jubal? She couldn't seem to focus, and her gaze kept returning to the spit.

A figure rose from a dais near the fire. Over the flame's ominous whispers, a voice from her dreams emerged. "Eily?"

"Ana!" She did a quick twist of her hand against the lead rope and broke free of Rann's grasp.

Without knowing how she'd passed between the clusters of people, Eily suddenly stood within reach of her sister. Ana's face, six years older than she remembered, looked like Eily's own reflection in the mirror. The almost-black irises, the glossy black hair, the smooth green skin. Eily's gaze flicked to the wide curve of Ana's abdomen before she crushed her sister in a frenzied embrace. "I can't believe you're alive!"

Eily breathed deep of her sister's familiar yet forgotten scent. She could hardly believe it, after all these years of thinking Ana dead.

Ana pushed away. "What are you doing here?"

Refusing to let go, Eily kept hold of her sister's naked arms. "I came to save you. To bring you home." She choked out the last words, realizing it was a futile promise. These cannibals would never let her or her sister go. She glanced at the staring faces surrounding them. "Is Jubal ...?" The rest of the sentence caught in her throat.

Just behind Ana, a man had risen to his feet. His shaven head bore the pattern of raised scars that marked a healer, but he held the spear of a hunter. His hooded gaze caught hers and he smiled, opening his arms wide. "Welcome, Eily! I'm called Sefe, King of the Taguan. Your sister has told me much about you."

Eily glanced back to Ana, who kept her chin high but refused to meet her eyes.

"Ana?"

"You shouldn't have come."

Without looking at her sister again, Ana turned and walked away.

Chapter Twenty-Three

Orange torchlight penetrated the darkness behind Jubal's eyelids, and he forced them open in spite of a numbing desire to roll back into sleep. A woman hovered at his side, a backlit shadow in the alcove where his pallet lay. Her breath fanned against his cheek, the scent of evergreen filling his nose.

"Eily?"

She pressed her open mouth against his words. The room spun in a nauseating wave. He struggled to sit up, but his limbs were bound.

A man's voice, "I told you, your magic's weak. Give him more."

The pressure of a palm against his forehead, and not-Eily's voice spoke against his ear. "Keep still."

Jubal opened his eyes wide, flexing his fingers as if he could stretch his way out of the bindings. The knuckles on his right hand stung.

Memories fought for his attention. Sefe's men pulling him off his brother. Rann betraying Eily's location. Sefe's declaration that Jubal should be restrained because he was obviously overwhelmed with grief about Pops. Ana kissing him until his eyes rolled back in his head. "Why are you doing this?"

A broad-shouldered hunter loomed over Ana's shoulder, the light from his torch making Jubal's eyes sting. The man said, "Sefe said to keep him sleeping until his father's feast is ready."

She leaned back but kept her hand on Jubal's face. "Don't tell me how to use my magic."

A deep snort of laughter bounced off the alcove walls. "Sefe has a new Spirit Healer. One with strong magic. Once you have this baby, he'll trade you to the Blood Eye."

The fingertips on Jubal's forehead curled into a fist.

Jubal focused his confused thoughts. They'd found Eily? How long had he been lying here? "Eily is my woman." His words felt thick, like he couldn't quite make his lips shape them. "I claimed her children."

"The laws are different for Flame Runnas," Ana said in a husky voice.

His pulse filled his head with flashes of light. "You're her sister. You have to help her."

The unknown man said, "Put him to sleep now, or I'll go to Sefe."

Ana bent to his mouth again. "We must all learn to accept the death of those dear to us."

As the king took Eily's arm and guided her toward two cages, her heart hammered so hard she could barely breathe. He wasn't rough, but it was obvious he wouldn't tolerate resistance. His palm seemed to burn into her skin. The people in the cavern melted away from his approach in a smooth wave.

He pointed to a cage. "You must look after your friend."

Inside, Pulo lay on his back atop a pile of dirty blankets. She searched for Wint and Jubal, but the second cage was empty. "Where are the others?"

"I do not want him to die." Sefe's dark eyes skewered her. He pushed her through the open door. Another man closed the bars and secured them.

She was a prisoner. Sefe was going to send her to the Fosselites. Blackness pressed at the edges of her vision. She should help Pulo, but all she could do was sink to her knees.

"You need these?" Rann thrust a hand through the bars. The pill box rested on his open palm.

She grasped his wrist, sending the box thudding to the dirt floor. "Don't send me to the Fosselites. I'll do whatever you want."

He tilted his head, upper lip drawn into a sneer. "I don't need your permission anymore."

"Where's your brother?" Her gaze flicked toward the firepit and her stomach roiled. Would Rann kill his brother to save his own skin?

Rann's face twitched, but his eyes softened. He jerked his hand free and turned to Sefe. "I've paid back your Flame Runna."

Sefe tapped his mouth with a forefinger, his gaze on Eily. "Mmm." He jerked his head in dismissal. "Take your brother and go."

The tightness in Eily's chest eased a little, making room for her thundering heart. Jubal wasn't dead. He wasn't the one tied to the spit.

But she was still a prisoner. Had the traders intended to betray her all along? Jubal had promised to protect her. He'd claimed her as wife. If he'd meant to hand her to Sefe he wouldn't have bothered with separating everyone and hiding her. So where was he?

Rann glanced at her one last time and pushed through the crowd, leaving her with a sea of staring faces. How could she escape from this?

She shifted her gaze to Pulo. Sweat beaded his face, and his eyes shifted rapidly beneath his closed lids. She placed her fingers against his clammy cheek. He showed no fresh bruises, only the black ones Rann had given him two nights ago. Had it only been two nights? If he hadn't been beaten or tortured, what was wrong with him? He should've overcome the alkaloids from the sunstorm by now.

"Where's Wint?" She looked up at the strange faces and remembered she was speaking to a crowd of cannibals.

"The weak one died." Sefe crossed his scarred arms.

Her face tightened as she battled tears. First Lisius, then Gid, and now Wint and Pulo. *No, not Pulo.* Not if she could help it. She snatched the box and opened it. Only three pills remained. Her mouth dropped open. "How many did you give him?"

Sefe shrugged. "The magic doesn't work."

The horror inside her burst into white hot fury. "You gave him an overdose!"

"Can you heal him?"

"He needs a Flame Runna Healer." She pulled Pulo's shoulder, trying to get him onto his side. Perhaps she could make him vomit the pills. "Someone help me. I can't do it by myself."

Sefe's mouth turned down. "Bring Ana," he said over his shoulder.

The crowd parted again, a murmur sweeping the cave. After a few moments, Ana appeared. She kept her eyes off Eily, staring instead at the wall behind the cage. "Yes?"

"Your sister needs your help."

Ana turned her head to speak to Sefe. "He cannot be saved."

Sefe only stared at her. One of the warriors opened the cage door and her jaw muscles flexed, but she didn't argue further. She stepped through the door, her beaded skirt swaying. The door latched behind her.

"Hold him on his side so he doesn't choke," Eily said. "I'll make him throw up."

Ana eased herself to her knees at Pulo's back and braced him. Eily pulled Pulo's chin down and thrust two fingers into his mouth as far as they would go. He heaved mucous and a few white fragments of pills over her hand. The pills were designed to counteract the toxic chemicals the chloroplasts produced under UV light. Eily wasn't positive about what an overdose would do, but the label said to take no more than five pills a day. There had to have been thirty-five or forty pills in the box.

"You can't save him." Ana stared at the mess.

Eily wiped her hand on the corner of a dirty blanket. Ana might be right, but her sister's hopelessness made the back of Eily's throat ache. Ana had lived like this so long, she'd forgotten how to fight. *I'll have to fight for both of us.* Eily reached out and put a hand against Ana's swollen belly. *All three of us.* But she didn't know how.

Ana's stomach muscles tightened beneath Eily's palm. Her eyes narrowed as if in pain. "Sefe wants Spirit Healer children."

In Ana's dark gaze, Eily saw terror. Desperation. How could she give her sister hope? The only chance for the baby was the Protectorate. "You need a doctor," Eily said, intentionally using the Haldanian word for Healer. Then she said, a little louder so Sefe might hear. "The baby will die without Flame Runna medicine."

To Eily's surprise, Ana's brows drew into an angry line. She lurched to her feet, her mouth stretched wide over her gritted teeth. "A girl child will live."

Arms crossed, Sefe stared at Ana with his lips pressed into a tight line. His scars made his emotion difficult to read in the firelight, but Eily knew Ana was afraid of him. Afraid of losing this baby. What would happen if she did? Eily wouldn't contradict her sister's claim in front of the king, but she had to speak to Ana alone. They had to get her out of here.

Ana pressed both palms flat against the sides of her abdomen, took a deep breath, and let it out through pursed lips. "A girl will live."

Sefe spoke to the man at the door. "Let her out."

The hunter opened the door, and Eily fumbled for an excuse to keep Ana with her. "What about Wint? Did he take these pills, too?"

Ana shrugged. She was breathing hard and tight lines touched her eyes. "I wasn't there. You'd have to ask your man."

"Jubal? Where is he?"

"He's safe." Ana turned away to face the cage door.

Eily could feel the crowd watching her every move. She needed them to go away. She needed time alone with Ana. She turned to Sefe. "I still need her help."

Sefe's mouth widened into a knowing grin. "And you wish to talk with your sister." He shifted his attention to Ana. "My consort may do as she pleases. Ana?"

In response, Ana doubled over, her arms wrapped around her middle. A small moan threaded between her lips. "Not now."

Eily jumped to her feet, both hands out to support her sister. A line of blood rolled down the inside of Ana's knee.

Ana closed her eyes and took an unsteady step forward. "It's too soon."

Eily looked up at Sefe. "The baby is coming."

What felt like a rock poked Jubal in the kidney, but he couldn't seem to gather the will to sit up or shift. The rattle of wheels over stone jostled his bones, and his stomach churned with the movement. He struggled to open heavy eyes, blinking slowly. Overhead, a lavender sky spun out of control, so he squeezed his lids shut again. The gurgle of a river whispered to his right. His head bounced, then the movement stopped. Something heavy settled near his left leg.

"This is the last cache? Loose that rope," Rann's voice at his feet.

Pressure on Jubal's midsection eased. A goat bleated near his head. *My goats?* "Mmmm," he let out, trying to move.

"He's waking up." Was that Rodi? Where were they?

"Good. He can walk," Rann said.

A rope snaked off his bare chest, leaving a slight burning sensation. Still trying to orient himself, he rolled to his right. He flopped to the gritty earth, the air exploding from his lungs. Blinking, he brought Rodi's face into focus.

She squatted next to him. "Are you okay?"

"Where..." his voice came out as a wheeze. He cleared his throat, pulling threads of memory back together. "Where are we?"

"I saved us. Take your pack," Rann said.

The familiar weight of his pack slumped against his elbow. He rocked upright to his knees. Unable to stop his momentum, he toppled over backwards.

"I don't think he can walk yet," Rodi said.

"Where's my staff?" Jubal asked. His limbs felt heavy. He wanted to go back to sleep.

"You can make a new one." Rann gripped Jubal's arm and jerked him to a sitting position. "You're lucky I got both packs."

A sick feeling settled into Jubal's gut. He sagged back, catching himself on one elbow. "Eily."

"Your rotting Flame Runna is gone." Rann returned to pulling rocks away from a cairn. "Now get up."

"You had no right to trade her, Rann." Jubal's supporting arm trembled, too weak to lift him higher. He refused to collapse again. "I have to save her."

Rodi cocked her head, her face a contrast of light and shadows. "Nonsense. Have you been eating amarantox?"

"He let her magic him. That's all," Rann said. "If it weren't for me, we'd both be roasting next to Pops right now."

"I claimed her children," Jubal gritted between his teeth. "She's not just any Flame Runna."

Rodi crossed her arms. "You swore you'd never take a woman. You sure she didn't magic you?"

"Rodi, you think I'd claim her lightly?"

"But she's a Flame Runna."

He sucked in a breath, steadying his fuzzy thoughts. "She's more than that. Special. I have to protect her."

Rann fished a stack of terra cotta pots from a hollow beneath the cairn and loaded them onto the cart. "It's too late now. Put her behind you. We have to go."

"I'm not leaving her." Jubal swallowed against the helplessness in his chest.

"I've already used up the whole day finding where you left our caches. Sefe could be after us at any moment. I'm not going to risk my life to protect a Flame Runna," Rann said.

"You love her?" Rodi asked.

Jubal nodded.

In a slow, soft voice, like she feared being overheard, Rodi said, "I may be able to help."

Rann snorted and threw a rope over the cart to tie the load.

Jubal took a deep breath and commanded his arm to push him to sitting.

Rodi scooted closer. "There are those at the Taguan who

oppose Sefe's hunger for Flame Runnas. He's lured too many hunters to join the One Tree, using Flame Runna magic as payment. Now the Taguan is controlled by men who take what they want when they want it. Men who force themselves upon us without claiming our children. Who eat our manna cakes without lifting a hand to harvest or store."

"We can't go back," Rann said. "He'll kill me."

Rodi continued speaking to Jubal. "We'd like to see the hunters gone. But as long as Sefe has Flame Runnas, they will come."

"Sneak the Flame Runnas out. We'll take them far away," Jubal promised.

Rodi shook her head. "Ana won't leave. She likes her position here." She turned to Rann. "I think she may have helped that first Flame Runna escape. To eliminate competition."

Rann stepped around the cart, hands balled into fists. "*She* let the Flame Runna free?"

"She came to your father every day after you left." Rodi said. "Supposedly to ease his suffering. One day I overheard her whispering apologies to him."

Rann glared at Jubal. "See?"

A pang of guilt entered Jubal's heart. Ana had freed the other prisoner and allowed Rann to take the blame? He recalled her cold, black eyes on him when he'd arrived with Pulo.

Rodi continued. "My people want Ana and all the other Flame Runnas gone."

Pacing in front of the cart, Rann seemed ready to explode. "She should be my slave. She owes me."

"We don't care what you do with her," Rodi said. "We've thought of killing her, but too many feared the ire of Sefe and his men. If she were to disappear now, he'd assume she ran away with her sister."

"What do we need to do?" Jubal asked.

Rann stopped pacing, shoulders slumped. "We can't go back."

"Sefe cannot deny your participation in your father's flesh-feast. That gives us a little time to work out the details."

Jubal shook his head. "He'll just get more, Rodi. He has Eily's box to call the flying machines."

Rann squatted next to them. "That's what I'm saying. We can't go back. Not even for Pops's flesh-feast. I took the beacon."

Rodi sucked in a breath. "You took it? How? I saw it on Sefe's platform when we carried Jubal out."

"I left the box. I just took what was inside. I wasn't about to let the man who stole my father have everything."

Jubal started to laugh. It was all he could do. "Of course you'd ruin this plan, too."

"I told you I didn't free that Flame Runna." Rann shoved Jubal's shoulder. "And I just saved your life. You should apologize."

The cold anger against Jubal's spine gave him the strength to rise to his feet. He longed for the support of his staff. "You betrayed me. Your own brother."

"You were going to leave me there. At least I didn't abandon you."

"You sold my woman into slavery. She's family."

Rann crossed his arms. "Not my family."

Jubal gritted his teeth. "Just give me the beacon."

"Fine," Without taking his eyes off Jubal, Rann stuck his hand into the loaded cart. He withdrew a leather pouch. Pulling back his arm, he threw it hard against Jubal's chest. The sack bounced and hit the ground.

Jubal bent and gathered the bag. Pulling open the drawstring, he shook the device out into his palm. The strange, brittle material had a jagged, open crack stretching from the button, over one edge, and down the other. Something inside the crack blinked red.

Jubal's insides tightened—the button was depressed. He looked up at his brother, eyes wide. "What have you done?"

Chapter Twenty-Four

Haldanian Protectorate

The com at Rael's bedside beeped. He opened one eye to the stars gleaming through the transparent roof of his bedroom. With a grunt, he rolled over and toggled the receiver. "You are waking an old man from his much-needed rest."

"Sir, this is Breden over at Com Ops. The beacon has been activated."

Rael looked at the clock. Midnight. If the reversions had activated the beacon because of the Fosselites, he didn't want to get in the way. He smiled. "Thank you, Breden. I'll deal with it in the morning."

"Yes, sir." The com cut off.

Rael stared up at the stars and tried unsuccessfully to sleep. By morning, his eyes burned, but he leapt from his bed anyway. He donned his best gold-link necklace and matching ear bands and called a skimmer to drive him to the office. The sun sparkled off the buildings. As they passed the Gardens, he glanced with contentment at the children playing inside the protected walls. Upon reaching the Leibert Building, he stepped out of the skimmer and raised his face to the sky, taking a deep breath of the cool morning air. He pictured a Fosselite hooked to a spinal shunt, those disgusting red eyes rolling back as the neurotoxin took hold. His city would soon have one less threat against it.

He opened the mirrored door and entered the climate-controlled hallway. At his office, he greeted his aide and set to work on his daily tasks and forms, humming under his breath as he worked. By afternoon, as the sun streamed in through the ceiling above the concrete-block walls, he leaned back in his chair and decided he'd earned a well-deserved nap.

What felt like moments later, his aide shook him by the shoulder. "Sir, you have an emergency call on line one."

"Hmm? Who is it?"

"The Holdout Liaison, Ijon. He says a member of the Doomseeds party has returned."

Rael sat up, blinking back brightness. *But the beacon is still out on the Reaches.* Eily must have left it behind with the reversions. He tapped a finger against his lips. Although he would have sacrificed her to the plan, her return eased his conscience. He toggled the com screen. Ijon appeared, wearing his usual sleeveless blue tunic in a ludicrous attempt to placate the Holdout tradition of modesty.

Rael chose a grandfatherly smile as he greeted the liaison. "Ijon. This is Councilman Rael. I hear you have good news."

"Sir, the native, Gideon Yoder, has returned to the compound." Ijon leaned closer to the camera. "He says the rest of the party needs help."

Rael hesitated for a moment, trying to recall Gideon Yoder. The Holdout man had barely registered on his consciousness when the party left for the Reaches. "What about the Reversion Specialist, Eily?"

"Mr. Yoder arrived alone." Ijon shook his head. "Well, not alone. With a party of cannibals. They want conversion."

Rael drew back. "Cannibals?"

"Four men and a woman, sir. Do you want them to enter screening here at the Holdout? Or should I send them to the main lab?"

Rael scanned his desk's blank surface, as if it might provide an answer. Policy was to offer conversion to any who didn't resist capture. But adults never surrendered. After Burn Ops did their job, the only ones left to convert were children. Children conformed well to Protectorate doctrine; they generally became acceptable citizens.

But these weren't children. What were these cannibals up to? He didn't have time to risk an infiltration plot right now. He had to finish the Doomseeds project. "Send them to euthanization," Rael said.

Ijon frowned. "But, sir, they laid down their weapons."

"We don't need to spend any more resources on people who will only turn into reversions."

Ijon didn't speak for a moment, his frown engraved on his face. He bit his lips together, then took a deep breath and raised his chin. "We have another, more immediate problem, Councilman. I'm afraid he spoke to people at the Gate before I was informed of Mr. Yoder's return. He says the others from his party have been taken into slavery and has confirmed that the cannibals are trading reversions to the Fosselites for guns. Panic is spreading through the Holdout."

Rael massaged his forehead. He couldn't let this rumor spread right before the Fosselite problem was solved forever. A shaft of daylight crept onto his elbow as the sun began its downward arc. The Fosselites'd had plenty of time to collect the reversions and retreat by now. All that would be left at the beacon site were cannibals. The kind who didn't volunteer for conversion.

"It's probably too late for the reversions if Mr. Yoder's story is true," Rael said. "I'll send you the beacon's coordinates. Put together two Burn Ops teams. I'll rally a third from here. Send them at first light. Oh, and warn them about the guns—tell them to shoot from above and offer no mercy. I want those cannibals eradicated."

The Taguan

Every fiber of Eily's being cringed as Ana collapsed back to the pallet, limp and haggard. Normally, a birth during a flesh-feast was considered lucky. But nothing about Ana's progress so far had been lucky. Labor had come on hard and fast, giving her sister no time to recover between contractions.

At least Sefe had relented and allowed Eily out of her cage. She reached out and stroked a sweaty strand of hair off Ana's cheek. Her sister's skin was unusually cold, and her eyes were sunken and bruised looking.

Two women hovered nearby, reluctantly helping as Sefe commanded them to boil water or bring fresh blankets. The rest of the cave's population had disappeared. The great cavern seemed to swallow all sound and light, as though life had been sucked away. Even the roasting spit had been removed. Eily was glad the sickening stench of cooking meat was gone. The smell of Ana's blood was bad enough.

The shorter helper-woman added a branch to the fire for the sixth time that night, sending shadows contorting across the cave walls. In the flare of light, Ana's blood-soaked pallet looked impossibly crimson. Eily took her sister's hand and choked back a sob. She'd not been allowed to help with births at the Holdout. The women considered her bad luck. But right now even she could tell something was wrong.

Ana screamed, curling in on herself with another contraction.

"If you're screaming, you're not pushing." Sefe stood at the foot of the pallet, leaning on his spear as if it was the only thing holding him up. He was marked as a healer, but so far all he'd done was offer words.

The contraction eased. Ana shook her head weakly from side to side. "This child will live."

Eily's heart lay like a lead weight in her chest. She resisted looking up at Sefe and stroked Ana's hand. "I'm sure you'll be fine. Just keep pushing."

Ana lifted her other hand toward Sefe. "Sefe, promise you won't replace me. Let her go."

He took an awkward step forward and knelt by Ana's side to take her offered hand. "My Ana."

Eily blinked in surprise at the tenderness in his voice.

Ana moaned, a contraction seizing her. Her eyes rolled back as she weakly tried to push. Sefe remained kneeling, his hand around Ana's.

"You're a healer." Eily's throat tightened. "Save her."

He didn't take his eyes off Ana. "I have no medicine for this."

"Is she dying?" Eily whispered, the dreaded words sour on her tongue.

The muscles of Sefe's jaw bulged beneath his scars. He lowered his chin, took a deep breath and let it out slowly. After a pause, he placed a palm on the side of Ana's abdomen. With his other hand, he drew a knife from his belt.

Eily's stomach lurched. She thrust her hands over Ana's belly. "You can't cut her open!"

He looked into her face and his lips spread into a line that might have been an attempt at a smile. His eyes glittered. "Sometimes what's best isn't exactly what we want."

She threw her body over her sister's. Some women at the Holdout labored for days. Ana only needed more time. A contraction tightened Ana's abdomen as Eily held her. Opening Ana up without anesthetic or antibiotics was no better than giving her the Knife. A savage's solution.

"Save my baby." Ana's voice brushed Eily's ear, a sigh of wind at sunset.

"I can do no more." Sefe's voice was almost as soft. "Would you waste them both?"

Eily shuddered, every muscle, every fiber, every bone crying out in denial. No wasting. The core philosophy on the Tox. This entire journey, Gid's certain demise, Wint and Lisius and soon Pulo's deaths, had been wasted. The baby had next to no chance at survival; Haldanian mothers exposed to UV during gestation almost always delivered stillborns. How could this be happening? Sefe couldn't be right. How much loss could one person take?

Ana's chest rose and fell as fast as a bird's. She lived, but her body felt oddly clammy and stiff. The scent of death rose from her. Eily groped for her hand. The fingers and wrist were limp and cold. Nothing but meat. A voice inside Eily's head began to wail. *No!*

Beneath Eily's embrace, a tiny ripple rose across Ana's abdomen, like a fish surfacing from a pond.

The wailing in Eily's head ceased. The baby lived. For now.

She pushed away from her sister and met Sefe's eyes. "No wasting."

Jubal hurried along the river trail back to the Taguan, plunking the makeshift staff's butt against the ground. The staff was merely a long amarantox stalk he'd stripped of leaves. A few broken pottery shards dangled from strings at the top, their noise more muted than he liked. The staff would be worthless in a fight or even to support his weight, but it would announce a trader's presence in the dark. His heart raced. If Sefe chose not to honor the staff, Jubal would die long before the flying machines arrived.

Rodi jogged next to him. "I don't understand this Flame Runna magic."

"Eily said the button calls flying machines. The entire Taguan is in danger."

"But how?"

"I don't know. But they could be here by morning." He shook his head, glancing up at the moon hovering over the tamarisk stand on the far bank. To his right, a long slope of rock formed the basin floor from the cave mouth to the river.

"If I had my son with me," Rodi looked back over her shoulder, "I'd leave with Rann right now."

His brother had gone the other way with the wagon. Jubal couldn't care less if Rann took all the goods and was never heard from again.

"I'm sorry," he said. "I have a plan to save you *and* the Taguan if we can convince people to listen."

"Flame Runnas burn everything. Are you sure your woman isn't setting a trap?"

Jubal swallowed, his breathing ragged as he climbed the slope. The wooziness was mostly gone, but he still felt worn out. He shook his staff again to calm his nerves. "I trust her. If we keep everyone inside the cave, away from Sefe and the others who will fight, the Flame Runnas won't burn us."

"That sounds like a trap."

Without pausing his stride, Jubal said, "She offered to stand with us, so if they send fire, she'll burn, too. Remember the rumors of children being taken? They're true. Small children don't run or fight back, so the Flame Runnas adopt them. Eily was such a child. She was born into the Under Stone tribe."

"Then how did she get Flame Runna skin?" Rodi's voice came from farther behind him.

Jubal paused to look over his shoulder. She stood with the moon at her back, one hand on her hip. "Keep up," he said. Once she continued walking, he answered. "Eily says they changed her skin to make her one of them."

"Will they turn us into Flame Runnas?"

"I don't know." Jubal shrugged. "But Eily hasn't eaten once since I met her. Flame Runnas never hunger. I think many people would like that."

"Sefe and his men will try to shoot the flying machines. Then the Flame Runnas will burn out the cave."

Jubal grimaced. Hiding inside the cave did seem dangerous. But so did standing outside, especially if Sefe's men were attacking. "Eily said she'd stand with us."

Rodi kept pace with him in silence.

As they drew near the Taguan, the gabble of a crowd met his ears. Jubal slowed. Was Sefe about to send men after Rann? A child cried, and a woman's voice floated over the others in laughter. Not a hunting party. "Why are they all outside?"

"Wait here." Rodi disappeared into the darkness.

Jubal eased forward until he could make out a clump of people sitting around a small fire. They were visiting and talking. Shadows moved about other glowing fires scattered up the Taguan's basin.

Rodi returned a moment later. "The Flame Runna is giving birth. They've moved your father's flesh-feast outside."

He glanced toward the cavern entrance. "Eily's inside?"

Rodi nodded. "I hear labor's not going well."

Jubal pursed his lips. "Where's Sefe?"

"Inside. He's a Healer."

"Gather your group. Let me talk to them."

Rodi reentered the crowd, and Jubal approached the nearest fire, shaking his staff gently to announce himself.

"Trader?" A man looked up over his shoulder. "I'm surprised to see you return."

"I would not miss my father's flesh-feast."

The group murmured to each other. A woman with braided hair spoke up. "Your father was a fair man. He's traded with us since I was a child. But he's brought ill luck on the Taguan this season."

Jubal squatted down between two men in the circle. "How so?"

"That Flame Runna of Sefe's is about to spawn more," the man beside Jubal said. The entire group turned to spit over their shoulders.

"What has that to do with my father? He didn't plant that babe inside her. Nor did he bring her here in the first place."

A heavy pause, then a young mother with a sleeping child on her lap said, "His flesh-feast is cursed by her birthing."

Jubal cocked his head. Births during a flesh-feast were considered good luck. The child was almost always named after the deceased. "How can a flesh-feast be cursed by a birthing?"

"It's a Flame Runna birthing," the man next to him muttered. Again, people spat.

A man with deep lines around his lips and eyes wiped his mouth with the back of his forearm, then pointed at Jubal. "And you traded more of the evil into Sefe's hands."

The man beside Jubal stirred the fire. The orange light exposed their frightened faces. Two new people joined the circle, a young man and woman holding hands.

"Has Ana been evil?" Jubal asked. "Has she brought the flying machines? Or killed your children outside the Hunger?"

"Sefe uses her to control the hunters," the old man said.

The woman with the child replied, "Not very well."

From among the other fires, Rodi arrived with her son on her hip. She brought with her three women and two men. They took places standing or squatting behind the others around the fire.

"How many of you are or were hunters?" Jubal asked, looking at the firelit faces. Most of the onlookers were women. None of the men had a hunter's peculiar braided beard or facial piercings.

A slight pause before a young man answered. "Not me."

The rest of the group muttered agreement.

The woman who'd spoken first said, "Sefe needs them to attack the Flame Runnas."

"Ana's a Flame Runna. Why does she help attack her own kind?" Jubal asked.

"She claims she was once one of us," one of Rodi's women said, "and the Flame Runnas gave her green skin. She hates them."

"But her sister's one of them," Jubal pointed out.

"I don't think she likes her sister much, either." Several people laughed.

Jubal's stomach soured. The hazy recollection of Ana's kisses prickled his skin. He was fairly good at reading people during trade, and while Ana had seemed regretful, she'd also been resolute. Eily was competition. And Ana had spoken of death. Was Eily all right? Ana'd helped the other Flame Runna escape. Maybe she'd help Eily. He could only hope. Right now he had to get the residents of the Taguan to safety. "Sefe is bringing the anger of the Flame Runnas onto you and your children."

"We're safe at the Taguan," said a lisping girl. Many in the group turned faces to the dark sky.

"Not out here, we're not," Jubal said. To the east, the sky and land had parted ways, light above and shadow below. Dawn approached. He had to get everyone inside. "Flame Runnas are on their way. They will be here with the daylight."

The mother let out a cry and lifted her child to one shoulder. The man next to Jubal shot to his feet, fists clenched at his sides. Others rose as well, muttering plans to run.

Jubal shouted over the rising noise. "Families moving through the amarantox will leave trails. The Flame Runnas will track us down and burn us out."

The mother sobbed along with her child. The young couple clutched each other, the woman burying her head against the man's chest. The crowd grew as word spread to the other fires. "How do you know they're coming?" a woman shouted.

"He brought them to us!" Other voices rose. "We should kill them all."

Jubal shook his staff, yearning for assertive metal chimes instead of the dull clunk of pottery. "A trader does not choose sides in wars between the tribes. I only bring news."

"If you didn't lead them here, then how'd they find us?" The old man pushed to the front of the crowd to face Jubal.

Guilt washed over Jubal, and he sidestepped the question. "They're hunting Sefe. Their magic leads them to the guns. I've traded with them, and they say their attacks are in response to hunters invading their home. They don't know the difference between tribes, between hunters and families. You must lay down your weapons." A memory of how Flame Runnas discerned friend from enemy poked at the edges of his attention.

An old man's voice rose above the shuffle. "I lived on the Tox many years before this and experienced many hard times. We've avoided the Hunger here. The Taguan's our home. Let Sefe fight them."

"Sefe's assaults have only made them more sure of their cause." Jubal said. "If he attacks them, we're all doomed."

"But they always attack first!" a woman wailed, throwing both hands into the air.

The flash of her pale palms in the dawn light brought the image of Gid waving his white flag. *A way to tell friend from enemy.* He blinked as the image took full form. Among the items the Holdout had traded him was a folded length of white cloth.

It was still on Rann's wagon.

Chapter Twenty-Five

Eily clenched her jaw as tears swam across her vision. Sefe hesitated, his gaze locked with hers. Then he glanced over his shoulder at the women. "Is there water ready?"

The short one nodded once. The other scurried to the fire.

"Pray to the Mothers for a girl child," Sefe said, knife poised above Ana's belly.

Before he could cut, a breathless warrior skidded into the cavern. "Sefe! That trader's back. He's causing a riot outside."

Eily's heart skipped a beat. Jubal had returned?

The king set the tip of the knife to Ana's midsection. "Deal with it."

"He says Flame Runnas are coming."

All the air left Eily's lungs. Jubal had used the beacon? Even with the danger to the Taguan? She looked down at her sister. Maybe the Protectorate would arrive in time to save Ana. She and her sister could go back to the Holdout. She had to act fast to get the duster's attention. To stand out from the rest of the people at the Taguan. She pulled her crumpled bonnet from her pocket and fitted it over her hair.

Sefe stopped his knife and looked over his shoulder at the warrior. “He’s lying.”

“He’s telling everyone not to fight.” Sefe’s man thrust his gun upward in one hand. “He wants us to stand there and be slaughtered.”

The woman who held the water dropped the bowl. She turned and fled the cave without a backward glance. The second woman gaped at the warrior, her face ashen.

Sefe lifted his eyes toward the cavern ceiling and let out a howl. Then in a single, deft stroke, he sliced Ana from ribs to pelvis, exposing muscle and blood and a thin layer of yellow fat.

Eily choked on a scream. But Ana never moved. Never flinched or made a sound.

He sliced again, this time more gentle and precise. The folded limbs of a baby slithered from the bloody mess, hardly bigger than Eily’s two palms. The mouth opened as if to emit a sound, but none came. Sefe grabbed the child by its feet and flipped it upside down. He cleared its mouth with a sweep of his finger. The child gurgled weakly.

“A boy,” he said, his voice flat. “Not green.”

The child lives. In wonder, Eily reached out and cupped the slippery body in her hands. A miracle for which she had no words. She didn’t bother to tell Sefe none of Ana’s children could be green. Converts could only have photosynthetic children if they implanted genetically modified embryos. Even then, many mothers ended up miscarrying.

She snugged the child into the crook of her left arm in an attempt to warm him. Her nephew. Her last piece of her sister. The boy was limp, not quite pink and not quite blue. The chances of the baby surviving were less than slim, but if the Protectorate arrived in time, perhaps they could save him. He whimpered, eyes squeezed tight as if in denial of this cruel existence.

Sefe twisted the umbilical cord around a finger and pulled taut before severing it with his knife. He flung the severed end back toward Ana. Something else moved inside her gaping belly. Sefe scowled. The flesh moved again, slight but sure. He slid a hand into the cut. A second, tiny body emerged, sprawled face-down across his palm. This one squalled, and Sefe quickly hung it to clear its mouth. A second boy.

The baby's flailing arms vibrated with his cries. Lusty cries. Sefe looked at her with dead eyes, his hand still clutching the baby's ankles. "Boys never live."

Eily thrust her free hand beneath the baby as if to catch it in case Sefe released his grip. "The Flame Runnas can save them."

Sefe's eyes narrowed and his mouth curled into a snarl.

"Let me try to save them," Eily said. She'd seen grief in his eyes when he'd looked at Ana. There had to be a spark of humanity in his feral soul. "These are your sons."

Staring at the bloody child hanging from his fist, Sefe's chest heaved. His arm trembled as if the child weighed too much. A heartbeat later, he thrust the baby toward Eily and addressed the waiting gunman. "Take this Flame Runna outside. Maybe the flying machines will avoid the women if one of their own is among them. Arm the men and get them to the top of the basin."

Eily settled the second child awkwardly into the crook of her right arm as the gunman prodded her with the tip of his rifle. She kept her eyes on Sefe, hoping what she was about to say was true. "The Flame Runnas know I'm here. They won't attack if you don't."

Sefe pushed up to his feet on his spear. "Flame Runnas

killed my parents. My brother. Broke my back so I could barely walk."

"At least call everyone into the cave." She struggled to her feet, fettered by the infants. "We'll be safe here until the fight is over."

"I've seen them fill caves with fire, leaving nothing but blackened holes. If you hide in here, no one will survive this fight."

Her blood chilled at the thought of being trapped inside while Burn Operatives blasted the cavern. But the Protectorate knew she was here. They wouldn't burn without checking first. She raised her chin, looking him square in the eye. "If we surrender, no one will get hurt."

"Flame Runnas have no honor." Sefe spat and stalked away.

The chill in her blood crystallized into daggers. Sefe could be right. Behind her, the gunman grabbed her shoulder.

Jubal scanned the eastern path. The sky glowed a hazy gold but the earth was still in shadow. How far had Rann gone, trailing wagon and goats? The Flame Runnas might arrive before he tracked his brother and the white cloth down.

A newborn wailed near the cave mouth, followed by Eily's voice. Like a ripple on water, the crowd grew silent and turned toward her. Jubal gripped his staff and raised himself onto his toes to see.

Eily stood at the threshold, her white bonnet glowing like a beacon in the early light. His heart swelled with relief. She was alive, and there was no sign of Sefe. Where was the cannibal king? Surely he wouldn't let her go, not easily, at least. There was no time for answers. Her bonnet could signal the Flame Runnas. He would have to use every trader skill he had to convince the people to stand firm in the face of what would look like certain death.

He pushed forward through the crowd. Eily was arguing with a man holding a gun, her back to the crowd.

"Let me through." He elbowed past a warrior, ducked around a woman clutching the hands of two children, and rose on his toes again. The warrior shoved Eily, sending her stumbling down the rock toward the crowd.

As she regained her balance, she turned to face the people. Her dress was smudged dark with blood, and in each arm she held a baby. She shouted, "The Flame Runnas will kill you all if you don't surrender!"

The crowd burst into an unintelligible roar. Jubal was borne sideways on a wave of moving bodies. His flimsy staff folded in half under his weight. Someone bumped him from behind and he went down. His necklaces of trade beads broke free while his right arm bent painfully underneath him.

"Flame Runna lies!... Kill her!... Sefe will win!..."

A heel connected with his temple, and stars shot across his vision. He rolled right. Someone stepped on his groin, turning the stars into a white-hot burst of agony. He rolled to his side and retched.

Rodi's voice roared over the clamor. "Jubal carries the trader's staff. Don't harm him!"

The scuffle continued, but a small space cleared around him.

"Can you stand?" Rodi spoke next to him. Her hands gently but firmly urged him upright.

Jubal swayed to his feet, panting through the pain. His palm was sticky, and he realized his arm was bleeding from an abrasion on his elbow. The crowd spread over the stone lip of the Taguan, easily two hundred faces, all of them speaking at once. Eily huddled on the stone, head bowed over the infants in her arms as three cannibals jabbed and slapped her.

His pulse roared through his ears. "Do not hurt her! We need her to communicate with the Flame Runnas. She can call Peace."

"We don't want Peace!" shouted a man with a gun.

"Sefe will defend us," a woman added.

"Do you really think Sefe can protect you?" Jubal bellowed. "The hunters will scatter when the Flame Runnas kill enough of them, and leave the rest of you to face the fires. Our only hope is to stop Sefe and declare a Peace with the Flame Runnas."

The people surrounding Eily ceased their attacks, but remained close to her. She hunched on the ground, not looking up.

Jubal strode through the crowd to her side. "Give me your bonnet."

Eily twisted her head to look up at him, her face contorted. "What are you talking about?"

He squatted beside her. "A white flag. Gid always waved a white flag. We can use your bonnet."

She sat up. One newborn squalled, and she jiggled it slightly to calm it. "One tiny flag won't protect all these people."

He reached over and yanked the bonnet from her hair. "The only way we're going to survive this is to prove to them we're more than cannibals."

"But Sefe's readying his men to fight."

Jubal rose to his feet. He had to find a way to stop Sefe—to overcome him if need be. Raising his voice, he addressed the crowd. "How many died in the last fight with the Flame Runnas?"

The crowd muttered and shifted. A nearby woman stepped up, her dark hair streaked with silver at the temples. "Too many. My boy was one of them."

"Will all of your sons take up guns and die for Sefe?" Jubal made eye contact with everyone close enough to see him. "For what? To own a handful of Flame Runna slaves?"

"Flame Runnas kill our families!"

"So do hunters, but Sefe welcomes them here—he *calls* them to join." Jubal pointed at the gunman standing in the entrance. "Is the One Tree a tribe of hunters? A tribe that breaks the laws the Mothers set down for us? Sefe stole my woman. A trader's woman. Soon no traders will visit the Taguan."

A man with a short beard and a bone spike through his nose hawked a wad of spit toward Eily. "Flame Runnas aren't goods. They're the enemy."

Several hunters wielding guns stepped forward to join him. People quieted and cleared a space around them.

Jubal drew himself taller. "Sefe treats his Flame Runnas as goods. He trades their magic for your allegiance. He trades them to the Blood-Eye for guns."

Rodi's shoulder brushed his arm as she called out, "And Sefe calls Ana his woman. Yet her skin is green. He makes or breaks laws at his whim."

People surrounding the warriors bristled. The space around the gunmen narrowed. Eily rocked back on her heels and clumsily got to her feet.

The bearded man widened his stance, shooting wary glances to either side. "Your brother traded them for his life. The Flame Runnas belong to Sefe now."

"My woman was not Rann's to trade." The only way to convince people to overthrow Sefe was to make this personal. He pointed to the young couple who'd joined him at the fire. "How long until Sefe takes your woman? Or your child? When I was a member of the Red Hand, our Big Man wisely sought the council of his tribe. When did my people decide to let one person rule without question?"

"Sefe makes the One Tree strong," said a voice from the crowd.

"He's turned the Taguan into a slave den. And now the Flame Runnas want revenge. Sefe can try to fight, but he'll only force them to kill us all."

"We have to run!" a woman screeched.

"Jubal," Eily leaned close to him. "This isn't going to work."

Jubal clamped a hand on her shoulder. "Eily, this is our best chance." He raised her bonnet high overhead and shouted to the crowd. "The Flame Runnas spare the people behind the lightning wall when they hold a white flag in the air. This is how they call a Peace."

Behind him, a man spoke, "That will be very useful in the upcoming fight."

Jubal spun, stepping around Eily to shield her.

Just inside the cave's mouth, Sefe pointed the long nose of a gun at Jubal's chest.

Chapter Twenty-Six

Eily peeked around Jubal's shoulder. Sefe stepped out of the shadow of the cave onto the stained rock, his hands around a long rifle. The crowd seemed to be holding its breath.

"Sefe, your people don't want to fight," Jubal said.

"I disagree."

In the crowd behind her, a few men jeered in agreement.

Eily spun to face them, her back to Jubal's. A handful of gunmen pumped their weapons in the air as they voiced support for Sefe. Men and women eased away from each warrior, pulling children close. Several children cried and mothers shushed them without success.

Sefe was going to end them all.

But what could she do? No one would listen to the words of a Flame Runna. She looked at the puckered faces of the babies in her arms. One of them rooted against her chest, mouth open wide in a useless attempt to nurse. Her eyes stung. She met the gaze of a young woman with an infant bundled against her breast. A young boy clutched the woman's leg. The mother looked so pitiful. Barely more than a child herself. Eily's heart ached.

Doubting anyone would actually hear her, she said, "We have to save the children."

The woman's gaze slid to the men behind Eily. A very short woman holding a little boy whispered something. Both women nodded. The short woman pivoted to face the crowd. "Sefe doesn't speak for me!"

The young mother joined her. "Or me."

One after another, mothers spoke out, then sons and brothers, the outcry gathering strength and momentum. A gunman in the crowd backhanded a thin woman next to him. The man behind her shouted in protest. Further back, another scuffle erupted between two men. People continued to speak out against Sefe, forming into solid groups.

An earsplitting crack echoed off the face of the Taguan behind her. Jubal's back slammed into hers. Both babies nearly toppled from her arms. She clutched them against her chest and braced herself.

Jubal collapsed against her legs.

"The trader! Sefe shot the trader!" A woman screamed.

Eily spun, half tripping over Jubal's out-flung arm. Blood welled from his left shoulder. Before she could see more, the crowd surged forward, driving her out of the way.

"Mambabarang!" a woman shouted beside her.

"Stop him!"

"He killed the trader!"

With both arms encumbered by newborns, Eily fought to remain upright in the rush. "Jubal!" she screamed, unable to keep him in sight. "Jubal!"

More shots reverberated against the rocks. People screamed in either rage or fear. To her left, a gunman yelped and fell to his knees as three women bore him to the ground. One woman wrenched the weapon from him and smacked it like a club against his face. Another of Sefe's men jammed the tip of his rifle into a graying man's gut just before being tackled from behind.

The short woman who'd first spoken against Sefe grabbed Eily's sleeve. "Come with me."

Eily peered through the crowd as the woman guided her. "Where's Jubal?"

"We got him out of the way."

People seemed to make room for the woman, unconcerned about the Flame Runna following her. Together they reached the Taguan's face and followed it to the edge of the dry stone wall. Next to a pile of rubble, two women, one with wildly curly hair, the other with tight, beaded braids, knelt next to Jubal. He lay flat on the ground while the braided woman pressed a blood-soaked cloth against his wound.

Eily cried out and sprinted forward. "Is he dead?"

The woman with curly hair turned and narrowed her eyes. "You brought the Flame Runna?"

The short woman said, "She's his woman. He wants her here."

"Rodi, did you find her?" Jubal struggled to sit up, and Eily exhaled in relief. The women pushed him flat before he could rise. His eyes were bright, feverish looking. He held out one hand. Bunched within his grasp he held her bonnet, stained crimson. "We can use a flag."

The short woman—Rodi—took the scrap of fabric between two fingers. "What do we do with it, Jubal?"

Jubal's brow furrowed as he stared at the bloody cloth. "I ruined it."

The top edge of the sun cleared the amarantox, sending blinding rays into Eily's eyes. She flinched, and both infants began to wail like sirens. "Can we move him into the cave?"

Jubal flailed and caught hold of Rodi's wrist, but his eyes were on Eily. "Not the cave. We have to prove we mean no violence. Like your Holdout."

She wanted to touch him, to comfort him, but her hands were full. "Sefe means to fight."

He lifted his head from the ground but the effort proved too much and he collapsed to the stone again, lips pale. His words were like breath. "The Flame Runnas won't stop with Sefe. We're all the same to them. All dead."

A chill shivered up Eily's spine. Jubal had a point. The Protectorate wanted to stop the Fosselites, or, at the very least, the cannibals with guns. And the Protectorate always got what it wanted. She and the reversions were collateral damage. The dusters knew they were approaching armed men. They'd attack first. Unless something stopped them.

She focused on the stained bonnet in Rodi's hand. During cannibal raids, the Order used their white hankies to signal the dusters so they weren't mistaken for attackers. Would Burn Operatives in the Reaches pay attention to a symbol from the Holdout? The tiny scrap of her bonnet would barely be visible from the air, even if it hadn't been darkened with blood. It wasn't enough. Not by itself.

She glanced down at her stained dress, then raised her eyes to scan the women. All browns and grays and muted natural colors. White was rare on the Tox, except for the yuvee trees during a sunstorm. Too much to hope for. But she looked to the sky, anyway.

The sun had fully cleared the horizon. Dusters would be in the air by now, Burn Operatives at the ready behind long-nozzled flame guns. Flashes of her childhood clouded her thoughts. Green faces and roaring flames and the horrific screams of her tribe. Ana clutching her tight, their small naked bodies cringing from the heat. Prickles of sweat broke out all over Eily's body, and the bodice of her dress felt too tight. Clothing always caught fire first and made it hard to escape.

Wait. Her undergarments were white. A seed of hope sprouted in her breast. Did she have enough fabric to signal the duster?

"Please, hold my babies." She lowered the infant from her right arm into the lap of the curly-haired woman. The woman instinctively put her hands out to cradle the newborn. Then Eily turned to Rodi and handed her the second.

Grasping the front of her bodice, Eily yanked at the closures, ignoring the pop as threads broke. She dropped the dress around her ankles. The morning air raised goosebumps on her arms and legs. She stripped out of the chemise and undershorts, leaving her in only dark stockings and shoes.

The women gaped at her. Eily ignored them. The underclothes were old and sweat-stained, but still white enough. Gripping one hem of the shorts, she jerked, straining to tear the seams in two. She repeated it with the chemise. If the flags were any smaller, they wouldn't be visible. But four flags were much better than a single small, stained bonnet. She held the rags out to the women. "Take these to the people. Make sure to spread them out and hold them high."

The braided woman rose and wiped her bloody hands against her thighs, then accepted the flags. "You must stand with us."

Eily's attention dropped to Jubal. Drying blood caked his chest. The wound glistened with a scarlet ooze. She fell to her knees beside him, finding it hard to breathe. Cupping his cheeks with both hands, she brushed her lips against his. His breath tickled her skin. She choked in relief. He still lived. But not for long if the dusters burned them out. "Hang on, Jubal," she whispered. "The Protectorate is coming. They have medicine to save you."

She rose and faced the women. Her bare skin tingled in the rays of the sun, usually hidden chloroplasts springing to life. She could shimmy back into her dress, but her green skin might stand out enough to make the dusters pause their fire, and she needed every advantage, no matter how exposed she felt at the moment. Raising her chin, she said, "All together."

Rodi handed Ana's baby back and swapped her own, heavier child to her other hip. She took a flag and left to join the mass behind them.

The curly-haired woman rose, Ana's second baby still in her arms, and took a flag. Her eyes locked with Eily's. "I'll hold this child."

Eily bit her lip. If these people were to trust her, she had to return their trust. She nodded. The woman strode away into the crowd. Eily was about to follow when the braided woman said, "You come with me."

The woman held onto both the remaining scraps until they reached the crowd, then she handed one off to another woman, giving instructions. The throng had already begun forming around the flags. Eily scanned the other groups, keeping her eye on the curly-haired woman carrying her nephew.

"What if they shoot first? We can't outrun fire," a gruff voice said.

Eily responded with more confidence than she felt. "They'll hold their fire."

Everyone vied for a spot near the flag, jostling shoulder to shoulder. Eily's infant mewed. Through the crowd, she caught a glimpse of one of Sefe's sullen-faced warriors, hands bound behind him, his nose torn and bloody where there'd once been a labret.

"What do they want from us?" asked a young man holding a gun in one hand.

The weapon made Eily's hammering heart skip a beat and

tighten. The weapons were a part of the plan she hadn't thought through. "No one can be holding a gun," she said. "If the Flame Runnas see them, they'll fire."

The young man hugged the firearm tight against his chest and glowered at her.

"Put the gun down," said an older woman, perhaps the boy's mother.

The boy scowled but elbowed his neighbor aside to set the gun on the ground. The metal barrel looked stark and dangerous against the pale rock. The crowd closed over the spot, but she couldn't chance even a glimpse of a weapon among them. A single gun could make the Burn Operatives assume these people were a threat. The Protectorate would need someone to blame.

Eily spun on her toes to see above the crowd. "Where's Sefe?"

No one seemed to have an answer. On the southeastern horizon, a glint of movement drew her attention to the sky. Fighting panic, she raised her voice above the noise. "Separate Sefe and his men from the rest of us! Lay the guns near them so the Flame Runnas know he's responsible!"

Panicked voices drowned out her command as other people spotted the specks in the sky. She grabbed the older woman's arm. "The Flame Runnas will think we all helped Sefe."

The woman stared at the gun a moment. Then she shoved her son. "Do as she says."

With agonizing slowness, the word spread, and the crowd expelled bound warriors toward the Taguan entrance. Most men had to be carried, but at least two walked on their own. Eily glanced at the sky. The dusters drew closer, flying in a V formation. More guns clattered to the rock as women darted out and dropped weapons in a pile against the nearby wall.

Four men lumbered out and flung Sefe's bald form in the

middle of the cluster of warriors. The ousted leader lifted his head, his teeth bared in a snarl, but seemed too injured to do more than choke out, "She'll doom you all!"

About twenty bound men now cowered at the Taguan entrance. Most were lying down or hunkered over with obvious injuries, but two were trying to move back toward the flags. Four women shoved them away, arguing. A short, broad woman jabbed the butt of a gun into a warrior's gut, doubling him over, then kicked him backward.

Against the nearby wall, the meager stack of firearms caught the morning sun. Eily shifted the infant to her other arm, surveying the crowd. This couldn't be all the weapons. The cannibals didn't understand that the Burn Operatives would be happy for any excuse to flash everyone.

A few miles east, the aircraft paused and circled tightly. One dipped below the amarantox while two others hovered.

She looked around in an attempt to find the older woman who'd helped before, but she was nowhere in sight. "If even one person holds a gun, the Flame Runnas won't heed the flags."

To her relief, Rodi rose above the crowd, held high on someone's shoulders. "This is our last chance. One person holding a gun will break the Peace."

The women fighting the upright warrior flung their weapons toward the pile and ran for the crowd. The bound warrior followed them, but no one stopped him. From the crowd, three more people scuttled out and dropped guns on the stack with a clatter. Bodies pressed close around Eily as everyone jostled to be near a flag. The remaining flag bearers took Rodi's lead and mounted the shoulders of others in the crowd, holding their rags high.

The dusters again formed a phalanx, rising high into the air to continue toward the Taguan. Silence enveloped the crowd like a blanket.

The flying machines arrowed straight over the top of the Taguan and across the river. Frightened faces turned upward, following the movement like a wave. Rodi swung her flag violently overhead. The scrap of cloth seemed fragile and insignificant as the dusters cut a wide return arc.

A child squealed, "They're coming back."

The dusters' nuvoplast siding reflected the rising sun as if the vehicles themselves were made of fire as they made a return pass. The pit of Eily's stomach burned, and she panted along with the others pressed tight against her.

On a third pass, one duster slowed and hovered high above the Taguan, a geyser of flame sprouting from its open side. A unified moan rose from the crowd around Eily. The other aircraft continued on their trajectory. The single duster rotated in a lazy circle. Someone on the ground screamed. Eily craned her neck to locate the other dusters. They'd split up. One now covered the path up to the cliff above the basin and the other hovered over the river.

"This is the Haldanian Protectorate," a voice crackled. From the duster's side, a tongue of flame licked out as if the machine itself spoke. "Surrender now."

Rodi's flag arm trembled, halting its frantic movement. "What do they want? We are surrendering."

Only the crush around her held Eily upright. Images of her past mingled with the present. The baby squalled, his little fists flailing as if he wanted to fight. Light-headed, she tried to form words with what little air she managed to gulp down. "I think they need to see me. I have to step away from the crowd."

A man gripped Eily's arm so hard it cleared the haze in her head. "You said you'd stand with us."

"I am." Eily looked around at the angry, frightened faces. "But the Flame Runnas need to know I'm alive."

Eily caught the eye of the young mother who'd spoken

against Sefe. Her baby's fist clenched against her breast as it nursed. In her own arms, Eily stroked the velvety skin of her nephew's foot. "This child is my blood." She held the newborn out to the woman. "Take him. If the Flame Runnas burn you, they burn him, too."

The woman's brows drew together, but she held out her free arm to take the newborn.

Rodi bellowed in a voice that belied her small stature. "Give her room, or the Flame Runnas will waste us all!"

With shuffling steps, the people parted by centimeters, then a meter and more around her. Eily looked up at the sky and waved her arms above her head. She had no white flag, but her naked green skin would hopefully be signal enough. "It's me!" she attempted to make her voice carry as well as Rodi's did. "Eily Kraybill! We call for Peace!"

The duster swiveled again, and for a moment Eily feared they would burn the other groups now that they had her location. Instead, the loudspeaker crackled again. "Clear below."

Without waiting for compliance, the duster descended, sending dust and debris scattering with the panicked crowd. The vehicle settled onto the rock and two men and a woman jumped from the open side door, flame guns in hand. The nearest cannibals screamed and fell back, but the mass of people behind them kept them from retreating far. Everyone ducked or crouched, shielding their heads with raised arms.

Eily swallowed and wove her way through the crowd toward the invaders. She held her hands out and open in the cannibal call for Peace. "We want to negotiate terms!"

As she drew near, one of the male Flame Runnas lowered his gun and grinned at her, his gaze raking her from head to toe. She halted, heat creeping over her naked skin. "Ijon?"

"Our girl in a dress has gone native, I see."

She lifted her chin and took in his bare chest. "I could say the same for you."

Ijon looked down and shrugged. "Didn't want to make myself a target by being different."

Eily raised her arm to point at the disabled warriors near the cave entrance. "There are the men responsible for the duster attacks."

The female Burn Operative swiveled her gun toward them. Ijon looked over the rest of the crowd. "Is this all one tribe?"

"They call themselves the One Tree." Eily moved toward the duster, hope flickering. "They're farmers, Ijon. They want to broker peace with the Protectorate."

Ijon cast a glance at the remaining two dusters hovering at either end of the camp. "We've got orders to flash everything."

Eily halted. To her left she caught the wide-eyed stare of a girl who was about the age Eily had been when taken. She reached down and took the girl's trembling hand, drawing her to her feet. "Then you'll have to burn me, too."

Chapter Twenty-Seven

Haldanian Protectorate

Rael frowned into the monitor at Ijon's face. Harsh sunlight backlit the man, and static made him difficult to hear. The councilman leaned forward to squint at the image. Ijon definitely wasn't in his office. Where was he? A white line of interference rolled down the screen.

"...white flags, sir. They've surrendered."

"Where are you? Who's surrendering?"

"The cannibal camp. We've found—" another haze of static.

Rael drew back. "You're in the Reaches?"

Ijon leaned off screen. The glare cut off and the inside of a duster resolved itself. The liaison's face appeared again. "I called in a favor with Panone. I used to work for Burn Ops."

Rael rolled his shoulders and sucked in a tight breath. Let Ijon play at Burn Ops. It didn't matter who went out—only that his orders were followed. "Report."

"I've got a med-tech with one of the reversions. Pulo, I

think. Eily's fine, if a bit rattled. I don't have details on the others yet."

Cold sweat prickled Rael's skin. The reversions were still there? He'd acted too soon. The cannibals hadn't traded with the Fosselites after all.

Ijon continued his account. "We're sorting out the cannibals now. Seems they had a coup just before we arrived. Most of them claim innocence in the duster attacks."

Rael scowled. "These are not citizens, Ijon. They have no rights under Protectorate law. Kill them before they turn on you."

"But they've surrendered the leader and his men. The rest are mostly women and children. I estimate we have over two hundred potential converts."

"We've got our hands full dealing with the Holdout. Our facilities cannot handle the extra load." Rael stared hard into Ijon's eyes. "Do everyone a favor."

Now it was Ijon's turn to scowl. "They're asking for peace. They may not be citiz..." Interference blurred the transmission. "...human beings."

A headache pounded behind Rael's left eye. He was tired of fighting soft-hearted civil servants. That's what he got for working so hard to shield Protectorate citizens from the reality of life outside; they would never see that these savages were irredeemable.

He sighed. The Board would likely take Ijon's side in this. But perhaps the cannibals could be useful when he released other Doomseeds into the Reaches.

Or be converted into Doomseeds themselves. The sudden idea made Rael's heart race. "All right. Bring them in for conversion."

The Taguan

Jubal's shoulder throbbed sharply. He opened his heavy lids to a blue sky. A man's green face loomed above him but didn't look down. The sky disappeared as the Flame Runna propelled Jubal up a ramp and into an enclosed space. Flame Runna equipment filled the area along with a strange, almost-scorched smell. Behind a clear glass partition, a handful of cannibals leaned against walls or sprawled on the floor in a smaller area. Sefe lay closest to the glass, one side of his bald head a bloody mess. His good eye stared straight out at Jubal, his teeth bared in a snarl.

The Flame Runna who'd brought Jubal inside pressed a hand to a spot on the wall, and the glass slid aside. Nearby, Eily's voice was raised in protest as Jubal was wheeled into the room with the other cannibals. "He's not one of them."

"This is where our med kits are located, miss," the man pushing him said.

"Don't let any of the prisoners near him." Eily appeared at his side, lips rising into a wan smile as she saw he was awake. "You're going to be all right, Jubal. Hang on."

He tried to raise his hand and found he was strapped down. "Are we safe?" His throat was so parched he wasn't sure she could understand him.

She brushed her fingers along his cheek. "They're flying you back to the Protectorate. I have to stay at the Taguan to oversee negotiations. But my Aunt Tula will meet you there. She's a doctor. Cooperate with her, okay?"

Something stung his arm, and he jerked. He tilted his chin down to see the Flame Runna man running his fingers along a thin tube up to a bladder of clear fluid. Wooziness flooded him. He again sought Eily, but she was gone.

His stomach lurched. Through the glass door and beyond, the ground dropped away with sickening speed.

They were flying. He was on a flying machine.

The green man thumbed Jubal's eyelids wide and blinded him with a ray of light. "You're one tough weed," the man said.

Jubal wanted to respond, but his chest felt like someone was sitting on him. A yawn built deep inside him, but he couldn't quite gather the strength to take a full breath. He closed his eyes.

When next he opened them, lines of light stretched across a flat ceiling high above. The smallest twist of his head sent stabbing pain into his chest and shoulder. He lifted his opposite hand to touch what looked like raw, wet skin. The shoulder was dry. Some sort of clear material sealed the wound, holding down the ragged edges of the puncture.

Being shot was his last real memory. Flashes of other things hovered just out of his reach. *Where's Eily?*

He turned his attention to the room, slowly, breathing through the pain. Vertical bars enclosed him in a cube of space. Beyond, more cages sat in neat rows. Some of the cages held people. The farthest walls looked like gray stone blocks. Where was he?

Someone coughed, the sound echoing around the cavernous room.

Cautiously, he rolled onto his side, then swung his feet off the low bench he was on and sat up. The room seemed to tilt sideways then steadied. By the Knife, he hurt. His cage contained a metallic basin, his bench, and nothing else. A man in a neighboring cage caught his eye and grinned at him, displaying a gap where several teeth should be. He was naked, including every strand or curl of hair.

"Strange, eh?" the man next door said.

"What happened?" Jubal asked.

"Sefe is making the Flame Runnas give us spirit healing of our own." The man grinned again and pointed to a cage across the way. Inside, a naked green Sefe lay sprawled on the bench. A circle of light bathed the raised scars on the man's bald head and body, and his glazed eyes focused on nothing as he stared through the bars.

Sickness squeezed Jubal's empty gut. Why would Eily's people make Sefe one of their own? He must have succeeded in using the flag to trick the Flame Runnas. But then what about Eily? Had her face been a dream as he was loaded onto the flying machine? Nothing was making sense.

"Jubal? Jubal, is that you?" Rann's voice echoed through the huge room.

Jubal turned stiffly, looking for the source. He almost didn't recognize the bald man several cages over. Rann's familiar, sneering grin creased the face. "I'll get my own spirit healing, now, brother."

The nausea in Jubal's stomach squeezed harder. "I thought you ran away."

"Not far enough. But that's okay." Rann moved away and sat on the bench in his cell. "Sefe got us a deal."

"Rann, you can't be a trader if you're a Flame Runna. The tribes'll kill you."

"What do I need to trade for anymore? Sunlight's free."

From the doors at the far end of the room, a woman entered wearing only a short yellow skirt and a collar of gold beads. She stopped in front of Jubal and glanced down at a flat rectangle in her hand. "Finally awake. Good. Are your friends filling you in?"

Jubal stared at her emotionless face dumbly. Here was a true Flame Runna, not a half-hearted one like Eily or even Ijon. This one was the kind who hunted the Tox. Who killed and wasted without mercy. Who didn't follow the Peace. Was this the aunt Eily had told him would help him? Goosebumps prickled his arms.

Gap-tooth stuck his arm through the bars and grabbed at her. "Do I get to go soon?"

Another man in a farther cage stood up. "I'm next. You said I am."

She pulled away, one side of her mouth curled. "We'll get to you. Now sit down." She stared at the man until he shuffled backward and slumped to the bench; then she turned to Jubal. "I need to check your wound. Since you're awake, we might as well get you prepped for conversion. Can you walk?"

Eily's voice telling Jubal to comply ghosted through his memory. He rose on trembling legs. His shoulder throbbed from the weight of his arm, and his head spun. How long had it been since he'd eaten?

The woman pressed a palm to the plate next to his door. A click sounded, and the door swung outward. She stepped back and pointed toward the opposite side of the room. "Come on, then."

He shuffled in that direction. She followed a few steps behind.

A man in a cage behind them shouted, "Why does he get to go? He's not even one of us!"

Jubal turned his head, and a wave of dizziness passed through him again. He'd been through hungers before, but never while wounded. Layers of weakness weighed on him like snow on a branch just before it cracks. He grabbed a nearby cage bar for support.

"Hurry up," the woman said, remaining several arm-lengths away. "Don't make me regret taking you out of order."

He dredged up enough strength to slide his feet forward. They passed through the doors, the heavy metal rectangles shutting with a thump behind them. Strange smells wafted down the hall, stinging his nose like smoke. He squinted down a long corridor with stairs ascending at the far end. Evenly spaced doors lined either wall. They reached an open door and Jubal paused. A familiar green man lay on a table inside. “Pulo?”

The big man turned his face in Jubal’s direction, wide eyes blinking and mouth slack. Before Pulo could respond, the woman shut the door and pointed to the next door on the left. “In here.”

Jubal let out a shaky laugh. If Pulo was alive, then Eily must be here somewhere, too. His footsteps felt lighter as he entered the next room. The hard white floor looked the same as Pulo’s room, with a matching narrow table. A hinged metal arm the size of a man hovered nearby, curled like a scorpion’s tail about to strike. Blue lights blinked from various points along the tail. A Flame Runna man sat on a spindly stool at a silver counter along one wall, his naked back to them. He glanced over his shoulder as they entered.

“Strap him there.” He hooked a thumb toward the table. “And go make sure the cages are clean. Rael’s bringing the Board by for an inspection.”

The woman scowled. “I’m not your janitor, Kess.”

“Would you rather be left alone with him in here?”

Her gaze slid to Jubal. “This one seems harmless.”

“Fine.” The man stood and shoved his stool backward. It came to rest near the scorpion tail. “You start his drip, then.” He eyed Jubal as he stalked past, brows drawn. “You sure this one’s well enough to withstand treatment?”

She shrugged. “He’s a weed. They’re tough.”

Jubal struggled to follow the conversation, reading their body language as much as listening to their words. He didn’t know what calling him a weed meant, but he didn’t think it was a compliment.

The man disappeared through the door, shaking his head. The woman pointed to the table. “Lie down.”

The lights on the scorpion tail winked at him like a trader in a shady exchange. His previous relief at seeing Pulo dissipated like fog in the wind. His feet were heavy as rocks, and he longed for his staff. Was he about to become a Flame Runna? The lure was there, the thought of no more hunger. The remembrance of the high he'd had making love to Eily. But remaining a trader would be next to impossible if he accepted green skin. How could he give that up?

You have a woman now. The thought was both frightening and exhilarating. He'd always sworn he would never take a woman only to leave her behind while he traded. "Where's Eily?"

"Please don't make me call security."

He turned to face the woman, hands up to show he meant no harm. "I need to see her."

"We only want to help you."

His head spun, his vision lurching in time with his accelerated pulse. "I'm a trader."

She spread her lips in the worst parody of a trader smile Jubal had ever seen. "You can trade your spirit healing however you want once you've got it."

The realization wrapped around him like a slaver's noose. It was one thing to kiss Eily and feel the high. It was another to be permanently as drunk as Rann on a bota of bitters—and probably just as stupid. He shook his head. "I can't."

The woman's smile fell. Her brows drew together, and she dropped her attention to the flat rectangle in her hands. "I'm not a Conversion Therapist, damn it. Just do what your leader agreed to."

His heart raced. This woman thought he was one of Sefe's hunters. Was that good or bad? "I don't understand what's happening."

"You don't need to understand." The woman lifted her gaze back up to him and shook her head. "Once you're converted, you'll never feel hungry again. This is a gift. We're making you stronger."

Eily had said the Protectorate would help him. He moved to the table, doubt burning through his bloodstream. They wanted to take away his very definition of himself. But did he have a choice?

Voices echoed in the hall and then the door swung open. A gray-haired Flame Runna was talking over his shoulder at several others as he led the way inside. He turned around. Jubal stiffened; it was the man from the floating image on Ijon's desk.

The old Flame Runna said, "Doctor, is everything all right?"

The woman nodded and smoothed a hand over her collar of beads. "Councilman Rael, you're early. I was just setting this one up for his pre-conversion drip."

Rael surveyed Jubal from head to feet, as if considering making an offer to buy him. "How many have we finished?"

"Eight successfully at this point."

A pregnant Flame Runna pushed through the others, her torso covered with a simple twist of blue fabric that matched the long skirt around her hips. "And how many failed?"

Failed? What did that mean? Apprehension spread through Jubal's gut.

The woman who'd escorted him to the room stood a little straighter, her gaze flicking toward the old man and back to Jubal. "The new strain is statistically effective."

"Dr. Macoby," Rael began.

"I want the numbers on record, Councilman," the pregnant woman said.

Rael pursed his lips and thrust out his bare chest, setting the beads around his neck swinging. "These men attacked our dusters. They ought to be executed. We gave them a choice, and they chose this."

"Knowing all the risks?"

"They're not citizens. They have no rights. We're offering them life."

The pregnant woman turned to Jubal. "What's your name?"

Pain and hunger weakened his limbs, and the conversation was making his head spin. He wavered on his feet, wounded arm throbbing, and choked out, "Jubal."

"Do you understand what's about to happen to you?"

He barely understood what they were saying, but he knew what they wanted. He leaned against the table. "They want me to become a Flame Runna."

"Dr. Macoby—" Rael interrupted. "These cannibals cannot possibly grasp all the nuances about conversion in such a short time. They'll come to understand through experience."

"Like the reversions did?"

Warning voices whispered in Jubal's throbbing head as the Flame Runnas argued. Eily had used that word–reversions. That's what she'd called Lisius and the others. The scorpion tail blinked its blue lights at him. He wanted his pain to go away. His hunger. He wanted to live in peace. Eily'd said the Flame Runnas wanted peace, too. He didn't have the strength to fight. He sat on the table and lay back against his elbows.

"When can I see Eily?"

The pregnant woman stopped midsentence and twisted her head to face him. "What did you say?"

"I want to talk to Eily. Is she all right?"

Dipping a hand into her pocket, Dr. Macoby retrieved a flat rectangle like the one the gold-clad Flame Runna held. She tapped her fingers against its surface and frowned. Then she rounded on Jubal's escort. "This man isn't one of the cannibals who attacked the dusters! Jubal helped my niece survive the Reaches."

The woman in the yellow skirt flushed. "I... I'm sorry. He

was brought down from the medical facility with the others. I just assumed—"

Rael held up a hand. "It doesn't matter. We plan to convert the entire tribe."

Dr. Macoby's mouth dropped open. "Certainly not with the Doomseeds strain?"

Jubal had no idea what they were talking about, but the word *Doomseeds* sounded ominous. And the pregnant woman had called Eily her niece. The gold-clad woman wasn't Eily's aunt? He sat up. *Focus.* A trader who didn't get all the facts was likely to end up with rotten goods.

One of the other Flame Runnas spoke. "Rael has assured us this newest version is safe."

Jubal squinted at the group of green men and women. "Does that mean the old version wasn't safe?"

The old man's mouth flattened into a thin line. "I think we should continue this conversation in private, Dr. Macoby. You're needlessly frightening our convert."

Jubal sat up straighter and balled his fists. "Is that why Pulo is sick? And why Wint died?"

A Flame Runna woman with tightly shorn hair frowned. "I was led to believe cannibals killed the reversions."

Rael turned around to face his people, his jaw muscles flexing and bulging. "We have a larger threat on our hands. Who knows how many other cannibals the Fosselites have subverted or where the next attack will come from? We have to fight back."

"Are you suggesting this entire tribe be sacrificed to attack the Fosselites?" Eily's aunt asked.

Jubal let out a breath. His fingers and toes went numb. "Eily was right—her own people used her as bait."

The group muttered. A lanky man raised his voice. "This isn't a handful of reversions we're talking about, Rael."

"We have to consider the welfare of our citizens first." Rael crossed his arms.

"While I agree the Fosselites are a threat, your strategy is unproven. And it could set back our mission to bring peace to the Reaches." The short-haired woman raised her brows. Her gaze moved to Jubal, scanning him from head to toe. "This tribe represents a new horizon for the Protectorate. A huge step to end violence and the starvation that causes it. We shouldn't waste our resources on hundreds of converts who only end up dying."

"That's not my goal—"

Eily's aunt thrust a finger against Rael's naked green chest. "You sent my niece into a dangerous situation—"

"She was going out there anyway."

"She's a civilian! A citizen of the Protectorate!"

Rael spoke through his teeth. "The Protectorate is at war. We need weapons."

"These methods are unethical. Completely contrary to our larger mission."

"You're letting your personal feelings get in the way of our goal, Dr. Macoby." Rael pointed toward the door. "You need to recuse yourself from this committee."

Lifting a hand in protest, Jubal was cut short by the lanky man in the group of Flame Runnas. "The Doomseeds program will only lead to further mistrust between us and the very people we seek to improve."

"Do you have a better solution?" Rael asked. "We don't have the resources to defend new territory. If we accept these cannibals as converts and don't use the Doomseeds strain, we leave every one of them vulnerable to Fosselite harvesting."

Jubal slid off the table, catching himself against the scorpion tail when his legs buckled. "The Taguan can defend itself."

Rael ignored him. "There are thousands of tribes in the

Reaches. Let's address the Fosselite threat first. Then we can worry about creating true converts."

The Flame Runnas weren't looking at the councilman, though. They'd all focused on Jubal. He maintained eye contact with the lanky man. A good trader wasn't afraid to stand by his claims.

The man flicked a glance at the gold-clad woman. "We have eight Doomseeds conversions so far. How many of the aggressors are left in Confinement?"

She scanned the flat rectangle in her hands. "Assuming everyone in the cages is guilty, we have nine more."

"I move that we continue the Doomseeds strain on those already in captivity, then put conversions on hold until we can make a decision."

"Second," said the short-haired woman.

Rael's eyes flashed. He shook his head and stalked toward the door. "You have your victory, Dr. Macoby. I just hope it doesn't cost us everything."

Jubal sagged against the scorpion tail. "What about me?"

Dr. Macoby moved to his side. "You get a choice."

Chapter Twenty-Eight

The Taguan

Eily clutched her torn bodice about her and paced the ground near the Taguan. Inside the duster, Ijon was speaking to the Protectorate via the com. Jubal and the babies had been rushed to the city for medical attention, but there had been no news of their conditions. The cannibals sat in silent groups against the rock wall of the Taguan, watching the Burn Operative guards with sullen eyes. The narrow looks they cast her direction were filled with distrust, reminding her of her early days at the Holdout. She felt more alone than she ever had, trapped by a collision of three cultures yet truly belonging to none.

She watched a Burn Operative who patrolled the clear area between the duster and the huddled crowd. The way his finger tapped his flame gun's trigger guard made her queasy. He passed the girl whose hand she'd taken when she'd given Ijon her ultimatum, and the child's hopeful eyes locked onto hers. These people had trusted her. Some still did. And look where they were. *At least they aren't dead.* But the future yawned before them like the Hunger come to life.

Com reception was erratic here in the basin, making negotiations difficult. Ijon had been in and out of the duster multiple times, talking with Eily, Rodi, and the other new Taguan leaders. With the sun well past its high point, the liaison and his crew were likely to be the Taguan's guests for the night. How would Ijon feel about that? How would the people of the Taguan feel? Rodi, another woman, and a man sat cross-legged on some nearby rocks, ready to parlay when Ijon returned. They looked much calmer than Eily felt.

The duster's door slid aside and Ijon emerged with a grim face. "They won't budge. They insist on children first."

Her throat tightened. While many of the One Tree were excited at the prospect of no more hunger, they wouldn't be happy being separated from their children, let alone sending their young to be initiated into something their parents weren't yet part of. "There are plenty of adult volunteers. Why is the Board insisting on children?"

"Many on the Board think adults aren't capable of learning to live peacefully."

"Removing a tribe's children is as good as killing them."

He sighed and sat at the door's lip, allowing his feet to dangle. "They'll be safe in the Gardens with the other Protectorate children."

She raked the fingers of one hand through her hair and surveyed the tribe spread out across the bleak rock basin. Within the larger clusters of people, small family units were obvious, as children clung to their mothers or fathers. In the Protectorate, all young were raised communally inside UV-protected domes called Gardens until they passed puberty. "Cannibal parents don't even send their children to school. How are they supposed to bear years of separation?"

"The Holdout manages."

"The Holdout doesn't send all their children to the Gardens. They get to choose who goes." A rush of wind showered them in dust, and whipped Eily's skirt around her legs.

"The Board doesn't want another stalemate treaty. They want converts, both body and mind." Ijon rubbed his eyes with the heels of his hands.

"Ijon, the One Tree aren't like other cannibals. They're farming. Did you tell the Board that?"

"If the cannibals won't accept, the Board says no deal. You know what that means."

Burning. Would Ijon really order his duster crew to incinerate two hundred people? "This is their final offer?"

"They say they will consider further negotiations while the children are being converted."

"It's not much of a negotiation if the Protectorate gets everything their way."

"They're viewing this more like a victory."

Eily couldn't argue with that. The Protectorate had the advantage. Starting with the children, they'd reeducate everyone until the Taguan became no more than another pocket of Flame Runnas. She asked softly, "What promises will the Protectorate make?"

Ijon turned toward the spread of people. "They won't kill the children."

Eily boarded the duster along with a dozen youngsters, all old enough to volunteer on their own, but young enough to be considered children by the Protectorate. She'd done the best she could to provide safety to the older members of the Taguan but feared it wasn't enough. Ijon had agreed to include one adult for every twenty children, without consulting the Board. Easier to ask forgiveness, he'd said. Rodi was in a second duster with another group. She was small enough to pass as a child at first glance, anyway, and if they could set a precedent, it would make including an adult chaperone for future groups that much easier.

As they lifted out of the Taguan basin, an eerie wail arose from the rocks: mothers crying for their loved ones. The sound resonated in Eily's ears well past when she could actually hear it.

Sunset painted the sky in neon shades as the duster approached the city. They landed among streetlights flickering to life. Her new flock stayed close as the piercing lights transformed dusk to daylight. Faces turned up to view the orbs, but no one made a sound. The children were accustomed to the need for silence on the Tox. They pressed close about her, gripping her skirt and hands. She nearly tripped several times as small bodies bumped against her while the group moved down the ramp onto the tarmac. Heat radiated off the pavement in spite of the cooling air. The area swarmed with Burn Operatives. They kept their weapons pointing down, but all it would take was one aggressive move and these children would go from volunteers to prisoners. Or worse.

She glanced across the street at the Med Ops building, sick with worry about Ana's babies. There'd been no word on them or Jubal in the day they'd been apart. All com activity had been between Ijon and the Board. What if they'd died? She walled off the thought and focused on the Leibert Building ahead. Once she'd seen these children safely into Confinement, she'd check at Med Ops.

Down several steps and through the double doors, several Med Techs and more armed guards waited. The children slowed as they descended. She pushed them gently forward toward the techs. "These Flame Runnas are healers. Do as they ask."

One little boy looked over his shoulder at her as he was led toward Sanitation, where he'd be deloused and profiled. Big, fat tears washed down his cheeks, and his bottom lip trembled, but he complied.

The oldest girl latched onto her hand, holding tight as a male tech attempted to pry her away. Lines of terror cut deep into the child's face, and she bared her teeth. A soft, high-pitched moan streamed from her mouth. Like water breaking through a dam, the rest of the children began to cry. A nearby guard shifted his gun, eyes on the girl. Behind them, the doors opened to admit Rodi and her group. The noise in the small receiving area swelled.

"It's okay," Eily said, stroking the girl's fingers with her free hand. Her heartbeat roared in her ears. She turned her gaze on the tech. "You don't have to force them. They're volunteers."

The tech cocked one eyebrow and released his hold with exaggerated slowness. The girl's hand trembled, her grip around Eily's fingers painful. Eily pulled the girl close and rested her chin on her head. Rodi's group now mingled with her own. Children clung to each other in panic, resisting techs. One young boy kicked a female medic's shin. The guard warned, "Hey!"

Eily caught Rodi's eye. The small woman sucked in a huge breath. "Keep the Peace."

Like magic, all noise cut off and the children froze. Eily took a few lungfuls of air, willing her racing heart to slow. Then she gently pushed the girl she held away. She looked into the child's flushed face. "No more hunger."

The girl drew a shuddering breath, her eyes wide. She straightened her shoulders and turned to the tech. The tech nodded once and swept an arm in front of him to direct the girl toward Sanitation. The rest of the children watched in mute terror.

Eily tapped a tech who'd paused to consult his gamma pad. "Can we process them in pairs?"

"That's against protocol." He turned back to his notes.

Eily resisted the urge to slap the gamma pad out of his hands. "This entire situation is outside protocol."

The tech shrugged. Before Eily could speak again, Aunt Tula emerged from the opposite doors. Eily's limbs weakened with relief. Tula would help. Elbowing past the tech, Eily wove her way between grasping little ones. "Aunt Tula!"

Tula found her in the crowd. "Eily, I'm glad you're here. You need to go to the nursery. Now."

Eily's skin turned cold, and she froze in midstride. "What's happened?"

"Don't allow them to move forward with conversion until I get there."

Without another thought, Eily turned to flee back up the stairs.

She burst through the doors and dashed over the tarmac, past startled Burn Operatives to the Med Ops building. Visiting hours were over, but surely she'd be allowed to see her own babies. Ana's babies. The distinction blurred beneath the intensity of her worry.

Someone near the duster shouted. Without stopping, she glanced over her shoulder. The cause of alarm wasn't easily apparent, but it wasn't directed toward her, so she flung herself with renewed vigor toward the double doors. Her cheek slammed against a solid, warm chest, and she reeled, blinking. A common blue shirt and suspenders filled her vision. A set of scarred hands reached out to steady her. She recoiled in disbelief. She'd know those hands anywhere. Tilting her chin up, she looked into Gid's scarred face and her knees gave out.

He tightened his grip on her shoulders before she collapsed. "I've been praying for you."

The harsh cadence of the Order's language falling from his lips—his living, breathing lips—brought tears of joy to her eyes. She threw herself into his arms. "Gid! You're alive!"

He patted her hair, then took a step back and pulled her clothing tighter around her front. "I told you God had a mission for me."

For a brief moment, she simply immersed herself in the fact he was alive. His scarred face was more weathered, but he looked the same as he always had. Steady.

"Where's Ana? Did you find her?" he asked.

Too choked up to answer, she only managed a fierce shake of her head. She had so many questions, but right now she had to get to the nursery. Taking Gid's hand, she pulled him down the hall to the maternity unit. At the door, a med tech at the desk stopped her. "Can I help you?"

"I have babies in there," she choked out.

"I'm sorry, the maternity ward is a quarantine area. Newborns have no immune systems during conversion."

Her eyes widened. "You have to stop the conversion."

The tech frowned, taking in her torn clothing and then looking at Gid. "You're that girl from the Holdout."

"Yes. And those babies are my sister's." She was breathing so hard, it was difficult to get the words out. "They're protected under the Holdout agreement."

He checked the gamma pad on his desk. "Ah. Gestated under UV exposure. I see. They're not well enough to accept conversion yet, anyway." He pointed to a large window looking in on a nursery. "You can see them through the glass."

Eily moved to the window, clutching the ledge to support herself as she searched for the twins. Green babies lay in rows of neat basinets. A naked man sat in a rocking chair holding a protein bottle for the child in his arms. He smiled up at her. Behind her, Gid grunted in disapproval. At the back wall, two enclosed neonatal units housed the only nonconverted babies in the room. The curve of the nuvoplast sides distorted the small, pink bodies inside, but the steady blinking lights on the attached monitors indicated that the infants both lived.

She pressed her forehead to the glass and closed her eyes. Tears of relief, terror, and exhaustion competed behind her eyelids. "All these years... I should have looked for her. I should have saved her sooner."

"No one believed she was alive. It's a miracle you brought back her children."

"But she's dead!" Eily choked, the words hateful on her tongue. She'd been telling herself Ana was dead for years, but only now could she fully believe it. She turned to Gid and buried her face against his chest.

He took hold of her wrists and slid them up his chest, inserting a distance between their bodies. Hands still wrapped around her wrists, he looked down into her tear-streaked face. "We will pray for them."

Prayer. The best Gid ever had to offer. Shudders rocked her as sobs erupted from her core. The sound echoed against the hallway walls. Eily sagged, freeing years of pent-up emotion. She longed for Jubal's strong arms around her. Where was he? She had to find him, but Tula's warning about the babies trapped her here.

From his station at the doors, the med tech cleared his throat. "Perhaps you'd like to take her to the visitors' lounge?"

Gid dropped one of her hands and, with the other, pulled her toward the exit. "She belongs at home."

Eily jerked away. "I'm not leaving."

"There's nothing you can do for them right now, Eily."

"Aunt Tula said to make sure they aren't converted."

"Miss," said the tech. "They won't be. I've put Holdout status on their notes."

She bit her lips and looked over her shoulder through the window. She wanted to hold them, but only nursery techs—screened and cleared of dangerous biotics—were allowed near the newborns.

"Come home, Eily," Gid said, his blue eyes solemn.

Eily swallowed. If she couldn't do anything for her nephews, it was time to find Jubal. "I have to check on Jubal."

Gid's face froze in a perplexed frown.

Her heart threatened to leap out of her chest. She rubbed a wrist where the coolness of Gid's platonic touch still lingered. "He got hurt defending me."

"He sold you to the cannibals." Gid's words were level and cold.

"It wasn't like that. He was just trying to save his father. In the end, he chose to save me." She dropped her gaze, catching sight of the torn edges of her bodice. The green skin between her breasts gleamed under the hallway lights. Jubal had seen her. Had touched her. Had loved her. How could she tell Gid? Should she tell him? For all she knew, Jubal was dead. Her chest constricted with that thought. No, he had to be alive. She looked into Gid's eyes again. The real question was—did she want Gid? If Ana's babies survived, Gid would be a good father to them. She could have a family.

But she didn't want to raise Ana's babies within the restrictive confines of the Order. And if she was truthful, she didn't want to spend the rest of her life with Gid. She wanted Jubal.

She licked dry lips and whispered, "I think I love him."

The muscles on Gid's throat tightened a moment, his nostrils flaring. Then he turned toward the exit. Eily's heart cracked, sending shock waves down her arms and legs. Gid deserved better from her, but she also owed him the truth. No more lies. No more pretending to be other than she was.

He didn't move forward, just stared down the hall at the double doors. His shoulders heaved in a sigh. "You're going back to the cannibals."

Eily glanced to the nursery window. "I've never fit into the role the Order prescribes for me."

He nodded. "And the Protectorate? What will they do?"

I'll be a reversion. She groped to support herself against the corridor wall. The Order had shielded her from the Protectorate for six years. If she left, she would be considered unremediable. The kind of reversion the Protectorate euthanized.

The air grew thick as she fought back dizzying terror. *They don't always euthanize.* The Protectorate had let Lisius and the others go. But there'd been an ulterior motive for that. And now the Taguan... So far the Protectorate had only agreed not to kill the children. She couldn't trust their intentions. Her mind spun with implications she couldn't fit together. Half blinded by her thoughts, she stared at Gid's back, his suspenders crossed over the blue fabric of his shirt. He looked the same as always. Ready to take his assigned place within the Order. She blinked. "How did you escape the hunters?"

Gid straightened his shoulders. "God directed me to bring His Word to the people on the Tox."

She blinked again. He'd used the cannibal word for the Amarantox Plains. "What does that mean?"

He turned around to face her. "I spoke of God's love, God's bounty, and the hunters asked to be baptized. They came to the Holdout with me."

Her thoughts flashed back to her own introduction to the Holdout, when she and Ana had been fleeing hunters with Tula and Levi. The Order had allowed Ana to be carried away before opening the Gate. "The Elders allowed them inside?"

"The Elders cannot deny a man's relationship with God."

The lines on his face deepened. "But the Protectorate is requiring conversion. That's why I was here, visiting while they recover."

Eily shook her head. Her entire world was shifting around her. "So they're getting green skin, and then they're being baptized into the Order. But they surely won't fit in to life at the Holdout. Where will they live?"

"I'll take them with me as disciples."

"Take them with you?"

"Back to the Tox."

Her mouth fell open. "You're going back out?"

He nodded. "As I am called to do."

The thudding in her ears sounded like the footsteps of a giant. One who could either crush her or lift her onto his shoulder. "The Order will let you? And the Protectorate?"

He shrugged. "The Order won't stop me. I have my mini duster. And my disciples will also be advocates for the Protectorate."

She held out a green hand to stare at the back of it. She'd been the first blending of two worlds, a disciple of both. But in her furthest past there had always been a third option. The Tox. The place where Jubal lived. Where she wanted to live. Could her worlds be brought into harmony with each other? Gid was already paving the way.

She lifted her chin to meet Gid's eyes. "I have an entire tribe who might be willing to listen."

Chapter Twenty-Nine

Jubal trudged down the hall with the gold-collared woman close behind. His wound throbbed, and her promises of relief if he converted still echoed in his head. Although the Flame Runnas hadn't forced him to make his decision yet, they'd also refused to set him free. No one had mentioned what might happen to him if he chose not to convert. He desperately wanted to talk to someone he could trust. He needed Eily.

As they passed Pulo's room, he strained to peer through the window, but all he could see were blank walls and cabinets. A muffled scream came into sharp focus as another door opened at his left. He jarred to a halt and turned to look inside as a green man exited the room. Inside, a naked cannibal lay strapped to a table with tubes and wires sprouting from his arms and legs. The skin at the crook of one elbow had blossomed with a strange yellow color that crept in splotches across the man's skin as Jubal watched.

The cannibal let out another scream, his back arching against his straps. The green man scowled at Jubal and clicked the door closed behind him. The gold-collared woman nudged Jubal from behind. "Keep moving."

Heart thundering, Jubal shuffled his way back through the door to his cell. Was that what conversion was like? Eily had said it hurt, but the argument he'd just heard between the Flame Runnas made him think not everyone survived the process.

Rann and the other three unconverted cell occupants rose and stood at their cage bars. "How much longer?"

"You'll have to wait." The gold-collared woman dropped her gaze to the rectangle in her hand. "I want to make sure I get the order right."

Anxiety tightened Jubal's chest. Rann had been counted as one of Sefe's men. "Wait," Jubal reached through the bars. "That's my brother. He's not one of them."

The woman shied away. She glared at him and kept walking to the door without reply.

"You can't convert him! Tell Dr. Macoby!" Jubal shouted after her.

"What are you doing?" Rann asked. His face was bright red, and even from several cages away, Jubal could see a vein pulsing in his brother's forehead.

Jubal pressed himself against the bars. "The conversion—the green skin—it's dangerous. They—"

"You won't take this away from me. You can't." Rann spat out, his eyes narrow.

"Rann, listen to me. I don't understand it all, but Wint died because of his skin. And Pulo—"

"Pulo's fine. I saw him in the hall."

"But he could have died."

Rann sneered. "Look around you—lots more Flame Runnas live than die. It's worth the risk. I'll always have something to trade. And you can't complain I'm using up the goods."

"Don't trust this trade," Jubal pleaded. "The Flame Runnas are up to something."

Turning his back to Jubal, Rann leaned against the bars and sat on the floor. "Now that Pops is gone, he can't make my decisions any more. And neither can you."

Icy dread seeped into Jubal's veins. As angry as he'd been with Rann, they were still brothers. "At least ask them about Doomseeds."

Rann didn't answer.

Jubal pressed his forehead against the cold bars, staring at his brother's back. "You want to die like Wint?"

"I want the spirit healing."

Jubal had no reply. Rann had been on a path to destruction since Momma took the Knife. Nothing Jubal could say would change his course. He lay down on his bench and closed his eyes, but didn't sleep.

Some time later, the gold-collared woman returned. She quietly passed Jubal's cage and opened Rann's door. The other cell occupants complained. Jubal didn't rise. He watched his brother pass by in silence. Rann turned his head only long enough to sneer in Jubal's direction. And then he was gone.

"Jubal." Eily's voice was soft and her hand was warm against his cheek.

Without opening his eyes, he grasped her hand to keep it close. He'd been dreaming of her, a disconcerting flow of images folding over each other like cloth blowing in the wind, sometimes dark, sometimes joyful and light. After a moment, he opened one eye to verify she was real. She knelt beside his bench, her dark eyes full of worry. "You're here," he whispered.

She smiled, her lips pink against her green skin. "I've come to take you home."

Together they rose and exited his cell. She took his hand to lead him toward the double doors. He resisted the pull. "Wait..."

Over his shoulder he sought his brother's cage. Within a circle of light, Rann slumped against the bars, his eyes half-lidded. His skin was a deep, muddy green, like algae on a sullen pond.

Jubal's throat tightened. "Rann's here."

Her eyes widened as she spotted him, then her face went hard. "He tricked me."

Squeezing Eily's hand tighter, he looked back at her. Memories of his childhood, before his mother died, wisped ghostlike through his mind. "He's still my brother."

Her face was stoic, but softened when she looked at Jubal. Nodding, she released his hand.

He took the few steps to reach his brother's cage. "Rann?"

Rann's eyes fluttered, but he didn't speak. Jubal crouched next to the bars and thrust an arm between them. Grasping Rann's forearm, he squeezed the cool flesh. Rann still didn't respond. A silvery line of drool etched a trail from the right corner of his mouth.

Jubal turned to Eily. "Is he going to be all right?"

She shrugged. "Most converts are. Do you want me to get a doctor?"

He considered, then shook his head. Rann had chosen his path. With a sigh, he released his hold and stood. "Goodbye, my brother. May you find what you're looking for."

When he exited the room, he didn't look back.

Rael stared steadily into the red eyes on his com screen. "This is my final offer, Torin."

The Fosselite curled his upper lip so his teeth showed in a snarl. "Your asking price is preposterous. And you're requiring us to do all the work."

The asking price *was* preposterous; Rael was demanding enough telomerase to keep the Protectorate running for ten years. But if he made trade too easy after the long embargo, the Fosselites would be suspicious. He had eleven viable Doomseeds converts, each with a GPS chip. They were to be taken out to the Reaches and released, far from the Taguan and its new converts. He had to be sure they fell into Fosselite hands.

He leaned forward to rest his forearms on the desk. "Giving you reversion tracking codes could mean the end of my career."

"Then why are you making this offer?"

"Anti-euthanization activists are allowing our population to be overrun with reversions." He truly couldn't care less about reversions or what happened to them, but he'd met enough purists to play the bigot. Let the Fosselites think what they would about him.

Torin shook his head. "Your terms are still untenable. Leaving our base to gather reversions isn't an option."

"You have trade contacts among the cannibals. Use them to hunt the fugitives."

"If we're going to rely on cannibal trade, your tracking codes are useless." Torin let out a derisive snort. "You're releasing your reversions anyway. We'll simply let traders bring them to us as they find them."

Rael swallowed against the rapid beat of his heart. The new converts at the Taguan would provide an easy target for cannibal mercenaries. But with so few Doomseeds carriers, the chances of the correct reversions reaching the Fosselites were minimal. He had to see the Doomseeds plan through to the end, now more than ever.

Pulse pounding in his ears, he looked down at the back of his green, age-spotted hand. No Protectorate duster pilot would fly within range of the Fosselite base defenses. To get the reversions there, he'd have to transport them himself, even if it meant driving a sand skimmer all those miles through cannibal territory. He'd make sure he had a dose of the toxin for himself in case the Fosselites turned on him. If it cost him his last breath, he'd see to it the Doomseeds plan worked. "I'll make sure the reversions are dropped on your doorstep."

The Taguan

The rhythmic thump of Gid's mini echoed through the sky, and Eily turned her face upward, searching the blue horizon. Near the neat stacks of felled amarantox to her left, three women talked while they split the canes and scooped manna larva into baskets. A green-skinned Rodi glanced at her and grinned. "Go."

Eily returned the grin, wiped her chapped hands on her apron, and raced toward the lip of the Taguan basin. At the edge, she was met by a cloud of grit kicked up by the mini's thrusters. Before stepping onto the narrow trail down, she paused to blink her vision clear. The sound of the mini cut off abruptly, replaced by the muted murmur of a crowd. The lack of children's voices resonated like an echo across a canyon.

Sight regained, she skittered down the narrow path, searching the crowd below. At the open door to his mini, Gid stood directing the offloading and greeting his flock with handshakes and nods. As always, he'd brought with him a photo of the Taguan's converted children. Women passed the sheet around with wide-eyed excitement, each searching for the faces of their own little ones within the group picture. A twang of guilt shook Eily as she thought of her nephews, fostered with Aunt Beth at the Holdout. But her hands were full overseeing the Taguan. The boys were better off there.

Gid caught her eye, his brows drawing together as his gaze took in her gaping bodice, open to better allow the breeze to cool her skin. Out of habit, her hand flew to the open clasp. He shifted his gaze back to the man unloading a stack of empty baskets. With conscious effort, she lowered her hand, leaving the bodice open. Seeking Gid's approval was a difficult habit to break.

As missionaries at the Taguan, Gid and Eily's teaching was much the same, but in some areas they disagreed. He wanted to be strict with the Order's ways, while she argued that the Taguan needed to adopt its own set of rules. Unlike the Order, most of the people at the Taguan wanted conversion. Modesty had to give way to necessity, and exposing green skin to sunlight was the surest way to avoid the Hunger.

At least she and Gid agreed on the fundamental issues of love, charity, and peace. The cannibals, especially the women, seemed eager to swap aggression for the promise of plenty. The Taguan had already accepted several new members from out on the Tox who'd come to trade and decided to stay.

But there were many who followed Gid's more stringent ways. His mini was magic to them. Two cannibal women in Order dresses stood near him now, beaded braids peeking from beneath their bonnets. One had a green face, the other, tanned. He could have his pick if he wanted a wife. But he treated the women no more or less fondly than the men.

He shut the mini's door. The men nearest him ushered him toward the cave mouth, green men with hunter piercings wearing cotton shirts and suspendered-slacks. With only their arms and faces to absorb sunlight, they would be hungry when winter came. What would Gid do when they turned to the Knife again? She prayed he would come around in his teaching before then. Smiling, she realized he probably prayed the same about her.

Happy as she was to see Gid, he wasn't the one she was looking for. She scanned the milling people, searching for Jubal's sun-browned face. He was leery of conversion after his scare in the labs and had elected to remain unconverted, at least for now.

An arm wrapped around her waist from behind, lifting her in a circle, and she squealed. Jubal's voice tickled her ear. "Miss me?"

She twisted about in his embrace and threw her arms around his neck. "How was trade?"

In order to support their treaty with the Protectorate and to qualify for adult conversions, the Taguan offered what goods they could to the citizens in the city. A surprising number of people craved tokens from the Tox. And it turned out the protein in the manna beetles was a perfect complement to photosynthesis.

Jubal nuzzled his cheek against hers. "Those Flame Runnas can't get enough manna meal. I think we may have enough credit to start building a Garden here soon."

She hugged him tighter, savoring his warm scent. She missed him when he left, but at least he traveled safely with Gid in the mini. "I'm glad." She pressed her lips to his ear. "We're going to need it soon."

His body stiffened. Pulling back just enough to look into her eyes, he flicked a glance downward to where their bellies touched. She nodded.

His face broke into the most beautiful smile she'd ever seen.

Life on the Tox was good.

THE END

Dear Reader,

Thank you so much for reading! Would you like to read the heart-pounding tale of how the apocalypse happened? The full-length prequel, **AMARANTOX**, will leave you thinking long after you put the book down!

With croplands failing, a mother is forced to choose between her ideals and her teenage daughter's life. Get your copy to keep reading now!

Tam Linsey

P.S. Indie authors like myself don't have a huge budget to spend on marketing like the big name authors do, so your support means everything to me. If you have a moment to leave a quick review of Doomseeds, I'd be eternally grateful!

P.P.S. Get your copy of Amarantox here.

Glossary

- *Amarantox* — a mutation of a common weed, which secretes toxins into the soil to prevent other vegetation from taking hold. Largely responsible for the Botanicaust.
- *Bann, The* — a roster of those being shunned within the Old Order. A punishment just shy of excommunication.
- *Blattvolk* — what the Old Order call Haldanians. Literally "leaf people."
- *Blow Out* — a sandstorm.
- *Botanicaust* — an event 400 years ago during which invasive weeds wiped out most plant life on Earth, including the major food crops.
- *Burn, The* — a five-mile radius of scorched earth around the Haldanian Protectorate, maintained by Burn Operatives to keep both cannibals and plant life at bay.
- *Cannibal* — people roaming the Reaches and beyond who survive by not wasting any food opportunity.

They do not specifically prefer human flesh, but will not waste their dead.

- *Confinement* — the prison where captive Cannibals are kept prior to conversion.
- *Convert* — one who has undergone genetic therapy to insert chloroplasts, as opposed to those born with the gene.
- *Days of the Prophet* — what the Old Order refers to when speaking about the Botanicaust.
- *Duster* — a silent aircraft powered by electromagnetic engines used by Burn Ops to keep the Burn cleared.
- *Flame runna* — what the Cannibals call the Haldanians.
- *Fosselites* — a group of scientists who have found the secret to eternal life.
- *Gamma pad* — electronic palm pad and stylus. Various versions exist, such as a simple, indestructible one for children, and more complicated versions capable of higher computations.
- *Garden* — the nuvoplast houses where Haldanian children are kept until they finish puberty and can withstand ultraviolet light.
- *Gotte's Wille* — God's Will.
- *Haldanian Protectorate* — the government formed after the Botanicaust by the scientists who developed conversion technology. Mission statement is to offer conversion to the population of the world in an attempt to minimize humanity's need for food.
- *Holdout* — the Old Order name for their protected community.
- *Hunger, the* — cannibal term for time of food scarcity.

The Hunger generally occurs during winter months, but may be "called" at any time of year when food is required.

- *Hunter* — cannibals who have abandoned tribal ties and banded together to actively seek human flesh. The most dangerous group on the Tox, they have been known to ignore the scars of the Knowing.
- *Integration* — the heavily supervised time period during which converted children acclimate to their new environment and society.
- *Knife, the* — ritual suicide in which cannibals offer their bodies as sustenance for the rest of the tribe. Usually performed by the old or infirm, but sometimes forced upon healthy tribe members during the Hunger.
- *Knowing, the* — cannibals who retain certain kinds of knowledge, such as healing or locating water. They are marked by scars to keep them safe from other cannibal tribes.
- *Mark of the Beast* — an Old Order belief. The green skin of the Haldanians is the obvious sign that someone is marked.
- *Native Haldanian* — one born to parents already expressing the chloroplast genome.
- *Nuvoplast* — a bio plastic grown and used by Haldanians to build everything from gamma pads to sand-skimmers to the walls of their dwellings.
- *Old Order* — a remnant Amish society who survived the Botanicaust by erecting electric fences to protect their hand-cultivated acreage.
- *Ordnung* — the set of earthly rules believed to be sent by God which are followed by the Old Order.

- *Reversion* — a convert who regresses to cannibalistic ways. Punishable by death.
- *Ripening* — a once common autoimmune condition among naturally born Haldanians in which the body attempts to purge itself of chloroplasts. The faulty gene has been largely eliminated from the population, but still appears as a random mutation in one out of ten thousand births.
- *Rumspringa* — a time during adolescence just before a young person chooses to be baptized into the Old Order. Literally "running around."
- *Sand-skimmer* — a land vehicle used by the Protectorate to cross portions of the Burn.
- *Spirit healer* — someone with the ability to affect the minds of others. An art feared among the cannibal tribes, and believed "lost" to their healers.
- *Sunstorm / UV flare* — a short period of time, more common in autumn and winter, when the atmosphere allows excess ultraviolet to reach the earth. Largely due to improperly tested herbicide use during the Botanicaust, which created gaps in the ozone layer.
- *Telomerase* — an enzyme that prevents genetic deterioration by replicating the telomere regions of DNA strands during mitosis. Used by the Fosselites to extend life indefinitely, although telomerase cannot pass the blood-brain barrier and therefore does not function on neural DNA.
- *Tox, the* — the cannibal name for the vast continental plains once known as the Breadbasket of America, now consumed by amarantox and other non-edible weeds.
- *Verification of Consent* — a signed document required

for cannibals or other potential converts over the age of sixteen in which they express their desire and reasons for becoming a convert. Outlined in Ordinance 317 under the Protectorate Mission.

- *Yuvee tree* — a genetically altered tree originally introduced to "fix" nitrogen in cropland and reduce the need for chemical fertilizers. Later discovered to foretell an incoming ultraviolet flare by the rapid leaching of color from its leaves. Called mgunga tree by the Fosselites.

Amarantox Sneak Peek!

JANUARY

The Tox didn't start with a plant. Or a seed. Or even a gene. The Tox started with an idea.
—The Histories

The murky gleam of a full moon reflected off the greenhouse roof as Jaide crept across the circle of bare earth surrounding the dark building. Ahead of her, Trevor's shadow halted with a hand up. After a pause, he dropped to his belly against the icy ground. She mimicked the action, her heavy daypack slamming against her spine. Her heartbeat rattled against her ribs. The brim of the baseball cap she wore to hide her face from cameras blocked her view of the greenhouse, so all she could see was the gated lane. To her right, Cindy panted as though she'd just sprinted a mile, gulping and gasping for breath.

An engine rumbled from the greenhouse parking lot. Headlights winked on, casting shadows across the rocky soil. She pressed her cheek against the frigid dirt and held her breath, willing herself to be one with the Earth.

The car backed up then proceeded down the lane toward Lafayette. Jaide exhaled a foggy sigh.

Once the sound of the engine had faded, Trevor rose and began his skulk toward the greenhouse again. Jaide scrambled to her feet, fingers and toes numb from lying flat against the January soil. The one-gallon can of gasoline in her pack seemed to weigh fifty pounds, but the real powerhouse for tonight lay against her thigh in the pocket of her jeans—a flash drive loaded with Trevor's computer virus.

She reached the side of the building right behind Trevor, core trembling with cold. He pulled his cordless Dremel out of his pocket. A high-pitched whine filled the air as he started to cut through the polycarbonate wall. After only a minute, he pulled a section of panel free and ducked inside.

Jaide crawled in next. Humid air, thick with the scent of soil and greenery, buffeted her face with warmth. The low drone of the circulation fans vibrated in her ears, and potted plants made shaggy shadows in the moonlight.

"I'll find the climate controls," said Trevor in a low voice. "You two look for the offices and lab equipment."

"Do you think any of these plants are dangerous?" asked Cindy, holding back against the wall.

"Nah," said Trevor. "This is only a level one bio-safety facility. Otherwise there'd be more guards. TelomerGen's probably just testing herbicide resistance so they can sell more poisons."

"So there's poison on the plants?"

"Jesus, Cindy." Trevor shoved a pair of wire cutters at her. "If you're so worried, you find the climate controls and cut the wires. I'll handle the lab equipment."

Cindy held up her gloved hands, refusing the tool. "I'm just having second thoughts about what I'm getting into."

Jaide took Cindy's hand and gave it a reassuring squeeze in

spite of her own misgivings about this operation. But someone had to do something to stop corporations from shoving genetically modified food down humanity's throat. Soon there'd be no options left for those wanting to eat as nature intended. "This is for the future." Jaide thought of Flora, her eleven-year-old, asleep in her bed back home. "We're protecting our children's children's children."

"I don't have kids."

Many members of the Coalition never planned to add to the human population problem. At seventeen, Jaide hadn't known better. But she'd never regretted it. "Every animal and plant is one of Earth's children—one of our children—don't you think?"

Cindy nodded, and Jaide let go.

Trevor shoved the wire cutters at Cindy. "I saw some ripple vents on the exterior to the left. Go see if the controls are on the inside over there. Jaide, you search the side rooms. I'll go right and circle back toward you, okay?"

Jaide set out to find a computer terminal, sliding her feet along the concrete in the dark. Flashlights would be too easily spotted through the glass walls. She was careful to avoid touching the stainless steel tables or the Frankenstein plants on either side of her. Corporations like TelomerGen claimed they were using genetic modification to end world hunger. In reality, they were adding to it by taking away self-sufficiency; farmers weren't allowed to save their own seeds, or even worse, the modified seed would be sterile. Corporations wanted to put a patent on life.

If she could, she'd torch this entire facility. But she'd only brought enough gas to damage the computers and other hardware. The fire was to be a decoy anyway; the real damage would be done by the virus, corrupting the research so TelomerGen couldn't repeat this particular atrocity any time soon. Hopefully the infection would make it all the way to their back-up servers before their IT discovered it. Once the climate controls were out of commission, winter would take care of the plants themselves.

She reached the end of the row and squinted toward the far wall. Two doors led presumably to the offices, lab, and staff rooms. On her right, Trevor's feet scuffed against the paved floor. She tried the door on her left.

Locked.

Dropping to a squat, she fished in her pocket for the tiny flashlight she'd brought for just this event. The bulb was red, so it was less likely to be noticed by someone observing the facility. Standard doorknob, no deadlock. She retrieved her tension wrench, inserted it and the rake, then jiggled until she heard the pins drop.

Thank you, YouTube.

Twisting the handle, she pushed. The door swished open. A scent like wet pennies greeted her as she slipped inside. From large pots on the concrete, foliage reached toward the ceiling in graceful arches. Taking a chance, she shone her light upwards, curious. Atop the high stalks hung bags covering seedpods or flowers—she wasn't sure which. They reminded her of heads held upright in a hangman's noose. A shiver raced down her spine as she recognized the leaves. Amaranth, one of her go-to foods. These were freakishly tall from whatever DNA the scientists had inserted.

The need to eradicate these Frankenstein plants burned through her veins. Not yet. These amaranth were only prototypes. The project could be easily repeated unless she destroyed the data. Then she would come back and torch the specimens.

Moving carefully between the leaves, she looked for another door. Sweat rolled down her back beneath her hoodie in the muggy heat. At the back wall, she found two office doors. She turned the knob on the one to the right, pleased when it swung open and doubly pleased at the whir of a running computer. A wiggle of the mouse woke the screen, showing the progress of a data process. Good. She wouldn't have to hack in to upload the virus. With a few keystrokes, she aborted the program and inserted the flash drive, overriding the protocols the way Trevor had taught her. The machine hummed again as it accepted the new code.

The constant drone of the fans ceased. She smiled, but then a chirruping beep—more alert than alarm—filled the greenhouse. From the main room, Trevor shouted, "Alarm! Get out now!"

She clenched her teeth. Dammit, of course there was an alert on the climate controls. She would've thought of that if Trevor had given her a chance to plan. But they'd been out of time; tomorrow, the Coalition would be announcing a call to protest, and once that happened, the company would increase security or move the tests to a new facility. The corporation couldn't be allowed to keep its data.

Only twenty more seconds to complete the upload. She drummed her gloved fingers on the desktop. She couldn't leave the flash drive behind as evidence. Ten seconds. Another, much louder alarm joined the first—a burglar alarm. Someone must've opened the main door.

The computer screen flashed once, telling her the transfer was complete. She yanked the drive free and dashed back the way she'd come. Careening through the room with the towering plants, she underestimated a turn, and the weight of the gas can in her pack threw her off balance. She slammed into the high stalks, toppling several over. The flash drive flew from her gloved grip amid a volley of falling leaves.

She regained her balance, heart in her throat. If she stayed to search in the dark, she'd be caught for sure. On trembling legs, she bolted for the door. Her feet tangled on a fallen stalk, and she fell, landing on her outstretched palms. Fallen leaves and crushed paper bags rustled against her face as she scrambled upright and kept going.

She veered left toward the exit. Behind her, Cindy's footsteps slapped against the concrete. "Sorry. I didn't know they'd have an alarm on the climate system."

Jaide shook her head, breathing too hard to reply. Cold air blasted the sweat from her face as she burst out into the moonlight. Ahead, Trevor's form scrambled over the top of the six-foot chain-link fence. In a few more steps, she hit the cold metal and dug her toes into the gaps to hoist herself up and over, Cindy right beside her.

They caught up to Trevor as he crossed the dirt road, and together they ducked into a windbreak along the neighboring field.

"That was close," Trevor whispered. Frozen branches crackled underfoot as they crept along in the dark. At least there was no snow in which to leave tracks. They'd parked nearly a mile away and had planned their escape via Google Earth. This line of trees would lead them straight to their car on the other side. Jaide had to scramble to keep up with Trevor's long strides.

Cindy fell behind, mincing through the leaves like a timid deer. "Did you get the virus uploaded?"

"I didn't have time to hack in," said Trevor.

Jaide shot Trevor a glare he couldn't see in the dark. "I did. Barely." Her elation at finding an open computer was bittersweet. "But I lost the flash drive."

He stopped walking. "You what?"

She stopped, too, and turned back his direction. "It flew out of my hand while I was escaping. I couldn't see in the dark."

Trevor threw his hands into the air. "Well, that's just great," he hissed, steam rising from his mouth in the moonlight. Behind him, a police siren wailed. He thrust his hands back into his pockets and shoved past her. "Jesus Christ, I should've handled it all myself."

Jaide's temperature rose in spite of the icy air. "Well, the police wouldn't be arriving quite so soon if you hadn't busted through the main doors. The climate alarm would've only alerted the greenhouse manager."

Cindy caught up and slid an arm through Jaide's, hugging herself close as they walked. "They must sell tens of thousands of those drives at every outlet mall across the country, right?"

Jaide nodded. She didn't want to think about FBI cybercrimes technology at the moment. She just wanted to put the greenhouse behind her and get back to her daughter and her normal life. "Yeah, we just need to lay low."

"And destroy my computer and everything on it," Trevor added over his shoulder. "The FBI can hash the ID from every file on the drive and trace it back to the source. Thanks a lot." His anger radiated like heat through the darkness.

"You're the one who insisted we had to take the risk," said Jaide.

Trevor blew out a sharp breath and picked up his pace, leaving her and Cindy behind.

Jaide clutched Cindy tighter and stumbled through the darkness.

Ready for more? Get your copy of **Amarantox** now!

Acknowledgments

A special thank you to my wonderful critique partners, who weathered my ups and downs, and were never afraid to be honest with me; Jennifer Bernard, Molly Gray, Brooke Hartman, Kellie Doherty, Mike Robbins, Louise Willis, and Lizzie Newell. I'd also like to thank my amazing editor, Joann Dominik, for telling me what a sick imagination I have, and still loving my book.

About the Author

Tam Linsey is a lifelong Alaskan who is obsessed with self-sufficiency. In spite of the rigors of living in the High North, she grows, hunts, or fishes for much of her family's food needs. She believes that we should have the right to choose what we eat, and therefore is also a GMO labeling advocate (not to be confused with a GMO opponent.) When she is not writing, she'd probably in the garden or the kitchen, exploring Alaska with her husband, or preparing for the zombie apocalypse. She also loves wine and hard apple cider, is mediocre at crochet, and has an adorable 12-pound bunny named Abigail.

Join the Botanicaust Tribe and get a free book by signing up for the newsletter at http://geni.us/tam-linsey

www.ingramcontent.com/pod-product-compliance
Lightning Source LLC
Chambersburg PA
CBHW070810180626
46818CB00001B/198

* 9 7 8 0 9 8 5 9 0 1 3 4 9 *